BEAUTIFUL SNARE

BOOK ONE in the SPIRITED WOMEN SERIES

LAURIE JAMESON

Seven Oaks Publishing
Llano, Texas

©2012 by Laurie Jameson
No part of this book may be reproduced or transmitted
in any form, or by any means, electronic or mechanical,
including photocopying, recording, or by any information
storage and retrieval system, without permission in writing
from the publisher.

ISBN: 978-0-9630829-8-5
Library of Congress Control Number: 2012911641

Cover and interior design by Sonya Unrein

Published in the United States of America

Seven Oaks Publishing
Llano, Texas

www.sevenoakspublishingco.com

For Bekah and Her People in Celtic Britain, circa 80 A.D.
May Their Spirits Heal and Live On

"These are the ravens of my soul,

Sloping above the lonely fields

And cawing, cawing.

I have released them now,

And sent them wavering down the sky,

Learning the slow witchery of the wind,

And crying on the farthest fences of the world."

—William Oliver Everson

BEKAH

BEKAH

I am Bekah. Hear my story. Hear my story for it is the story of all women. I am the voice crying in the wind at night when you cannot sleep. I am the pain in your ear because you will not listen, the aching in your throat because you are afraid to speak. I am the one who gives and takes away, the power that heralds the ravens sitting in the top most places. Darkness comes as a messenger, the raucous cawing of war, the deadening stench of bodies forgotten in the fields. Unburied. No longer loved. I am the voice of the dogs barking before dawn that calls the warriors to waken and the trumpeters to arise. I am the light that splits the darkness and the darkness that splits your soul. When you walk the tracks alone and frightened, tears running down your cheeks, icing in the cold, I am the pain that follows you everywhere, the silent weeping for those taken away, never to return again. I am the sword that severs your head from your shoulders when you are unaware that danger is even near. I am the dagger hidden within the bodice when I come at night to seduce you to my bed— and there, when you have settled into the warmth between my legs, I am that dagger driven into your back. I am the presence of revenge, the acknowledgment of anger, a rage so beyond comprehension you will be sorry I ever came out of the cave, out of the rock, out of the water, out of the stars in order to change the course of human history. You will not be allowed to go. I will hold you captive with my words. You will listen because I am Bekah. I am the voice of the women crying over their men slaughtered in the fields. I am the voice of the orphaned children. I am the voice of the wind that moves over every heart swaying that spirit to be open or closed, to be full of light or to suspend itself in the darkness. When I come for you, you will not know if I am enemy or friend; if I mean to bring you pleasure or pain; if I am destined to be your guiding hand or the hand that slays you. You will not know. That is your plight; the plight of all men because you have forsaken me and taken power that was not yours. You have misused and abused and been led by greed and gutlessness. Where are my warriors? Where are the men who bowed at my feet knowing that the worship of the divine female was the way to the Otherworld? You will not give my power back to me, so I have come to take it. With my sword. With my words. With my pain. And in those moments when the pain strikes you, you will feel my presence. Then the hollow emptiness of losing everything that you loved. Just as everything was once taken from me, now I take it from you. Everything. What you love. What you fear. I will be everywhere, taking back what is mine. I am Bekah. Hear my story or die.

THE FLIGHT

YWAIN

L eading my Lady's horse deeper into the trees, I searched for a place to stop for the night. The gloaming was upon us and soon it would be too dark to find our way. Not that I knew for certain where we were. Even after many hours of hard riding south and west of Muirray, the haze of smoke from its firing by Roman soldiers added to the early darkness of autumn. I dared not think too much about what we had left behind in our flight. If I allowed my mind to return to the mass confusion, the screaming, swords clashing, horse hooves pounding, the smells of burning and blood, I knew rage would consume me. I dared not think of my Lady's daughters or the rest of the household. I thought only of her hanging onto the thick mane of her silver mare, her other hand still clutching the spear I gave her only this morning when we set out to hunt as the sun was tipping the dawn clouds over the sea with rose-tinted light.

I glanced back. My Lady slumped in her saddle, her fair hair, unbound from its braids by tree limbs and wind, covering her face in waist-length tangles. Her bloodied staghound limped behind, his nose nearly in the soft duff of damp pine needles. We needed to stop, even if I still did not know if we had been spotted and followed. I searched the growing darkness for some kind of fortification and like an answer to a prayer, a natural ring of tall stones emerged vision-like behind a screen of thick brush. I stopped. My Lady's mare bumped her forehead into my gelding's rump.

"What is it, Ywain?" Her dead voice sounded pale and low as a ghost's.

"A place, my Lady, to rest."

She sighed, a groaning exhalation much like a last breath. I listened a long time. There was nothing else. Just the sweeter sigh of the night wind building, and, not too far off, the melodic trickling of water. The sound brightened my sagging spirit, and I urged my horse forward, pulling the mare along.

A good place, there was enough space for the five of us to huddle with some protection from the chilling breeze. I wished for a fire, but knew I could not risk it even with the scent of smoke already in the air. Somewhere along our hectic path my Lady's cloak had been torn from the saddle ties. As I helped her slide from her mare, she shivered. Prying open her right fingers, I released the spear and leaned it against the rocks. Still she did not raise her head and for that I was glad. I could not bear the sight of her eyes and everything they held. She had not spoken except for those four words since I had grabbed her mare's reins and spurred us into an all-out gallop away from the slaughter.

The staghound paced, whining, turning within the stone circle. "Here, Pet, here," I whispered, and when he came I told him to lie and lowered my Lady to his side in the dense grass. She leaned back against the rock, her legs curled to the side. Pet licked her knee and she reached out to touch his head. Like a sleepwalker, she drew back her hand and stared at the smear of blood on her palm. I brought my wool cloak and spread it around her.

"Care for the horses," she said.

"I will, my Lady."

"Now."

"I will, my Lady."
"I am fine. It is all right to leave me."
"Yes, my Lady."

I unsaddled. Then, gathering wads of tall grass, I rubbed the drying sweat from the horses' hides and led them in the direction of the sound of water. As they drank, taking turns at the palm-sized spring, I rolled up my sleeves and scooped water from the singing, pebble-lined overflow, drank, and splashed my face clean of dust and tears. When the horses had had their fill, I left them to graze, dragging their reins, and walked back for the horn cup in my saddlebag. My Lady was lying on her side, her back to the stone, Pet tight against her breast, her arm over his back. I whistled low and Pet raised his head.

"Come," I gestured, and he rose with pained awkwardness and followed me to the pool and lapped while I filled the cup.

I led the horses back and weighted their reins with rocks, and they stood nose to rump, heads down to doze, but ears up, alert as guards. When I tried to lift my Lady to give her water, she pushed me away.

"Nay, my Lady, you must drink."
"I hate you," she said.
"I know. Still you must drink."
"I had rather die."
"I know that too."

I reached out to pull the hair from her face and she sprang at me, flailing, and Pet lunged, going for my throat. I barely got my right arm raised to catch his snarled bite on the leather guard protecting my wrist. For a moment all was panic: the horses trying to rear, Pet barking and growling, my Lady beating me with her fists as I tried to hold her back.

Then, just as fast, she pulled me to her, kissing my face and neck, murmuring "Down Pet, down Pet."

"No, my Lady," I said as gentle as I could.

"Yes," she said, pulling at the leather tie that cinched my vest, pulling my shirt from my trousers. "Yes, Ywain."

I gathered her to me, kissing her hair, knowing it was not right, knowing it would only bode ill for me on the morrow, knowing even more how many years I had longed for this, for the chance to touch her, to hold her. But never had I allowed my thoughts to go beyond that, into the realm of having her, of loving her.

I tried to calm her, but she pushed away, clawing at her clothes, a sound like a mewling kitten escaping her lips. In frustration she flung back her head and hair, and I saw her face as if for the first time. Streaks of dirt clotted with dried tears on pale cheeks, her lips swollen and sore. Her eyes, vacant as the wind-swept moor in winter, began to blaze with a mad gleam, an internal fire that was neither delight nor fervor. It was the fire of the forgotten, the left behind. The fire of anger and betrayal. A fire that would consume her, and me, if I touched her again.

"Love me," she said.

It was not a request. It was a command.

"My Lady," I said, lowering my eyes, reaching for her hands that fumbled at my throat.

"Love me," she ordered and flung herself at my chest, throwing us to the ground.

I tried to be gentle, to go slowly, to honor our passage, but I could not. She would not allow anything but a fevered, insane, pushing, grabbing, biting, kicking, moaning race. She drove me, whip and spur, until I could no longer think, no longer maintain any control, until I rolled naked and sweating over her and under her, our bodies forced together, not by love or desire, but by primal need. I commanded my shut-tight eyes to open long enough to see that the horses, still tethered, stood with heads high, nostrils flared, with Pet cowering near them, only long enough to see my Lady transformed into a fury, nothing of her light goodness, her sweet temperament remained. There was only white flesh and fire arcing between her hands as she reached out for my head and shoved my face to her breasts.

When next I was aware, she was on all fours, her face buried in the grass, her rump raised, and I was deep inside her, thrusting, my hands on her shoulders so I could feel her shuddering until she came apart, her heart exploding, her skin melting, until I too was released into a blazing light.

We lay there, spent, flat out, my heaviness driving her bones into the sod. I gathered every ounce of strength I had left to push up on my elbows and my knees so I would not crush her. But, still, we were coupled, my hardness eased but not gone. With great tenderness I rolled sideways, bringing her with me, cradling her in my arms, my lips against the back of her head. I wanted to say something. Tell her I loved her. Tell her she was beautiful. Tell her how long I had wanted her, desired her, needed her. But my mouth was full of dust, the dryness of peat, the realization that this would ruin us.

And then, with a gigantic inhalation like a baby's first breath, she began to cry. Not a soft, sad sobbing, but a hard, deep, wrenching, whining scream that twisted her limbs. I held her, pinioned her arms with mine, forced her legs between my own. As she keened, I eased out of her, letting the fluids we had exchanged run between her thighs. She turned ice cold, her body shaking, her teeth grinding, and still she wailed, the sound echoing around the ring of stones and floating upward into a sky spangled with stars. I did not worry that anyone might hear, for the sound was nothing human, nothing of that time and place.

It was something altogether wild unleashed from the earth. I cringed. I, who feared nothing, was afraid.

Finally, she slept. I rose for the cloak to cover us and comforted Pet. Bid him come lay with us for warmth. So with him on one side and with me on the other, we passed the night guarding our Lady. Though tired in every cell, I did not sleep. I stayed awake to hold her, keep her safe. And whenever she roused, sometimes shouting "Get me my horse" or "Bring me a sword!" I would shush her as one would a child plagued by nightmares. I patted and soothed her and kissed her. When the stars began to fade, she woke, rolled to face me, touched my broken lips with her finger, and said, "Ywain, we must fight. You will help me fight." It was not a command. It was a request.

"Yes, my Lady," I said. And she slept again.

MORNING AFTER

YWAIN

When I woke, she was gone, the spot where she had slept in my arms empty, the cloak tucked around my shoulders. I flung it off and tried to stand, eyes searching everywhere. The horses gone, the dog also. Numb and aching, my legs would not stand. I had no strength, no balance. The world reeled around me as I reached for my shirt and trousers that had served as a pathetic pillow. How could she have gone without my knowing? When had I fallen asleep? I scrubbed sticky fingers over my sand-crusted eyes and stubbled cheeks and smelled the musk of her flesh and fluids.

The sharp tingle of returning sensation in my feet rushed up my calves and thighs to pulse in my groin as the memory of ecstatic joining pierced my brain. Struggling with clothing, with a recalcitrant erection, with boots that would not pull on over swollen feet, I fought to stand, to find my belt and dagger in the tall grasses that kissed the stone. I heard an odd humming and thought at first it was my shame battling the delicious delight in my heart; then I realized the sound was seeping through the mist-hung air from the spring. Crawling on all fours, I made my way to the break in the circle of rocks, and peered around the corner.

In the near distance, the saddled horses grazed. Pet lay between the pool and me, his head turning slow to take in every sight, sound, and movement. When he spotted me, his one good ear perked further and he made to rise. I gestured to him to stay and he relaxed but still stared, watching me as I clawed myself upright using the tall standing stone to lean against. New sun swirled through the fog. A slight breeze blew trailing wisps up from the damp earth toward the treetops. My Lady stood facing the slanting rays, her arms raised, her head tilted back so her finger-combed hair hung past her naked knees. She murmured notes and words in a strange mix of chant and song, a melody laced with invocation and imploring supplication. Though barely a whisper, the sound speared through me, raising gooseflesh on my arms. Her eyes closed, her palms open, she began to turn with studied deliberate grace, her toes and heels inching a circle as she sang. Her arched throat and taut breasts sparkled with leftover droplets from washing, as did the dark thatch between her thighs. I tore my eyes from her nakedness to search her face. She had taken mud and smeared lines across her forehead and cheeks, the marks a warrior paints on his visage before going into battle.

The singing stopped. She lowered her arms and it looked like she was reaching for me, opening an embrace for me to rush to. I pushed myself from the stone to run to her, but her eyes opened and a fierce stare pinioned me. I stumbled backwards, my arms dropping, my manhood wilting. Lowering my head with uncertain deference, I waited, the outpouring of love and compassion for her staunched.

"Come forward, Ywain." She slipped on her filthy dress and pulled her hair over her shoulder to make a braid.

Pet thumped his tail against the ground, and I bent to pat his massive head, careful not to touch the lacerated remains of his left ear. Though everything within me ached to crush Bekah to my chest, I strode with caution. When I was ten feet away, I bent my knee to kneel.

"Do not," she said. "Never do that again. Never."

"Yes, my Lady," I said, standing upright.

"And quit calling me, 'my Lady.' I am no longer anyone's lady." Her voice sounded like a pestle grinding against an empty mortar.

"Yes, my—"

"You may call me Bekah."

"Bekah?" I asked sounding like an idiot.

"Short for Rebekah. You know this, Ywain? No, it is clear you do not. All these years, and you've never spoken my everyday name."

"No, my—"

"It is not that hard, is it? It is only a name. Try it once and see."

Her half-mocking, half-teasing tone tinged with laughter. She stared at me, waiting, and I saw a softness melt the panic and grief in her eyes.

"Bekah," I offered and heard my love for her sing in those two syllables.

She closed her eyes and her body began to collapse. As I reached to keep her from falling, she forced energy into her limbs and straightened, trembling, like a lance jammed into the ground. Recoiling, I stepped back, stumbling over the spears laid side by side near the trilling water.

"You smell like a rutting buck," she said. "Wash and drink and then we will go."

"Go? Where shall we go?" I asked.

"Where were you taking me?" she asked.

"I do not know. Somewhere safe. Somewhere far away from what happened."

"I see," she said. "Well, we are going to go back."

"Back, my Lady?" I said as she frowned at me. "Surely we cannot go back. Let me take you to the far shore where we can send word to your husband."

"My husband is dead." She swished her arm outward in a gesture of release.

"No, Bekah. Surely not."

"Surely yes. I saw him murdered in my vision as we rode from Muirray. Do you think the enemy would have dared approach if he were still alive?"

The implication beat warring thought against warring thought. He was gone. The man I had worshipped, as a son worships a father. The man who had trusted me with the care of his wife and children when he went to war. She was a widow. She was free. I could love her without guilt and fear. We could go somewhere together. Start again. Begin a new life.

"Do you think I would have allowed you to touch me if he were still alive?"

Shame stained my face, then anger blanched it away. Was I so little to her that she could speak to me this way?

"Save your remorse for something more worthy, Ywain. Save your rage for the vermin we will face when we get back. I do not need a lovesick boy trailing after me like a whipped pup. I need a man who will fight with me, who will rally warriors, who will instruct and guide as well as listen and obey. Will you or will you not follow me as you followed my husband? Will you or will you not do as I bid you?"

"I will," I said trying not to smile at the vehemence that both tickled and unnerved me. "Haven't I always done your bidding, Bekah?"

"You have. I am glad you will. I need you now, more than ever. The first thing you must do is wash. I cannot think clearly when you smell that way. And stop looking at me like that. What happened between us last night never happened. Wipe it from your mind. Do you hear me, Ywain? Erase it as I have done. And hurry. We have no time to waste."

As I stripped, she turned her back, walked to the horses, gathered the reins, and led them toward the stone circle with Pet limping at her heels. Yes, my Lady. Of course, my Lady. Whatever you say, my Lady. I will take this mud and scrub you from my skin. I will take this icy water and rinse you from blood. I will take this sun and burn you from my mind. I will take this wind and blow away the ash of what it felt like to throb deep inside of you. I will hold these battered hands against my ears so I will not hear you begging me to take you, the growling moan of the pleasure I gave you. But, no one, not even you, can order me to expunge you from my heart. There you will stay as long as I have breath to breathe.

THE SPEAR

BEKAH

I saw and felt your death, my husband, as if it were my own. The hillside shrouded in last light, the bloodied earth rising to meet crimson clouds. The screams of horses and men, of iron blade against blade, the softer sounds of insects whirring in the grasses, the laughter of children, the singing of the women all left behind along with the purling of the river, the lullaby of the wind at night against the cliffs. I know your last thought as if it were my own. It was not a thought of me. Or your daughters. Of the land you had fought so hard to save. Of the ancestors, the spirits who wove around your head, more than memory, more than guardians sent to help you raise your sword again and again as you slashed your victims to the ground already piled high with corpses. Your last thought, your last thought before the sailing spear pierced under the left shoulder blade and ripped through muscle to explode your heart before exiting your breast, was of your horse, his head rising then flopping back down, his guts spilled around your feet like trembling hot snakes, his eyes rolled white with fear, the panicked guttural sound wheezing from his gaping mouth like nothing you had ever heard before. Not whinny nor neigh nor nicker nor huffing sigh. A blood-icing, skin-crawling, desperate attempt to live while his life slowly exhausted with each exhalation. Your thought was this: in a moment I will end his misery. In a moment I will slice his throat and stop the agony. In a moment, as soon as these curs quit appearing from nowhere to taunt my sword. In a second as soon as—

Then it was over. Seeing the shock in your eyes was far worse than seeing the spear thrown, seeing the jagged point and wooden shaft enter and exit your body. Those eyes, darker than the deepest blue in the depths of the sea, harder than the flint you taught your daughters to chip, those eyes that I could soften with a touch, melt with a kiss, those eyes flared in disbelief before the lids shuttered, then ceased moving.

I will miss you so much, my darling. The way you made me laugh and sigh. The way my cries always brought you into the wildest part of the man you were. The way you looked at me as if I were the most beautiful and cherished creature on earth. The way you loved to fondle my free breast when I nursed your children. The way we hoped and dreamed and planned and believed in a better world for them. I will miss your hands, the great crushing strength of those hands. But, most of all, I will miss your eyes. The way they held me with more tenderness than any woman deserved.

Rest, my love. Your fight is done. Mine is just beginning. If you leave me anything, leave me your courage. Let me be your incarnation. Let me take up your sword, your stalwart purpose. Not only to avenge your murder, or to scrape some small sacrifice to leave our girls, but a peaceful future for all the people. Give me your great heart, a heart made to lead, to protect and save. Let the enemy not see a frail, pale woman. Let them see you in my visage. May the Goddess grant me this one power, the magic of your countenance blended with mine. May the brief bit of goodness that is left in this world bear your spirit high into the sky you worshipped, far into the earth you loved. I will not think of what the sun and scavengers will do to your precious flesh. I will think of you soaring with the sea eagles. I will think of you coming home to me. Forever, I will think that, in time, you will still come home to me.

THE RETURN

YWAIN

"Bekah," I said, but she did not hear me. The odor of horse sweat hung in the hot air. Pet trailed farther and farther behind. Bekah led, I followed. How did she know which path to take? I had fled yesterday with no thought of direction, my only purpose to get us far away. We had scaled ridges and crossed streams I did not remember. She forced us to travel at such a hard trot that the exhausted horses stumbled along the dusty trace, and the sun was only mid-way across the sky. We had not eaten for thirty hours. My stomach rumbled its discontent.

"Bekah, we must stop and rest the horses. Let me see if I can find us something to eat. Pet cannot keep up at this pace."

"What?" she said coming back from the far distance place in her mind.

"We must stop or we defeat our purpose."

"Yes, of course. There is a rill around this bend with grass and berries. We will stop there."

I wanted to ask her how she knew that. This was not country we frequented, not an area that I recalled. I wanted to ask, but was afraid of her answer. I knew she heard things I could not hear, that she saw things from the Otherworld as her mother had before her. It used to intrigue and entertain me that she knew where to find the deer or could sense a storm days before it came. Now, the power she held frightened me. It could not bode well for any of us in the end. My idea of escape, of beginning again in a safe place, had been ignored. She was taking us back to our deaths. How could I go with her? How could I not?

Water rushed beneath a moss-clothed shelf of stone and formed a thin silver snake winding through the grass. Pet plopped with a splash and created a dam that backed up the flow, and from this the horses drank, their ears twitching back and forth with each gulp. I dismounted and searched for my horn cup, but Bekah had already lain belly-down to dip her whole face and suck in the wet sweetness like the horses. Unpredictable and untenable. How was I ever going to do what she expected of me?

She sat sprawled in the grass, her legs akimbo like a girl who doesn't yet know to keep them close together. Plucking a wide blade, she held it between her pressed thumbs and blew softly. A squeaking whistle pealed forth, and Pet leapt to his feet as the horses threw their heads high. She laughed. It was a sound I thought I would never hear again. Noticing the way I glanced around with nervous expectation, she said, "There is no one around to hear, Ywain. Sit down. Relax. Rest. We have a long way to go still."

"We cannot make it back in one day, Bekah. The horses are spent."

"If we keep on steady and slow, we will be fine. We must return before sunset."

"Are you not afraid of what we will find? You saw the slaughter over your shoulder."

"It will be the mostly ghastly thing I will ever have to face, but face it I must. My daughters are there, Ywain. Not going back is not an option."

"I know. I fear for you when you find them."

"No, do not fear for me. Fear for those who have done what they have done. This I know: the girls are buried deep in some dark place where they cannot be seen or heard. A blind one watches over them while a creature with many spines guards the door."

"How do you—" I began.

"I have seen it and I know."

I silenced my tongue, and as much as I wanted to stretch out on the welcoming sod and feel Bekah nestled in the curve of my arm, her head on my shoulder, her breath on my neck, I could not sit. Instead, I placed my spear alongside hers, which leaned against a tree that sheltered the rill's source. I dipped my cup and drank, allowing the overflow to run off my chin onto my clinging shirt.

"Ywain, I have never seen you seem so afraid. Tell me. What do you fear?"

I could not say, "I fear this great wrongful love I have for you," so I said, "I fear your knowing. Not that you know, but how you come to know. It is beyond my ken."

"It is only beyond you because you are not open to it. You can know as well as I."

"There is a huge burden to knowing before we are meant to know."

"No. That is not true. Knowing is a gift that prepares us for what is to come. Now that I know my husband is dead, I know what I must do. If I did not know of his death, then I would be spinning in circles like a leaf caught in a whirlpool not knowing when and how I would be sucked down. Now, because of the vision, I have done my grieving, I have set my purpose."

"Do you always know what will happen? Did you know that what happened yesterday would occur? If so, you never would have gone on the dawn hunt with me."

"True enough. I did not know. Yet, I had not taken the time to ask, to be still and receive. I was happy and distracted by the idea of spending the day with you among the woods and the deer. I did not attend to my morning prayers as I should have."

"Did you know last night would happen?" I asked and then regretted the words as soon as they left my lips.

"Nay, my love, I did not," she spoke so softly that I was not sure whether I had heard or imagined the endearment.

"Come, now," she said. "We must go. Today the enemy will have retreated to care for their wounded and attend their dead. By tomorrow they will be ready to return to loot whatever they did not carry off immediately. We have only a small window of time."

As Bekah spoke, she pulled half-dried berries from the bushes, shoving what she could into her mouth and gathering more for the pouch she made by tying up part of her dress. I followed suit and poor Pet gallantly nibbled the ones I flung at his feet. When we mounted again, my Lady's palms and mouth were stained purple-red. Together with the dried mud streaked on her cheeks and forehead, the wild hair once again escaped from her braid, she looked a terror, like a wraith escaped from an early grave.

THE RECOVERY

YWAIN

The sun had long since set when we made our way through the last patch of forest, headed for the tucked away cove where the fortress walls met the sea. I could hear the boom of the waves, smell the salt and seaweed. Strange it seemed that no gulls screamed overhead. I braced myself for the sight we would see in the gloaming. Knowing he was close to home, Pet reclaimed his place in front of the horses. Bekah's mare whinnied, a long shrill question that hung in the heavy air. We had not talked again. The miles covered had been ground out with stoic and solemn silence. It felt more like a funeral procession than a homecoming.

"Bekah," I whispered. "Let me go first alone. Then come back for you."

"No, from now on we go together. Rein up. Walk beside me. We will face it together."

I eased forward and her mare's shoulder touched my gelding's. Our legs brushed and sensation laced up my spine. Bekah handed me her spear, her hand shaking. Then, reconsidering, she took it back. With the horses still walking side by side, she dropped her reins and drew her arm back as far as it would go and released the weapon high into the silver dimming light. It made a slicing trill through the sky and disappeared from view. From the rampart where the castle wall joined the cliff face, a falcon lifted off, sharp wings creating a silhouette before it tucked and dove, the bells on its jesses tinkling a celestial lilt.

"We are safe," Bekah said, setting the spear in my hand. "Lilith would never come if a stranger were present." She raised her outstretched arm, fist clenched, and the falcon opened her wings at the last moment and settled, light as a feather on the surface of water, before she clenched her talons into Bekah's flesh. I started to protest, then realized that the piercing pain would prepare her for what was to come. We came upon Bekah's still shuddering spear and I stopped to wrench it from the earth.

Rounding the curve of the last hillside, we saw the first bodies scattered at random, struck down as the people, women and children among them, had tried to run. With outward calm, Bekah steadied her horse and walked to each corpse, pausing a moment to say a blessing, using the names of the persons she knew well, thanking them for their service, for their love, before moving on.

"Count the dead, Ywain," she said. "There will be an accounting."

The numbers rose as we made our way into the fortified yard where the heavy gates, battered and hacked, hung like drunks on their hinges. Fires still smoldered among the thatched ruins. The hazy smoke lifted a dull stench into the approaching night, but the main dwelling, though ransacked, stood, its one lofty tower reaching as high as the cliff's wall. We stopped the horses to stare. Bekah released Lilith and the falcon found the air to make ever-widening circles above our heads. Tears pricked my eyes and I swallowed back a howl of despair, my throat working like a dog trying to vomit. I had seen my share of carnage in skirmishes, but nothing before could prepare me for the sight of people I had known and loved piled one across another in haphazard disarray as if they had been toppled by a gigantic sea wind and drowned. In vain, I searched for my mother, my wife and child.

"See if anyone lives," Bekah said. "I will search for the girls."

We tied the horses to the wreckage of a cart near the gates. Pet followed me, alternately whining and growling, sniffing each person as I knelt to feel for pulse or breath. I tried for each one to repeat the prayer I had heard from Bekah's lips, though the words sounded empty and without feeling. My count had passed two hundred when I heard a startled shout and ran toward the stone enclosure where the horses used to be stabled.

I found Bekah pulling at fallen timbers ten times her size. "Here, Ywain. Here. The storage cellar. The spiked creature guards the door."

I dropped flat and saw Pet's dead litter mate pin-cushioned with Roman arrows.

"Wait," I said, pushing Bekah away. "Stay and wait. Let me get the horses and some rope."

She shoved against me, panic widening her eyes. I shoved her back, raised my hand as if to strike her.

"Wait," I ordered. "If they are alive, a few more moments will not hurt. If you tumble the rest of the structure they will be buried alive and it will take days to dig them out."

Stumbling backwards, she sat with a crash on the ground. I pulled Pet from beneath the beams and set him panting at her side.

"Do not move," I said, and she nodded.

It took long minutes to do everything methodically, to select and remove the timbers one at a time until I had the doorway clear and relatively safe. At last, I took the dead staghound by a hind leg and pulled him away from the threshold he had given his life to protect. Then I wedged a lever between the thick plank doors and heaved, again and again, until I broke the bar that was fastened on the inside. When I could move one door inward slightly, I called into the black hole, "No harm. It is Ywain. Who is here?"

The wailing cry of two girls and a woman came floating up, bringing Bekah to her feet as Pet barked and howled.

"Quiet," I murmured. "Hush. Pet hush. Alanna, is that you with Jenna and Morgan?"

"Yes," I heard.

"What blocks the door?"

"The casks. Keenan and I rolled them into place."

"Is Keenan there with you now?"

"He is alive, but not conscious."

"Is he in the way if I set the casks rolling? Can you move him and the girls aside? All of you out of the way?"

"Yes. We will try," Alanna said.

Bekah joined me at the door, her ear pressed to the crack. I thought she would speak, say something to her daughters, but her bloodless lips were pressed into a grimace, her teeth clenched.

We heard tugging and huffing, muffled words and scratching. Then, "All right."

"Stand back." I laid my shoulder to the door with a gentle thud. With each succeeding blow I shoved harder until Bekah joined me. We counted in unison and then threw our combined body weight against the wood. With each attempt we could hear the casks slide a bit against the packed-earth landing. Then, in one thunderous rumble, they spilled down into the darkness and the door sprung inward, casting the last of the day's light into the tunnel.

"Alanna," Bekah said. "Can you hear me?"

The girls began screaming "Mother, Mother" as Alanna shushed them. "Yes, my Lady."

"Take the cloth of your dress and tear two strips. Bind the girls' eyes. Jenna, Morgan, do not be afraid. You have been in the darkness where you can see nothing. I do not want you to see what is here when Alanna brings you up to me."

Silence was interspersed with the sound of ripping fabric and the hushed words of the young girls. Then, step by step, coming up out of the blackness, Alanna led them, one by each hand, until Bekah was on her knees and had them gathered in her arms. Alanna threw herself into mine, and I held her, letting her sob against my chest as Pet licked her drooping hands. When all settled, when the tears eased, I put Alanna next to Bekah, and entered the dim chamber to bring Keenan up from his grave.

"Sir," Alanna said, stopping me.

"Yes," I said.

"He lives, but they tore out his eyes. He got us into the cellar and the door barred before the pain took away his senses."

FIRST NIGHT

YWAIN

Full night was upon us by the time we had eight-year-old Jenna in Bekah's saddle with six-year-old Morgan holding on behind, their delicate hands gripping mane and waist, their eyes still shadowed by the strips of Alanna's dress. We wrestled Keenan's inert body across my gelding and boosted Alanna behind him.

"Try to keep him steady," I told her. "If he begins to slip, call out so I can catch him before he falls. This will be slow, but the moon rises and soon we will be able to travel faster, especially once we reach the track going north. Agreed, Bekah? North to your sister's."

"Yes," she said taking her mare's reins to lead the girls.

We wound our way through the maze of bodies and out of the yard into the fields, turning away from the soothing voice of the sea into the darker woods. An owl hooted and we stopped until the haunting cry echoed against the cliffs, then disappeared. We stayed long enough to take the blindfolds from the girls' eyes, the difference in darkness only the outline of the trees against the sky.

"Here." I handed Bekah a sodden loaf. "It was all I could find."

She adjusted the spear slung over her shoulder, switched the reins into her right hand held high to carry Lilith, and hesitated as she took the bread.

"Go on," I said. "There is enough for all of us. If you lose your strength now, what will the rest of us do?"

She tore her teeth into the ground meal and handed the loaf back to Alanna who passed it to Jenna who passed it to Morgan who said, "Please give mine to Pet."

"Eat yours, little one," I said. "I will get a bite for Pet."

"Where's Pal? Mama, where's Pal? How come Pal did not come with us?"

Bekah shuddered next to me.

"Pal's with Papa. Now, no more talking. We are going to see who can be the most quiet tonight. Then, tomorrow, after we have stopped to rest, we can ask questions."

I reached over and squeezed Bekah's shoulder and she nodded her head. "Ywain," she whispered, "how can I bear to go without laying out the dead?"

"Your prayers will have to be enough. There was no time. We dare not take the chance of being caught."

"The wind's speaking. Do you hear it?"

"No," I said.

"Listen. It is their voices chanting. All of them calling my name. Rebekah. Rebekah. Someday, I will return to soothe their spirits."

"Mama," Morgan said, "You are talking."

FULL MOON

Ywain

We found what we thought was a safe spot in the shelter of thick trees many miles from Muirray. The girls whined, weary of trying to stay in the saddle, and Alanna said she could not keep hold of Keenan a moment longer. Bekah and I settled everyone the best we could, tying the horses, keeping our spears close. Keenan roused for a moment, long enough for me to give him water and reassure him we were safe, then he slipped again into unconscious sleep. Bekah snuggled Jenna on one side of Alanna and Morgan on the other, and we covered them with our cloaks. We slipped off to the side of the fireless and foodless camp to watch and wait for dawn to come.

I reached for Bekah's hand to help her to the ground and she did not mind, nor did she leave go of my fingers, but drew me down beside her and said, "Will you stay close, Ywain? I cannot bear to be alone now."

"Of course," I said. "I wish I could ease you in some way. Forgive me for mentioning him, but I have to tell you how grieved I am for you, for the loss of your husband, the girls' father. I believe you now when you say he is gone, and when word reaches you from the southern shore, weeks from now, months perhaps, you will not be surprised."

"Thank you. No forgiveness is needed. You loved him too, and in some ways knew him better than I ever could. He was a rare man, was he not?"

"That and more, my Lady. Ah, do not scold me. Old habits are hard to break and even though you claim you are lady no more, you still are, to me, to many others. Allow us to honor you as we can."

"Did you find your mother?" Bekah asked.

"No," I said.

"Life is too odd for me, Ywain. Two days ago, the world revolved around taking care of the girls and waiting for Gordan to return. Besides my sewing and schooling, time with Lilith on the wing, and riding out with you to hunt, nothing occupied my mind. Now our world is gone."

"Changed, Bekah. Changed beyond belief, but not gone. You have the girls and other family in the north. You have me—do not, do not chastise me. No confession of love will come your way from my lips. I do not have to tell you my feelings. You have known them for years, and we have shared the best of times, been the best of companions."

"Yes, we have. I have been at ease with you from the start. I have always known that you knew the woman who lived inside my heart, the woman no one else could see, perhaps not even Gordan. Yet, now, when I talk of these things, you pull away, you fear the one you recognized and accepted."

"Maybe it is not fear." I released my fingers from her grasp, stretching my arm behind her shoulders and drawing her close to my chest. "Maybe it is just that I haven't experienced the things you see, the places you go. How can I know something that is not part of my experience?"

"Would you mind if I told you a story about it?"

"No, I would love to hear you speak, to hear what you have to say. It will help us pass the time that we must stay awake. It will keep me from trying to kiss you the way you kissed me last night."

"I thought we agreed to forget that."

"Your command, my Lady, not mine."

She sighed, a bone-deep inhalation that lifted her head and raised her shoulders as her lungs filled with the cool damp air. When she exhaled, it felt as if all the breath in her body had seeped away, and she slumped against me. When she finally spoke, I had to bend my head to hear her murmured words.

"Ywain, I had been trying to keep my promise to honor the full moon and do some small ceremony to acknowledge the old ways of my people as my mother had taught me. I had spent the last few days wondering how I should spend this past full moon day and night when I had been so consumed with Morgan being ill and whiling away my time waiting for Gordan to return. One thing I did know is that I could not allow the day to pass without recognition and time spent with the Goddess. The healer who came to help me after Morgan's birth, when I was so weak, had warned me, her admonition had been strong: *If you do not follow through with your promises, then the spirits will beat you up.* I have known of this visionary path and these obligations for some time, ever since I was a child myself, but it hasn't always been easy for me to make the time to do the work. Yes, prayers. Yes, thoughtful consideration. But the actual quiet time invested has been minimal."

Bekah yawned, squirmed closer to me and said, "I will surely bore you."

"Not at all. These things about you fascinate me. It is like seeing inside your skin."

"All right, then. Mid-day, after a hectic morning of getting the horses ready, I knew that the right thing for me to do was to go up on the mountain, to a high place. The most likely and familiar was Lovell Tor. So I helped make the evening soup, settled the girls with their indoor play, and then, with some unknown trepidation following me, I readied myself to spend the last hours of daylight in the hills.

"I went without knowing why. I went unprepared except for the desire to go and make good my commitment. I wore comfortable clothes and took along a heavy cloak. I took my leather pouch of ceremonial herbs and my prayer stone, but somewhere along the way I left them behind. Perhaps I forgot them when I stopped at the spring for a last drink of water. I do not know. I just knew that when I began to walk the deer trail up into the woods that I did not have them with me. That shows you how distracted I had been. But I was wearing the sacred bag given me by the healer and that was comfort enough. I tied the mare at the trail's end, when the way became too steep for her to climb.

"A storm brewed, thunder and lightning and the threat of more rain. Though sprinkles sifted down through the leaves and pine needles, somehow I knew that the main storm would go around me and that I would not have to worry. I met the beggar woman in rags—you know the one who came to help me heal Jenna—coming down and she warned me that it was not a good time to be up on the mountain. I said, "Yes, it looks like a bad storm," but walked on, regretting that I had no food or coin to give her.

"The vague mark of the foot trail wound tight uphill the whole way going through clusters of trees with wildflowers everywhere. The giant white evening primrose had a fragrance so heady I wanted to stop and do nothing but breathe in the perfumed air. The trail was still damp from recent rain, the drying puddles rimmed with the yellow dust of pollen. The air hung fresh, damp, clean and cool all around me so I was glad to have my woolen cloak.

"Do you tire of hearing me ramble?" Bekah asked.

"No," I said. "The sound of your voice soothes me. Go on."

"Soon the steepness of the trail took away my breath and forced me to stop. When I paused I said short prayers asking for guidance, because I really did not know why or where or how. I kept on climbing. The storm intensified, but it moved away to the east, going around the ridge where I stood. A hawk flew over, screaming three long notes. A good sign. The only other sound was my feet crunching on the trail, my labored breathing, the wind in the trees rustling the leaves and the far off barking of foxes. I had taken the left fork on the loop trail and knew if I kept on, I would eventually reach the apex of the ridge where I could walk out onto a grassy knoll and see the top of the tor and all the other hills in a circle—and even far out to the east, where, at some point, the moon would rise.

"Then, I was there on the top of the world, feeling badly that I had left behind my ceremonial stone and herbs. I stood with the world stretched out below me, already the lights of Muirray's fires glowing, a good breeze as the storm dissipated and some clear skies appeared in the north and west. I held onto my sacred bag and, turning to each of the directions, spoke to the Goddess, saying prayers of thanksgiving and asking for blessings for those I loved, especially for Gordan so far away. At the end, not knowing quite what to say or how to say it, I merely asked: if there is a reason or purpose behind my being here on this full moon evening, please give me a sign, let me know what I am to do.

"I hiked on, searching all the while for the sacred tree I had often seen in vision. I knew it was large and distinctive and not far off the trail. Every so often I had to stop to look all around, each direction giving me a different perspective so I would not miss it. On a patch of grass and pine needles, a squirrel appeared with his pointed ears and bushy tail. He was not afraid of my approach because I walked with peaceful intent. He simply stood there and was quiet, not even watching me. I stopped right next to him and said a silent greeting. There, behind him, was a small-diameter, slightly curved sacred tree, one the ancestors had tied as a sapling to make it grow in special ways. I smiled. I had seen this in vision and I knew the bigger tree was close by. Still I stayed to watch the squirrel. Moments passed in silence with no movement by either of us. Then he began to dig down into the needles and duff, scratching up a pile all around him. From deep in the earth he extracted something, held it in his paws and began to chew on it, eating his supper as if I was not there. Such a tiny natural act, but so light-hearted and entertaining. When he had finished but still stood there, I turned to walk on, my foot making a sliding-gravel sound on the earth. The noise startled him, as if he hadn't even known I was there, and he dashed away. I said a small apology for scaring him, turned and walked on down the trail, and there was the giant sacred tree.

"It was very tall with three arms, a thick trunk that rose twice as high as my head, and two large arm-like branches, going out at sharp bent angles that turned upward toward the sky. In the middle, one spiked dead branch went up as high as my shoulder. At eye-level, a forked branch with long needles soft to the touch and new pale green growth drooped. The ground all around was littered with broken branches, sticks, needles, and tiny plants. I thought only to touch the tree and say a prayer, and then go on. But as I reached out my arms and allowed my hands to grasp the branches, a tingling power came up out of the earth and flowed into my arms. I closed my eyes and said, 'Thank you for bringing me here.' I felt the need to stay, to see if there was something for me to see, to hear. I kept my eyes closed and listened to the sounds of the evening forest fade. My legs began to tremble, first the right, then both, and though my hold on the tree was light, my hands felt grafted to the bark. I felt the vision coming on strong and tried to remain calm."

Night falling. Through thick trees a fire burning. I approached, being quiet, wondering what was happening while knowing it was something important and perhaps something I should not see. The first image was a roaring bonfire in a clearing surrounded by trees and from the trees, looking as if the trees turned into people, there came a circle of men dressed in brown cloaks, hooded so I could not see their faces tipped down to the ground. They walked to a slow measured beat and there was a sound, not singing, not chanting, but a melodic humming that grew louder. Off to the side there was a huge tree with a hollowed out trunk, big enough for a person to stand in, and from inside the hollow there glowed a silver-white light that intensified as the men's humming did. From the light, a lady appeared, all in glowing white, shimmering, long light hair, some kind of wreath around her head. She took shape and walked from the archway of the tree's door into the darkening night.

"I became afraid. The word and images of sacrifice came into my mind. I stopped the vision. I did not want to see her die. Or did I fear for the men? All these things flashed before me, but then I realized that there would be nothing violent, and if I wanted to see what happened, something important, then all I needed to do was be still, to open my inner eyes again as my real eyes remained closed. I was still trembling. I tried to stop the shaking but could not. I heard a voice say, 'shall you see more' and when I answered 'Yes,' the vision continued."

The woman walked toward the fire, toward the circle of men. They opened the circle, moved aside, and allowed her to enter. There was great honor and worship. As they watched, still humming loudly, she walked right into the blazing inferno, but she was not consumed. She was still visible within the flames and smoke. She spoke. The men fell silent to listen. She went on speaking for the longest time, important words of wisdom, messages, direction, guidance, and one by one, as if they were filled with too much knowledge, the men fell in soft faints to the ground, until none were standing. The fire died down, her voice disappeared, and her person dissolved into the last flames and embers. Then there was nothing but the silence of the night and a few animal sounds. Morning was coming, dawn appeared in the eastern sky, and with great care and sleepiness, the men began to rise, not speaking, but stretching, yawning, lifting their hands in greeting to one another. Together they collected the ashes of the fire and carried them to the hollow tree. With great ceremony, they placed the ashes inside, handful by handful. When the work was done, they turned their separate ways, and faded back into the forest.

"Ywain, do you believe me?" Bekah asked.

"Yes," I said, "though I do not know what it means."

"The vision was over, but for a long time I could not remove my hands from the branches. I felt like I was grown to the tree. My feet would not move although my legs ceased trembling. I opened my real eyes and saw the ground beneath me, studied the twigs and branches, and heard the bird sounds of night coming on. I leaned my forehead against the tree branch and rested until some of my strength returned. I kissed the tree's gnarly bark and said thank you again. I asked if I could leave, if this was the reason I was brought to that place, and what I was meant to do next. The answer came from within the earth: gather strength, walk the trail, go home, bathe, seek your pallet and sleep.

"I was foggy and disoriented. I knew where I was. I knew the trail to walk, but it was hard to make my feet move or keep my eyes open when they wanted to close in sleep. I was drained of all energy, exhausted and uncertain in my steps. I did not know if I could walk the miles to get down off the mountain, especially before true dark came, but I also knew that I must try. One slow step at a time, cautiously, trying to focus on the plants and birds, I made my way, studying glimpses of sky for moonrise, wondering if I would see the full moon.

"I walked and walked. I saw no one and nothing, but from time to time a small rabbit dashed across my path, a sign that I was fine and I would find my way out before dark. I walked down among the trees where it was darker, among the big stones, the singing stream where I stopped to listen to the sound of the water spilling. I saw bear scat, small black patches on the trail. I saw old horse manure, fox droppings and fur, and the remains of a killed fawn. I was honored that the Goddess had given me this time alone. I was not afraid, just tired, very tired. I walked as the day disappeared, and the trail became hard to see. I came to the loop ending and the small creek crossing where I stopped to put finger dabs of water on my eyes, my throat, and my heart, and say another prayer of thanks. I untied the mare that whickered at my approach. I heard far off sounds, dogs barking and the distant voices of children playing. I saw the lights of the fires. And just as it became too dark to see my feet in front of me, I reached the boundaries of the Muirray.

"You know what it is like to come home when you have been away, do you not?" Bekah asked.

"Yes. It is a feeling like no other," I said. "Tell me the rest."

"It was full dark when I got to the house, having made my slow way being extra cautious of animals close to the trash heaps. Alanna was there to meet me. She took me inside, saying she would heat water for a bath. I went in to say goodnight to the girls and Jenna softly scolded me for being gone so long in the dark. I knew it was only love and worry. I told her I went to the mountain to say prayers for her father. I did not tell her the rest. She seems too young to know the other. Do you not think she's too young, Ywain?"

"Perhaps. You knew of such things when you were young,"

"I know, but I often wished I had not," Bekah said.

"Alanna poured the warm seawater over me. She washed my hair and scrubbed my back and listened to me tell all that had happened. She leaned over to kiss my cheek and thanked me, told me I was blessed that the Goddess worked through me. As I dried my body and slipped on my shift I was so tired, but energized in spirit and happy. Alanna rubbed my sore feet with scented oil and left the windows of my tower room uncovered so I could feel the moonlight as I slept.

"Are you like me, Ywain? Do you love the moonlight with you as you sleep?" Bekah asked.

"Indeed I do. It is a comfort to me," I said. "So did you sleep?"

"No. It was a restless night. I ached from the long miles. I could still see the woman coming out of the hollow tree and walking into the fire. Who was she, Ywain? Was she the Goddess? What was her message? Where is she now? Will I ever know?"

"I do not know," I said.

For a long while I waited to see if Bekah would go on with her story, but she stayed quiet, breathing as a child breathes in sleep, her head cradled in my lap, my hand resting on her shoulder. I felt the need to say something, to acknowledge her connection to the Otherworld, but the words rolled around in my head and could not find their way to my throat.

"Ywain," she said, "Do you think my mind is unwell?"

"No, Bekah. Not unsound. Chosen perhaps. Gifted."

"What does it mean? Who was she? Who were the men?"

"I do not know, my Lady. With time, perhaps, and trust in your power, maybe the answers will come to you. Try not to worry. Allow what is to come to come. Does that make sense?"

"Of course, but far easier to say and think than to do. Will you help me? There is so much I need to know and I cannot do it alone. I need you to guide me, to keep me safe, to keep me from the sadness so I can do what I must do."

"I will do whatever I can. I am pledged to you now. I cannot forsake you whatever may come."

"You promised you would fight alongside me."

The memory returned to me, but I did not want to claim it, did not want to allow that I had made the vow. Not that I feared the fighting for myself, but for her.

"Ywain," she said, sleepiness softening her voice further, "I asked and you promised. Say yes or no. Is that true?"

"Yes, it is true. I am not a man to go back on my word, but I do not see how—"

"Let us not argue. We will speak of it tomorrow. For now, will you hold me and let me sleep? Can you stay awake to guard the girls?"

I did not need to answer her question for those were things I was willing to do without reservation. As she slept, I allowed myself the pleasure of looking at her, of stroking her hair, of feeling her strong heart beating under the palm of my hand.

THE DOVE

YWAIN

I swear I was not asleep because my eyes were open and I could see the shapes of the trees against the brightening sky as the moon rose. But I must have been off in a love-induced reverie because the sound of a dove calling woke me. Bekah slept beneath my hand. It was so still I could even hear the girls and Alanna breathing in their rest. Again, the call of the dove, but it was the middle of the night with dawn hours away. There was no reason for a dove to call. Again, the mournful notes. There could be only one source for the sound. I slipped from beneath Bekah's thistledown form and laid her to the ground; then crouching, moving slow, I made my way to Keenan's side. I cleared my throat to let him know I was near before I reached out and touched his leg.

"They are coming. I can feel the horses' vibration in the earth," he said.

I took a breath and held it, listened hard, but heard nothing. I squeezed Keenan's leg once more.

"You cannot hear yet; only feel. Lie on the ground," he said.

So I stretched out, allowing my chest to hug the dirt and leaves. There I rested, barely breathing, until I too could feel the distant thunder deep beneath the sod.

"Their scouts will have dogs. Damn the traitorous southern tribes who have given way and joined the invading force. Even if the moon is veiled by the incoming clouds, they will find us."

I did not even give myself a moment to think before I was up saddling the horses. Bekah appeared by my side to tighten the cinches.

"Wake them as quietly as you can," I said. "Take the mare and Morgan. Put Alanna on the gelding with Jenna. Do not stop for any reason. Keep the moon on your off side. When you reach the river too wide to cross, stop there where it spills into the sea. Wait for me. If I do not come by moonrise tomorrow, go on without me."

"Ywain."

"There is no other way. The horses can take only four. Keenan is too weak to walk. I will remain with him. If need be, we will hold them back to give you extra time. Let me keep your spear for him. He may not be able to see, but he can hear and still hurl the haft."

"Ywain."

"Take Pet. I will keep Lilith back with me. You will ride better without her, and she is not apt to follow you in strange country."

"Ywain," she said.

"I know. Say nothing else. Get the girls."

I sent them on their way knowing they had a head start. When the noise of the horses moving through the trees faded, I took the spears and crouched next to Keenan to wait. There was a good chance that the party was not on our trail; that they did not even know we were there. It could be anyone, but the fact that it was a large group, moving fast, moving at night, was difficult to ignore.

"Are they still coming, Keenan?"

"Aye. A bit slower than before. Leave me. Go on after the women."

"I cannot."

"There is not much left of me to save, Ywain. I am old anyway. Ready to die. I knew that when they tore my eyes."

"All the more reason to return the same to them."

"Do not make foolish choices where life is concerned," Keenan said. "It is too soon gone. Save yourself and the women. Let me serve as foil."

"If they find you, they will torture you. If they do not find you, how will you go on living? Either way, it bodes a slow death."

"Well, then, if you will not go, do you have a plan?"

When I said nothing, Keenan laughed.

"So I figured," he said. "It is hard to be so young, eh?"

When I did not reply, he said, "Tell me where we are. Describe everything. How far off the track? Does the trail split anywhere near? Did we come across a stream, a low place?"

I told him everything with as much detail as I could recall. Then, for a long while we were both silent.

"They've stopped," he said. "That is good, it gives us time. How long do you think before dawn?"

"A couple hours, maybe less."

"This is what you need to do. Find a high spot on the track where it runs directly east and west. If it is bordered by trees, tightened by brush, all the better. Then come back for me. Before you go, give me the falcon. She'll keep me company."

I untied Lilith from her branch perch and waited while Keenan unwound the bandage from his eyes and wrapped it around his hand. I settled the bird there and left him stroking her breast feathers, murmuring love words to her hooded head. I had no idea what the old man was up to, but he had a plan and I had none, so I did what he asked of me.

SUNRISE

YWAIN

The sun rose raw, oozing orange light through the trees. I had found our high place. I had led Keenan by the hand, the spears slung over our shoulders, the haughty falcon riding his free fist through the last of the night. We had been waiting by the side of the road, tucked into a thicket of brambles, for some time. As we gathered sticks and stones onto the open cloaks, Keenan kept me informed about the horsemen's progress: how close they were, how fast they were moving. We could hear them plainly now, the creak of leather and jingle of metal against metal along with the heavy trotting hooves. The horses' steps were laden and in time; these were armored men riding in formation. We saw the first helmeted heads top a rise below and watched the columns dip down into a low-lying swale. I tried to count, but lost the number after seventeen. I tried to calculate the odds, but no matter how I looked at it, there were way too many men for us to take on.

"Ywain, we have two things on our side," Keenan whispered. "Surprise and the Goddess. Do not underestimate either."

"I have no idea what you are planning. Tell me, so I will know."

"No. You will do your best without thinking. Do as I say. Trust me in this."

He spoke to the bird and removed her hood. He allowed her a few moments to adjust her eyes to the light, to stretch her wings and resettle on his hand. He said, "They are all in the shadow now. It is our time. Crawl to the middle of the road at the highest point. I will follow."

I snaked out of the brush and wormed my way forward dragging the bundle of objects to throw. From this vantage point, I could hear the approach of the party, but could see nothing.

"Prepare your spear. When I give the command throw it, then the sticks and stones, and do not stop throwing," Keenan whispered as he hunched in a tight ball, the falcon primed on his fist.

The sound of the horses became deafening. Blood pounded in my ears. I heard the clink of sword and shield. I heard men's voices, the horses' heaving as they began trotting the steep rise. I could feel the hot sear of the rising sun on my back, the pebbles of the track biting into my elbows and knees.

"Now!" Keenan shouted. He bellowed out a guttural cry as he launched the falcon at the horsemen just as the sun spilled over the hill into their eyes. I let go of my spear, then threw a stick, then a stone, then another, and another. Keenan felt his way, slow, but throwing true. Lilith screamed as she dove over the heads of the lead horses. They reared and spooked. Our weapons found their marks. And then there was such a melee of dust and shouts and falling men and running horses that the scene before my eyes was like something from a horrific dream.

"Come," Keenan said, "Time to flee." He reached out a hand to me and I scooped him up like a child and ran, first down the other side of the hill on the track, and then into the woods, zigging and zagging my way between the trees, turning north as soon as I could find the sun on my right shoulder. When I could breathe no more, when numbness stole my legs, I stopped in a copse of oaks and lowered the old laughing man to the ground.

He looked like a wraith. Pale and icy as a corpse. The blood-crusted sockets of his eyes squinched tight, but his mouth open in a huge O as chortled sounds spilled forth. I heard the falcon call and was surprised she had managed to follow us.

"Help me sit up," Keenan said, and I lifted him and braced his back against a gnarled trunk. He raised his arm and Lilith floated in, her feathers ruffled, her eyes wide. Keenan greeted her with words I did not understand, and when he was done sweet-talking her, he turned to me and said, "Well done, son. Well done. Can you even imagine what they thought seeing our figures burning with the sun on that hill, with the bird and the spears and sticks and stones raining down on them? Oh. Oh. Oh." Keenan laughed until I could not help but join the contagious hilarity.

"What a way," Keenan said, "to go. My prayers are answered."

His head and arm dropped, and I took Lilith from his hand, settled her on a low branch and tied her. I searched for her hood in Keenan's pocket, found it, and slipped it over her beautiful head. Taking the cloak from his shoulder, I leaned him forward to remove his belt and knife. Then I sat down beside him and gathered him into my arms, but he was already gone, the last breath sighing from his lungs. I did nothing for some time but hold him and listen to the doves and robins greet the day. Then I rose and built a rough scaffolding for his body in the branches of the oldest oak and laid him there. I placed his hands on his chest and covered him with his cloak. I searched the ground for two like acorns and set them in the hollow sockets of his eyes. Repeating the prayer I had learned from Bekah, I said the only words I knew to say, then strapping on his knife belt and taking the falcon on my fist, I walked away.

THE TRACK NORTH

BEKAH

On the track, the hours passed in a kind of suspended animation. I was so tired of riding, I walked, leading my mare with Jenna hanging onto her milky mane. Morgan had quit crying and Alanna had quit complaining a long while ago. We were all so weary, we were no longer afraid. The trees far off in the river bottom rolled by with strips of orange and yellow and brown, the leaves changing with fall, with the passing of season to season. Miles slipped by leaving the southern seacoast behind and moving farther north to mountains and memories, the scraps of dreams blown this way and that by old winds that never ceased. I walked and thought. They were there. I rode and daydreamed. They were there. Not as nightmare. Not as pleasant passing of time. Not quite torture, but enough pain to be acute. The ache of another time, another world. One where the notion of aloneness was pervasive, like air, something that had to be breathed in order to stay alive and well. Something that poked and prodded like an idea waiting to be born, something that would have its own way with me whether I wanted it to or not. It said embrace me, but moved away. It said leave me be, but then circled back to touch me from behind. If I had to give it a name, I could not. Not alone, for I was never really alone. Not loneliness, for I did not feel lonely. Nor lost. How could I be lost when I knew where I was even if I did not know where I was going to end up? It did not matter that the trail was unknown, that the falling leaves had obscured the path and there was no time to move them aside and see which was the right way. I just walked. Letting my feet feel for some remembered foundation, some sense of dirt and stone that felt familiar, that spoke of other journeys where there was more fear but less knowing, less understanding. In the fear, there was caution and mistrust and wondering where I would be on the morrow. There were just the undulating uneven miles, passing without me, passing too close to me, passing the acres of trees caught by circumstance in the river bottom. Then the river turned and bent away from the course that even the trees thought they would be going on. Not even the trees knew what would happen to them. Season after season. The sap rising, like desire, a force unto itself, one not controlled or negotiated, one just from nowhere to nowhere. Only the trees knew that the movement in their veins and warmer weather meant new buds which surely, with rain, would turn to leaves, and the leaves too would change, ever dependent on air and temperature and storms. The clouds would cover them. The sun would bake them. They did not complain. Why did they allow all that to happen? Budding. Growing. Shedding. Dormancy.

Why not stay in winter awhile longer and feel the freedom of being in a trance-like death where there was no thought, no growth, no struggle, just resting, resting, resting, letting the wind rattle the leafless branches, saying over and over and over again, "I am not here, I have gone home to some other place. Do not look here. Do not trouble me with notions like alone or lonely or loneliness." I was free of those things. I was like the tree. Old. Older by far than the river's changing course, the shifting sand and the silt that fed my searching roots. Not older than stone or earth or sky, but old enough. Old enough to know that there was no reason to go on with the nonsense of constant search. Patience. Waiting. The trees did not know when it would rain. They did not know when the storms would come to blow them over, tear them up by the roots, bend them, break them, or force them to be different than they are. They did not cry out. They sang when they could and then they were silent. They allowed silence to be part of what they were. It was a silence that came when the leaves were gone and the wind was still and the birds did not light in their uppermost limbs to sing. This was the silence of acceptance and knowing that place and purpose could not be given or known; it just was. Just becoming what you were meant to become. Trees did not know right from wrong, lovely or ugly, bountiful or stingy. There was no capacity for judgment. For saying, "I am not what I should be. I have failed at being what I need to be." What if someone tried to tell a tree that it needed to be a certain height, a special width, this shady, this barren, this shelter, this place for things to come and find nurturing and safe place? Like a tree, I was only what I was. So why did my mind want more than that? Why search? Why ask? Why torture and tease? Why know the word disappointment and be angry when the judgment found fault, discovered that I had failed. The old healing woman had said "Peel away the layers of your illness like an onion." Each layer brought some new thing to pull away and discard, going deeper and deeper until the inner core was smooth and white, pure and sweet—yet still it made me cry. First the skin, flaky and yellow brown, or red, or white, then the outer layers, thick and fleshy and often cut or bruised or spoiled, beginning to rot from exposure. Once the skin was gone, the under-layers, thinner and paler, would appear with a silky transparent skim of wet juice separating one from the other. Interesting how each layer peeled away revealed another layer that was smaller than the last. Smaller and smaller and smaller each portion became, until there was nothing at all but the air, a knot of air and the beginning again of creation. I wanted to get there from here. I was weary of peeling layers. Weary of all the tears. Yes, things were whiter and purer and sweeter, but it seemed like a tedious and complicated process. So unlike the trees.

"My Lady, please," Alanna said. "Morgan is near to faint. Can we not stop a bit and rest?"

"Not yet, Alanna. We must keep on. See the sparkle of sun through the trees? There's the river where we may wait. We must push on to there before the darkness comes."

"We have lost Pet. He's no longer with us," Alanna said.

"He's lagged behind. He'll follow our scent and find us."

"Ywain will never find us. We have come too far. There are too many trails, and we have not kept on one, but keep shifting from this one to that. We do not know where we are. We do not have anything to eat. The girls are about to fall from the horses—"

"Stop it. Not another word from you. Not one. Do not ever question my judgment again. Would you rather be back at Muirray shot full of arrows like Pal or rotting in the sun like the others?"

I stopped in the middle of the road. I pulled my dagger and raised my hand as if to strike Alanna. The dull threatening tenor of my words drifted away. Whose voice was that? It was not a voice that I had ever heard before. Or was it? It sounded like Gordan dressing down his men, the hard-hitting consonants emphasizing his anger. Alanna clasped her hand over her mouth and her nostrils flared as if she could not breathe. Her green eyes blossomed with tears and against her breast Morgan whimpered.

"You may stay here if you wish. Or go back." I said. "I will take my daughter, but you may have my mare. Which will it be? Go with me or go alone."

It took her forever to form the words and say, "Go with you, my Lady."

I said nothing more. I sheathed the knife and pressed my cheek against Ywain's gelding's shoulder. Tears stabbed my eyes, but I refused to cry. I would not cry again. When I raised my head, Jenna leaned over and touched my hair. I patted her scratched, insect-bitten leg. She had lost a shoe somewhere. Clicking my tongue to encourage the horses, I walked on.

TWO GIFTS

BEKAH

We made the river before dark, and though we could not see it for the trees, the sea was close enough to hear the waves smash against the rocks. I closed my eyes, extreme fatigue willing me to leave them that way, but when I forced the wind-dried lids back up, there was a hare sitting several paces in front of me. Her long ears twitched, her soft nose wiggled, drawing in the scent of humans and horses. She lifted a hind leg to nonchalantly scratch, then she turned her head to stare at me. My dagger, flung haft first, flipped several times and clipped her between the eyes. She dropped, shuddered, then lay still. No one was more shocked than I. Holding my forefinger to my lips for silence, I handed Alanna the reins to the gelding and strode through the short grass and fallen leaves to claim her. More than stunned, she was dead. When I grabbed the body by the back feet and lifted my arm as high as I could, the velvet ears still dragged the ground. Convulsive delight seized me and I began to laugh and dance in a circle, the beautiful hare my graceful partner.

"We camp here," I said, breathless. "And eat. Alanna unsaddle the horses and let them graze. Girls, come on, we will go wash at the river."

I risked the barest fire in the thickest cluster of trees where the branches and leaves would diffuse the smoke. We ate the meat half-raw, hunkered down on our heels as the first stars appeared. Alanna had not spoken to me since our confrontation and the girls asked no questions, made no requests. Just as we chewed the last bits of sweet flesh from the hare's bones, Pet slunk into camp on his belly, tongue lolling. Morgan and Jenna looked at me for permission, then attacked the poor dog with a barrage of kisses and snuggles. I gave him the hare's remains, as well as her head, but I folded the hide flesh to flesh, then rolled it and stashed it in Ywain's saddlebag. The hare had been a gift from the Goddess, and I would tan the skin and keep it to remember how our hunger had been filled.

Settling the girls to sleep with Alanna, I kept watch over the dozing horses with Pet pressed to my side. I inventoried each night sound: bat squeak, the whisper of an owl's wing, the chirping of insects and the frog's off-key song. As chilly as the night became, I knew he would not sing much longer. I listened and waited for Ywain. I had seen someone walking alone. I had seen a man sleeping in the branches of an oak tree. And I had seen a falcon exploding out of an orange and gold ball of fire, her wings wide, her talons outstretched. I waited and prayed as the moon rose and began its silver arc across the sky. I tried not to sleep, but exhaustion sucked me to the ground. My eyes drooped, then flared open, drooped again. I would have to trust Pet to be on guard.

Out of the river's mist a man walked. He turned four tight circles around the cold ashes of the fire. He made four wide circles around the sleeping women. He soothed the horses with an outreached hand, then glided four circles around their hip-cocked bodies. He crouched and waited until the staghound quit growling and came to him tail wagging. He stayed a long time petting the dog's head and scratching its burr-laden belly. When the dog slept, he crawled on his hands and knees making four circles around the protector. He stood again and walked to where I lay curled into myself, the dagger under my right hand. Circling his hand over my body, he chanted without sound until the words and the rhythm entered my mind and heart. "Su-ni-ki-wa. Su-ni-ki-wa. Su-ni-ki-wa. Su-ni-ki-wa." Then he stayed, sitting beside me, his hand on my shoulder, until the moon fell and the stars faded and the first silver-rose hint of dawn colored spaces between the eastern trees' uppermost branches.

I felt his warmth leave my side and I woke, my first awareness the hard dampness of the ground, my second the piercing stiffness in my knees and hips. I opened my eyes and in the dim pewter light and lifting fog I saw the man walking away from me, his left hand wrapped in a bloody rag. Though I did not speak, I called out with my thoughts as I pushed myself up to sit. He turned, his cloak swirling around his feeble legs, to look at me. Beneath his hood, his face blazed like a bronze shield and he had acorns for eyes. Bowing his head, he placed his right hand across his heart, then pressed those fingers to his lips and released a kiss into the sparkled air. I opened my arms to receive the gesture and folded it to my breasts. When I looked again, he was gone.

"Good-bye, Keenan," I whispered. "Good-bye."

YWAIN

YWAIN

Had it been only ten years since Gordan had pulled me from the rolling, brawling, yelling knot of dirty boys playing in the stone-laden summer sand below the towering heights of Muirray with the cliffs raucous with gulls? He had just married and the community buzzed with rumors of the beautiful wife he had brought home from some place far to the north. Had he bartered for her? Had he paid a high price in money and horses and jewels? Had he won her heart with his strong stance and reputation for being a fierce fighter? Certainly it was not his looks or personality, for he was neither handsome nor charming. The people said he had the visage and manner of a great bear just wakened from hibernation: rumpled, unruly, surly, ready to fight and determined to find something to fulfill his huge appetite. When his parents had succumbed to the wasting sickness two winters before, he had assumed his father's power and prestige, but little of his mother's grace and humility. He was proud to a fault, yet protective and dedicated to providing for the people who had been trusted to his care. No one had ever seen him smile or turn an affectionate hand until he brought his wife home with him after a half-year's absence. Then, with her light as a white butterfly on his thick arm, he not only smiled, but talked and laughed. The woman known as Rebekah but always called "my Lady" or "my lord's Lady," had changed the whole cold, wintry mood of Muirray into one of constant spring. Gordan was fond of saying, "I saw her in a dream and went searching. I found her where the apple trees were in bloom."

    I was too young then to know more than the stir my Lady caused whenever she came into the yard, ventured to the stables, or made her weekly rounds to the wattle-and-daub thatched huts to see if anyone was in need. Everyone brightened and smiled, for she laughed at everything and she loved wholeheartedly, from the smallest child incapable of anything but drooling and grinning to the oldest infirm man who still hobbled about on crutches trying to make himself useful. Sometimes people stopped in the middle of their work because they heard the heavenly notes of her singing from the high window of her room far above the sea. If ever there was a blessing bestowed upon the people of Muirray, it was Rebekah.

    Whenever she floated by, trailing the sweet scent of lavender, a stiffening pain wakened in my groin. I did not know then the implications of love and lust, but I did know that her station existed far above mine. With my awkward shyness and sharp embarrassment, it fell easy on me to turn back to my work after I had offered the obligatory nod of my head, my hands hovering below my belt to hide the evidence of my adolescent desire.

    So, when Gordan had grabbed me by the back of my shirt and dragged me from the free-for-all on the shore, I thought he only meant to scold me and send me back to my mother's chores. Instead, he placed his meaty hand on my shoulder and directed me farther down the beach where we sat side-by-side on a jutting thumb of rock.

    "How old are you now?" Gordan had asked.

    "Twelve, Sir, going on thirteen come fall."

"You lost your father the same winter I lost mine?"

"Yes," I said.

A scowl hung on his leathery brow.

"Sir," I said and he smiled and patted my thigh.

"Brothers and sisters?"

"None, Sir. The wee one died just before my father."

"Your mother will come to the large house to help my wife. Will you come to me, work with Keenan and the horses, train with me for the fighting?"

Gratitude and apprehension rammed together in my throat. Finally, I was able to say, "Why me Sir?"

"Because you have a quick mind and a fine heart. I have been watching you for a while. I need a man to take over for Keenan, to care for things here when I am away, to watch over my wife and the children to come."

"But Keenan?" I asked. "Excuse me, Sir. It is not for me to question you."

"No, Ywain. It is appropriate to question, to ask, and to find answers. Keenan is not old yet, but the years are beginning to slow him down. It will take time for him to help you learn all you need to know. Ten years from now you will be doing all that he does and more. Will you come to me, to us, be part of our household? I am asking you a great favor. I am asking you to give up whatever skills you wanted to perfect for yourself, your hopes and dreams whatever they may be, to come and serve me and mine."

I took a long time to formulate an answer, but Gordan did not seem to mind. He sat with me and watched the waves crest and break, his hand on my thigh in a gesture of camaraderie, of brotherhood. I loved him then for taking note of me, for wanting me to have a special place in life, for trusting me with the responsibility for his family. It was an honor I had never hoped to have, but also a weighty burden that I was not sure my young shoulders could carry. With great care I chose the words inside my mind and practiced several times before I stood. Gordan stood beside me and when he had risen to his full height, I looked up at him and said, "I am honored and humbled by your request, Sir. I would be blessed and pleased to come with you." Then I dropped to one knee and bowed. He placed his hand with heavy solemnity on the back of my head. I felt the sunlight burning through my scalp, or perhaps it was Gordan's power pouring into the receptive heart trying to burst from my chest. I heard him give a monstrous, growling sigh, then he ruffled my hair and said, "Go on and play for today. Keenan will come for you soon, and then there will be no more play."

Because there was no one to see my tears, I allowed them to trickle down my cheeks and off my chin as I walked, keeping to the trees and brush, avoiding any semblance of trail or road. I had no way of knowing if anyone followed me, but I doubted it. The traces Keenan and I had left on the hill would show the presence of two men, one being carried, when we fled the skirmish. Instead of bothering to track us, the enemy would have seen to their own wounded and dead, then carried out the mission they had been so intent on when we struck them at sunrise.

Who did I cry for? Myself, certainly. For the father I had lost so young. For the father Gordan had been to me. For the grumbling friendship of Keenan. For Bekah's unimaginable loss. I knew for certain that Gordan was gone because I no longer felt his guiding hand on my head or my shoulder. His presence had left the world as I understood it to be. Perhaps he and Keenan walked together now in some uncertain void I could not begin to grasp. The small weight of Lilith on my fist kept me from pure despair. I had to return her to Bekah. I had to keep us both alive for our Lady's sake.

Dusk found me too far inland and miles from the river where I had asked Bekah to wait for me until moonrise. Weak with hunger, thirst, fatigue, and the loss of blood from a jagged tear on my thigh I did not recall receiving, I stopped in a lone glade that supported a colony of willows and cattails, a sure sign of fresh water. When a pair of ducks flushed from the reeds, I whipped the hood from Lilith's eyes, pointed her in their direction, and sprang upward to lift her into flight. If I could not eat, perhaps she might. Within two-dozen wing beats she had bested her prey, striking one into the other until they both fell end-over-end trailing feathers. I threw my cloak above the pond's edge and loped toward their descent, arriving just as the falcon settled to the ground to hop over to one bird. I dropped to all fours and crawled where the other one, stunned, flopped in the tall grass. A quick twist of the neck and I had dinner in hand. Trusting that Lilith would not go far on a full stomach, I left her plucking breast down, drank deeply from a sandy spot where a spring bubbled, gathered the cloak I had left, and retreated into a thicket for the night. I ate the duck's warm meat raw, savoring the heart and liver, then buried the entrails and bones so scavengers would not be drawn while I slept. For it was sleep I needed most, and the sleep that came to me was like a drug taking me beneath conscious thought, deeper even than dreams, into the untracked realm of fantasy and fearlessness.

Mid-morning sun struck me full in the face and the heat and brightness jerking me upright. The smell of the duck lingered on my fingers. The smell of Bekah's back and tangled hair, the feel of my rough hands on her smooth shoulders, the skin of her neck in my teeth as I slid into her assaulted my drowsy senses. "Love me," I heard her say, pain twisting her voice into a snarl. "Ywain, love me." What had that been between us? Rage, anger, grief, loss, despair, lust. Whatever it had been, it was nothing like the daydreams I had had as a boy about my Lady—nothing that hinted of tentative kisses, longing sighs, the gentle explorative touching that would bring us both satisfaction. Our coupling had been a brutish passion, a honeyed poison. I could feel the after effects of it in my blood urging me to seize her again, throw her to the ground and shove my burgeoning flesh into her again and again until she moaned her pleasure and groaned her pain. Shaking my head with vehement dismissal, I crawled from my haven listening for the sound of anyone or anything that might be a threat, but there was only the melodious greeting of blackbirds calling to each other.

I washed my face and flung water over my hair and shoulders, slung the cloak over my shoulder and whistled two long notes for Lilith. She ghosted from the top of a tree several hundred yards away, settled on my upraised fist and chirped over and over again, turning her head from side to side to make me notice her.

"Lonely, eh? I understand. It was a long night and a long way yet to go. And by the way, thank you for getting me my supper last evening. You are a treasure. How lucky I am to have you travel with me."

THE RIVER

BEKAH

"Girls, it is mother," I whispered, shaking each body with a light touch. "We must go." Pet moved in beside me licking faces and arms. Alanna stirred first, sighing and stretching, rumpling her hair and rubbing sleep from her eyes. She saw the horses saddled and waiting though the sun had barely peeped over the horizon.

"I thought we were meant to wait for Ywain," she said, then added as she lowered her head "with respect, my Lady."

"We must go on alone. He said wait until moonrise. He did not come. That means he has been delayed."

Seeing the unuttered question in Alanna's eyes, I answered for all their sakes, "He is alive. I see him walking. He will find us in time."

"And Keenan, my Lady?"

"He walks with the others we've lost. He came in the night to keep us safe. He will come again whenever we have need. All we need do is reach Lynnmer. Hurry, it is still a long way."

"Mama," Jenna and Morgan said in unison, "I am hungry."

"I know, so are Alanna and I. Even Pet. But we have not time now to hunt or fish. Can you be brave souls as Papa taught you? Are you strong enough and brave enough to swim the river so we can get to Graham and Gwendolyn at Lynnmer?"

"I am," Jenna said.

"I am," Morgan echoed.

"You are not," Jenna said shoving her sister, "You are too little. Papa said you had to eat boar's heart to be strong and you never would."

"I am. I am. I am," Morgan cried.

"Girls. Girls," Alanna said, stepping between them. "We need your help, not your arguing. Be quiet. Go into the bushes to do your morning work, and I will take you to the river to wash. Quick now."

"Thank you," I said. "Forgive my harshness yesterday."

"There is nothing to forgive, my Lady. All is different. None of us knows what we are meant to do, except for you. The Goddess speaks to you and reveals what you need to see so you can help all of us. It is I who needs to ask for forgiveness."

"Well, we might as well forgive one another as I have no forgiveness for those who destroyed our home."

"What will happen to us, my Lady? I cannot even think of Keenan without crying for the way he sacrificed his eyes for us, then his life."

"I do not know, 'Lanna. I only know we cannot go back to what we were."

We wandered upstream for hours before I found a place I thought might be safe to cross. Still, the mulberry-colored water stretched wide and forbidding. Wavelets lapped debris along the banks. I could not see the bottom; I could not judge the distance the horses would have to swim. I only knew that this was the place to cross, and the time to go was now, while the sun was high in the sky and the day was warm enough to dry our clothing once we reached the far side.

"Listen," I said to my daughters as I slipped off my mare and motioned for Alanna to get down as well. I loosened the cinches a little to give our mounts more room to breathe and continued, "Once the horses lose their footing and begin to swim, all you have to do is hold onto their manes. All right? Nothing else. Do not let go, no matter what. Alanna and I must slip off and hold to their tails so they will not have to carry our extra weight. Hold tight. When they reach the other bank, they will leap and clamber to find their footing. That is when you grab the reins and pull them in. Practice now. Say *whoa*."

Their small voices spurted *whoa* in harmony, and the horses flicked their ears back in response.

"Good." I tied the long reins together so when Alanna and I dropped them mid-stream to float behind, they would stay looped around the horses' necks. "No crying, no screaming or hollering. The horses will go better if you are quiet. Ready?"

Neither girl spoke, but each gave a solemn nod as Alanna and I swung up behind them. I gave none of us time to think. I reached around Jenna's sides to gather the reins, jabbed my heels into the mare's flanks, and she splashed into the stream. Aiming her toward a clearing on the opposite shore, I glanced back in time to see Alanna's white face above Morgan's wide eyes. The mare snorted as the river bottom disappeared from beneath her feet. I squeezed Jenna once, said *hold tight* and allowed myself to float free, grabbing first the cantle on the saddle, the strings holding our rolled cloaks, and then the white streaming tail. I allowed myself to drift back to avoid the mare's hind feet. The river's current sucked me downstream as I made a double wrap of tail hairs around both hands.

This must be the way it feels to move from life to death, some unknown power sucking you down, pulling you feet first from the earth into darkness, where the sweet sounds of the world are replaced by an ungodly roar, water grinding against stone, pebbles scraping against sand, the haunting break of water through the gills of the fish, the swaying dance of aquatic plants, the twist and tumble of silt and insects and miniscule debris as the current turns around the face of a boulder, the great sucking noise of being washed away, of forgetting all else except the sensation of wet and cold and the bombardment of sun spots overhead. I heard the hollow thump of the mare's heart as she labored to swim the distance set before her, and I tried to measure the kick of my feet to hers so I would not be a dead dragging weight.

"Rebekah. Rebekah. Your strength fails. Your lungs fill. You must choose. Let go and be released from the fate that awaits you. Or hold tight and live, but face the enemies that lurk in the shadows. One choice is easy: just open your hands. The other is difficult: fear, pain, sorrow, defeat. You know this already. You have known since you were a child playing with your wooden sword as your father taught your brothers how to thrust and slash."

"Who speaks?" I asked.

"I am the source of the stream, the wife of the water god, the eternal giver and taker. With me everything lives, without me everything dies. I am the voice of the river, the wonder of the rock, the arranger of the stars. What is your choice?"

"I am Bekah," I shrieked as the voice disappeared and the stream swept me into a soundless, aphotic place of no sensation.

Ceaseless howling and keening brought me back, a slow rising as I thrashed my way toward the light. I could not raise my arms or open my eyes, but a bilious eruption of water spurted from my mouth as I shouted "Silence." Alanna, chafing my hand, still sobbed. The girls, huddled and shivering with Pet between them, leapt onto my chest. I let them stay, clutched to each other, clutched to my shoulders, and turned my face to the stretch of river we had crossed. The purple-black of the water shone silver with sunshine and reflected back the myriad colors of the grass and leaves and tree trunks and sky. I listened, but heard nothing more than the girls' whimpering, the wind's soothing whisper around us.

"Shhhh," I sighed. "Shhh. We are fine now. Help me up. We need to go."

"We had to pry your hands from the mare's tail, my Lady, after she hauled you over the rocks. You had no breath, no pulse. You were white as death. We thought—"

Then she gulped the rest, but would not let go of my hand.

"I am fine. Let us move from this place. Bring me my horse. Help Jenna and Morgan get on. Tighten the cinches first. We might make Lynnmer by nightfall if we can keep a steady pace."

LYNNMER

BEKAH

The old arrangement of the trails intersecting the track no longer existed. In my mind's eye, I could see the way it used to be when I was a girl, before I had gone south to be Gordan's bride, but nothing was the same any longer. Ten years had altered the face of the landscape in ways that seemed unreal. The day stayed light and sunny. The wind wicked our soiled clothing dry. If nothing else, the river had cleansed us, had given us all a serious dunking and scrubbing. The crossing returned over and over again: What I had seen and heard reared high above me, then crashed down with shattering fury. While the wave of memory built, then broke, the aftereffect spilling in all directions, I had to stop and shudder savagely, like a near-drowned dog trying to rid its coat of water. Stuck somewhere between waking and dreaming, between this world and the other, my mind seethed, a steaming welter of confusion and indecision. The choice I had made stabbed me with uncertainty. Unable to focus on our destination, barely able to stay balanced in the saddle, I said to Alanna, "I cannot trust myself to know. You must take us the rest of the way."

"But I do not know where we are. I have never been this far north," she said. "I do not know where we are going except to your sister at Lynnmer. How am I to know the way?"

"Why do we not ask somebody?" Jenna said. "I know what aunt

Gwendolyn looks like, and I know how Lynnmer appears because you told me, Mama."

The directness of a child. The common sense of a girl. Why did life not allow us to stay in that aura of innocence, that state of simplicity?

"Good idea, sweet one," I said. "You help Alanna. Together you will get us there."

"No one knows us here," I said to Alanna. "Stay on this main track bearing north and east. You are bound to cross paths with someone. Do not mention Gordan or Muirray. If they do not know who we are, they have no reason to harm us."

The sun scalded the skin on my arms and legs and burned the top of my scalp. I melted inward, all my energy collecting in one command: "Hold hard to the saddle horn." I knew if I fell from the horse, Alanna and the girls would never be able to lift me astride again.

"Jenna. Morgan. Mind Alanna. Do as she says without question. You are all I have now."

The words slurred from my lips as pounding blackness overtook my eyes with a humming like a hundred hives of bees. Slumping forward, I ordered my hands to grip tight as Jenna's arms came around me to grasp the reins. Somewhere, a woman began to sing, the rising and falling of her chanted notes soft as spring water purling over mossy stone, soothing as a lullaby, comforting as the sparkle of the first star in the evening sky. Night. Darkness. Sleep. Dreams. Rest. No thoughts. No pain. No tears. No guilt or shame or remorse or sadness. No arguments, or anger, or fear, or uncertainty. No loss. Just silence, slumber, and Ywain's warm arms holding me, the succor of his hand under my breast holding my sore throbbing heart.

"Two days, my Lady," I heard Alanna say. "When she could no longer ride, we waited by the road until the peddler with the cart came and brought us here."

"She talked the whole time," Jenna offered. "But we could not hear what she was saying. The words were all funny."

"She was mad at someone because she was arguing," Morgan added. "They made her cry."

"All right. Let us let her sleep," the woman who had been singing said. "We will all go down to the garden and get something to eat; then all of you will sleep as well."

"Gwen," I tried to say. "Gwennie."

I tried to lift my hand to reach for her, but my mind was not connected to my body, and I could not make it obey. Tears traced a slow pathway toward my ears. Fragrant cloth dabbed my cheeks. Cool lips pressed my forehead. The bed beneath me breathed in a shallow breath and sighed. Then the bees returned, bringing their humming blackness.

TRUSTED SISTER

BEKAH

I wanted to call for you, Gwen, but I am not yet able to talk, so I am speaking to you in the language of thought and waking dream instead. Do you remember when we were girls how we spoke to each other all the time without words? We had a magical childhood, did we not? I wonder if mother knew what would happen to us, the choices we would make, the men we would marry, our lives separated by distance and desire.

I do not know what all this thinking means, and I do not have the strength to try and understand it. Confusion. Resistance. Struggle. You said yesterday when you sat at my side that we had work to do. I acknowledge that; always have. But I have been timid and resistant because this will not be easy work for me, and it will change the direction of my life. I admit to being afraid, terrified even. The task is daunting and I feel incapable of taking it on, as if someone is asking me to carry a load that is way too much weight for me to bear. I have many questions and no answers. Many things to do and no direction. I keep reminding myself I only have to do one small step at a time, and that this work will not be done in a month or a year. I know already that it will take the rest of my life. And, when it is done, I will be free to leave. Part of my fear is that when I walk between the worlds I am uncertain how to find my way back alone. I have had times when I have known that it was my choice to stay beyond the veil and not come back to this time and place. There are many fears, but that one seems the most striking, the most prevalent.

It seems whatever I try to do to get well, the pain returns and keeps me from healing, from living with ease. It is like the old pain I had as a child. I never knew what it was and still do not. I feel like I have been going around in circles, spinning, with no true direction for the path since I came here.

Yesterday, you asked for mother's wizened healer to come help me. She brought with her the fresh cold air of the moors. Invigorating. Refreshing. I remember her. She does not speak. She works only with her hands and eyes. I did not know what our time together would bring. I hoped for some easing of the pain.

She took me back, not very far, but enough to hear voices. At first the sound was distant, a universal humming. "Live the life of the Goddess," they said. "Go now back to the old memories. Search. Find out. Live her life." When I argued I was not strong enough, the voices said nothing else mattered—not missing lovers, not dead husbands, not children, not wars in progress. This was the life I was meant to live. When I argued further, the voice became more imperative and it was no longer a universal voice, the great conscience of people speaking together. It was one voice, her voice. "Live my life. Tell my story. You have been chosen. You have no choice. If you refuse, I will send the pain until you die from it." It was not a cruel voice, but demanding, giving no quarter, allowing no excuse. It kept on and on. It would not stop. Every time I tried to shift my pattern of thought, the voice was there.

She gave Ywain to me. She sent him, his warrior spirit, his skills, and his opening heart, to be my protector. I must learn to trust him implicitly and allow him to take care of me. He will be the one who makes me rest and eat. He will be the guardian at the door when I go to walk the Otherworld, and it will be his voice calling me back, his love that brings me home again. I need not be afraid because he will defend my back and be there to keep evil from me. You, trusted sister, will keep company with me at times; at others, I will need to be alone.

I could not come back easily from the other side. The healer was talking, not through words, but through thought, telling me she had to leave. She told me to stay and rest, take my time getting up because I could not move. I could barely move my lips to speak. All I could croak was that I was fine. I would be all right. She could leave me. I would call for her later if I had need. She told me she was honored to share the Goddess's blessings with me. I thanked her for helping me. She said she would come later to check on me.

When the old woman left, it was a long time before I could move. Even sitting up was a terrible effort. Alanna came in, chatting. I could not chat. I tried to be polite and answer her questions, but I was not present, just barely back from the darkness and trying to ward off the human words. Every sense was heightened to a trembling. I made myself rise and go outside. I drank from the spring and searched in the storeroom for some dried berries and fresh yellow roots. Walking across the inner yard, the sunshine and wind felt like nothing I have ever felt before. I could not see well, but I could see things I have never seen before. Every glimpse was sharp and radiant. Every sound piercing. The noise of Graham with his men and horses was unbearable.

Alanna had followed, ghosting behind with arms outstretched as if to catch me if I fell. I asked her to bring me tea with spice and honey, something hot and sweet. I could not bear to be back inside, so I stayed out and sat on the wall and listened to the music Jenna and Morgan made as they played with your sons. My strength came back gradually. The pain was gone, only an empty hollowness left and shadows where it had been. It was hard to stand, to walk, even to move my eyes. Each raven croak, each dog bark, seemed too much on my ears. Each step demanded an effort. And I was so tired.

All the while the voice of the Goddess kept talking. I tried not to listen. Impossible. Tried to switch my thoughts. Impossible. Simply, she sounded like a harridan and I did not like being badgered. And I do not like where she wants me to go and what she wants me to do. It doesn't seem like much of an honor to be chosen by her. It feels like a curse without any blessing at the end. If there is any goodness to her, it is well hidden from me. I know we are going to argue and fight. But she is going to win the course of my destiny. Surrender is part of my role in all this, and a giving up of power and pride. Sigh. If you are laughing, smiling, I understand.

I made my way back to the beautiful room you had prepared for me, so depleted that I needed to rest. I lit the fire and candles, burned herbs, drank water, closed out the daylight, collapsed on the pallet with fur cloaks to warm me, and, finally, I slept. Some things returned to me, loud and clear. No matter what happens to me, you must promise that you will never allow anyone to touch me or take me away. If something does happen, have Ywain take me to a high place and leave me alone to re-gather my soul. If you ever choose not to be part of this, all you need to do is tell me. At that time it will be clear to me, somehow, whom I am meant to turn to. Ywain is not bound to this either. It is a choice for him, as well. It doesn't seem like a choice for me.

You and Ywain are free to talk about this with me or without me. You will have your own relationship. He may never engage at all. That is permissible. But he needs to know there is someone he can turn to if things become too difficult. I know only that he has been given to me for now, and that he will take care of things.

He seems willing to take this on, but he also needs to know that if he ever wants to be released from this commitment, he is free to go at anytime. The same is true for you. This is a demanding task I ask you to share with me.

This is all I can say now. I am so tired. My ears hurt from listening to her voice. My throat hurts from her trying to speak through me. I have no idea if this makes sense or not. My thoughts are so jumbled. I know I can be honest with you. I do not have to pretend or hide things. But, Gwen, I worry that I am mad. I get goosebumps, then the horrible trembling, and then stark fear. None of that is natural.

I can do no more. I have no strength. But tomorrow I will join Graham and his men and go about the work she has commanded me to do.

GATHERING MEN

YWAIN

I did not mind that Bekah came to me in my dreams, her voice calling, "Ywain. Ywain." It seemed right, with all we had been through together and all we had shared, that she would appear as she had that morning at the spring, her nakedness exuding a sparkling aura of white light as she sang. This nymph, this natural essence rising from the earth and water, seemed as familiar and ordinary to me as the woman I had called "my Lady" for many years.

There had always been an earthy girlishness about Bekah, even after she had had her children and motherhood softened her angles, filled out her curves, and enhanced her breasts and hips. She took childish delight in daily life, exclaiming over a flower, a butterfly, a just-born colt, a different recipe for bread, or a new method of dying fabric. Sweetness and light. That is how I thought of her, felt about her. My days as her personal attendant—the man who saddled her horse, took her hunting, helped her train Lilith, watched over her and the girls as they picked berries or played in the sea—were as pleasant and uncomplicated as anyone might hope life to be. Each dawn I met with Gordan and the other men to train with spear and sword, and when I mastered the skills, I began to teach the younger ones as Gordan and Keenan had taught me. Each night I would meet with Gordan to tell him of the day's events. It was an odd mix: my life with the men and my life with Bekah and the girls. I, alone, seemed to be blessed with the joy of both worlds.

Now I welcomed Bekah coming to me at night in my dreams while I slept. It was the next best thing to possessing her, to having her in my arms. But, truth be told, it alarmed me when I began to hear her voice during the day on my long walk with Lilith to the north. And it was not the kind and appealing voice that I had grown used to over the years. It was the voice of an enraged woman, a harpy, issuing orders, making demands. At first, in my fatigue and semi-delirium, I thought it was Lilith speaking to me—terrifying moment when I believed a bird might utter words, might insist that a man do her bidding. Gooseflesh riddled my skin and a wash of virulent nausea shoved me to my knees to puke in the dirt. Then, I heard her again, Bekah's voice, softer now, pleading: "Ywain, please, listen to me. Do not be afraid. If you take time to be still and listen, you will hear my thoughts across these long miles. I implore you, stop on your way and gather men. Tell them what you saw at Muirray. Tell them about Gordan. Ask them to join us at Lynnmer. Ask them if they are men enough to want to stay the flood of evil descending on us, men enough to want to protect their lands and families. Ask them to come."

No. I did not want to seek out my own kind. I did not want to stop to tell the story of the horror I had seen. I did not want to ask anyone for anything. I wanted only to be alone with my grief, with my belief that if I kept walking I would find my way back to Bekah and the beauty that surrounded her. Still, her voice came to me. She would not stop talking. It became a constant din that made me dizzy and ill. Finally, in a desperate attempt to save my sanity, I simply plopped in the dust in the middle of the trail and said, "All right. I will. I will do what you ask. Now, please, go away." Lilith chirruped, shook her head and flexed her wings before settling herself into slumped posture to sleep. "Fine," I said to the trees. "Fine," I said to a squirrel that had chattered out to the end of a long branch and, hanging by its facile toes, stared at me. "I will do what she asks, if for no other reason than to silence the jabber in my head."

Sitting there, the dust drifting down, sun streams pouring through the trees, my leg aching, my heart breaking, I began to laugh. I laughed because Keenan had died laughing. I laughed because the memory of Bekah and her daughters chasing sea gulls and splashing in the waves made me happy. I laughed because I was fast becoming a lunatic and there was nothing to keep me from being wildly foolish and giddy. I laughed because if I allowed myself to start crying, I would never stop. When I could laugh no more, I stood and resumed walking, talking to myself, preparing what I would say at the first habitation, altering my course to take me back into the lives of other men again.

In every place, I stood in stoic silence until some man came to me and asked what I wanted. Usually, they greeted Lilith first, honoring her with love talk or baby talk, before addressing me. It was true that men would speak to your horse, your dog, your falcon, even your herd of cattle or sheep, before they would speak to you directly. Perhaps it was a way of breaking the strain between strangers. Perhaps it came from the time long ago when we spoke to the animals, and they heard us and answered and we understood. I made a study of the habit and learned a great deal. It gave me something to focus my thoughts on, a reason to look men in the eye without fear or malice. In every place I spoke to one or two souls and asked them to pass the word, to let the news spread. It could not hurt us now that Bekah and the girls were safe at Lynnmer. I knew this because my Lady would not be asking me to do this job if she were in danger or off-track lost in the woods. It was funny about the knowing, how things came to us, seemingly out of nowhere, when in fact it had to be a deeper kind of thinking, of putting things together in their proper place, of discarding things that made no sense. When the men tried to follow me, I said, "No. I am not a leader. I cannot have a throng trailing behind me. Go on your own to Lynnmer. Take your horse. Take your spear, your sword. Take your courage and your resolve and go to Lynnmer. There Rebekah waits to tell us what to do." Many flinched when I mentioned a lady's name, and I was quick to throw Graham's name into the mix so they had to think they were amassing for the greater good through him now that Gordan was gone. Men are an odd lot. They come from woman. They yearn their whole lives to go back to woman. And yet, they struggle with dominance, with being over woman, above her in sense and sensibility, above her in strength and daring, above her in command and control of the world.

"What would happen," I asked Lilith, "if we simply did what we were told to do: what our mothers asked, what our wives asked, what our daughters asked, what our lovers asked, what the divine Goddess asked?"

The falcon screamed and beat her wings, trying to fly, but I held her jesses tight and tried to calm her.

"Ah," I said, "You are trying to tell me we would all be free. You give me a great deal to think about, fierce one, that you do."

The closer I came to Lynnmer, the more animated the people became when I told my story. They had heard of Bekah's arrival with Alanna and the girls. They had heard that Graham was setting up a large camp at the south end of lake in the lee of the great stones that shielded the glen from the harsh sea winds. They had heard that a man and a falcon came as messenger and friend. At every place I was welcomed, asked to rest and eat, so that by the time I saw the glisten of the lake's face surrounded by green fields and rolling hills, I was strong again in body and spirit. My leg had healed. My heart was healing. I had found my purpose, the correct direction, and I accepted that my fate was inexplicably bound to Bekah's. Whatever the Goddess brought to us, we would face it together.

GWENDOLYN

YWAIN

When I noticed a woman standing alone near the gates to Lynnmer, my heart quickened as did my step, for I thought Bekah had come to greet me. But Lilith, unhooded, showed no recognition and the woman did not call out or exhibit any excitement. As I came close, I noticed her resemblance to Bekah, the long curling blond hair, the fine features and full lips worn a bit by age, a bit taller maybe, more stout, but as beautiful, if not more so. She smiled and my breath caught in my chest. An arm's length away from her, I turned aside so Lilith would be behind me, beyond reach, and I offered my free right hand. She clasped with firm determination and exceeding warmth as she said, "You must be Ywain. We have been waiting for you."

"And you, my Lady, do I guess right that you are Bekah's sister, Gwendolyn."

"An easy guess, Ywain, but right you are. Follow me and we will make certain to get you something to eat and something clean to wear."

"With your permission, my Lady, I would like to see Bekah first, despite my appearance. I need to see her to satisfy my knowing that she is here and well."

Gwendolyn paused, staring out across the lake where a gigantic welter of dust rose high into the sky.

"She is there," she said pointing, "but I am afraid you will find her much changed. Be prepared, for the woman you once knew is no more."

Raising her arm, Gwendolyn signaled to a boy working near the blacksmith shop. He ran to her as she said, "Bring the bay gelding that is kept with the white mare," and he turned midstride and raced toward the rock-walled compounds where livestock was kept.

"I am sure you have walked enough miles," she said to me. "Angus will bring your horse for you. Come and have a glass of wine, at least, before you join my sister."

I followed her into the garden where Alanna, Morgan, and Jenna were engaged in a game of rolling wooden balls on the grazed grass. Spotting me, they yelped in unison and flew at me like a trio of witches. Holding Lilith high above the squall, I took their hugs and kisses in turn, patting backs and ruffling hair as I always had. They sprinkled me with questions, but Gwendolyn shooed them away, saying, "You can ask him later. For now he needs rest and refreshment before he goes to find your mother."

"Mama wants to be a fighter," Morgan said.

"Not a fighter, silly, a warrior," Jenna said pulling her hair.

"It is the same thing," Morgan said pulling back her foot to kick her sister.

"Is not," Jenna said swinging her open hand to slap back.

"That is enough, you ruffians," Alanna said. "With your father's blood and your mother's blood, there doesn't seem to be much of a chance for either of you to live in peace, or me either."

"Either way," Morgan said with her hands on her hips, "We do not get to live with her anymore, but she promised she would come visit."

I looked hard at Gwendolyn. She shrugged and gestured me

to a stone bench set in the winnowed shade of some fruit trees. I set Lilith on a perch and tied her, then slipped on her hood, for she had seen enough strange surroundings for one day. We sat in companionable silence until the cups of wine and some fruit and cheese arrived. Gwendolyn said, "Bekah's convinced that the men will follow her into battle and she will avenge Gordan's death as well as win back Muirray. She says she is following the guidance of the Goddess who speaks to her through dreams and visions."

"Stranger things have happened to women who have lost their husbands, their homes, and nearly lost their lives. With time and patience and loving care, I believe she will heal and acquiesce, allow your husband and others to pick up where Gordan left off."

"I think not, Ywain. All my cajoling, all Alanna's pleading, all Graham's haranguing, has led to naught. The worst of it, perhaps, is that the men have taken to her. They hang on every word she says and believe she is directed by divine power. She is a seductress to them, a siren who calls and they come and do her bidding without question. The best of it, perhaps, is that Graham says she has a keen perception of warfare, an eye for terrain and timing, as well as a compassionate understanding of what each man is risking. She is not able to lead because she is strong; she is able to lead because she is loved. Within days this motley gathering of boys and men have come from all corners because they hear of her. Some say she is the incarnation of Boudicca. Some say she is the Goddess herself come to save them and renew their lives. People are hungry for answers. They want to find a way to hold on to their cherished beliefs and traditions. They know that if the enemy keeps gaining territory what we have known and loved will be taken from us."

Gwendolyn stopped speaking as if she had run out of breath. I had dropped my head into my hands to listen and concentrate on what she was saying. I raised my eyes and saw her watching the children playing. Her boys and a group of assorted dogs, including Pet, had joined the fracas.

"What future will they have, Ywain, if we do nothing but wait like sheep for the slaughter?"

"You are way ahead of me, my Lady. I have had no time to think anything through. This past week, or has it been now ten days, I have been consumed only with getting Bekah and her children here to safety."

"Call me Gwen, Ywain. Bekah has told me that you use her familiar name and that you have earned the right. She also told me of your infatuation with her."

Taken by surprise, I drained the cup in my hand and stood to take the reins of my horse from the boy who had been standing and waiting while we talked.

"Alanna tells me you had a wife and infant son?"

"I did. I do. I mean, I did not find them among the dead. Nor my mother. I believe they may be in hiding. As soon as things are settled here, I must go back to search," I said.

"I have no right to interfere," Gwendolyn said, "but I am afraid for you, for all of us, who have fallen under Bekah's spell. If you have not already given her your heart, do not do so. Keep it safe within. Steel it against the power she wields. Bekah is not the only one who has the gift of second sight."

I could not speak of Bekah in that way. Instead, I said, "Will you give Lilith into your falconer's care until Bekah calls for her?"

"Of course," she said coming to hold out her hand again as I mounted. "Ywain, forgive me for speaking with such frankness. Things are changing each minute. The world swirls with uncertainty around us. Our enemies, both Rome and the tribes who have allied with them, are formidable. I love my sister, but

I have reason to fear her as well. I will say no more. She will tell you everything you need to know."

"Thank you for the wine," I said, "and for the chance to sit in your peaceful, lovely company. You have renewed me in body and spirit. I hope I can return the favor at some point."

Gwendolyn threw back her head and laughed, the lofty sweet sound like chimes tinkling in a gentle breeze. When I tried to withdraw my dirty fingers from her translucent white hand, she would not let go. She held tight to me and sought my eyes. When I looked into the tear-swimming midnight blue depths, I saw us clutching one another as we drowned. Nodding my head, I reined the gelding with a sharp jerk, dug my heels into his side and galloped away.

GRAHAM

YWAIN

Reaching the far-flung camp of huts where men and horses tramped in semi-organized confusion, I searched everywhere for Bekah. I had not gone far before a man crossed my path with his sword and asked me what business I had there.

"I am Ywain," I said. "I have come to see Graham."

He nodded his scraggy head and pointed his sword to the slope of a hill where a mock battle was in full swing. Kneeing my gelding forward, I approached with caution so I would not disrupt the activity. Just as I arrived, the melee dispersed and men moved to the side, dismounted, and stood holding their mounts as two warriors continued to strike iron on iron. The aggression of the smaller fighter drew shouts and cheers from the crowd. The larger, older warrior defended himself blow for blow, but did not seem keen on taking control or trying to best his opponent. Whether luck or skill, who could know, the wiry one pushed forward with increasing speed until the old guy stumbled over a discarded scabbard, lost his balance, and fell with a thunderous plunk on his backside. The agile victor leapt over his body, placed a light foot on his chest, and held the point of the sword to his throat. The watchers went wild, whooping and dancing like they were at a clan feast instead of a training session.

Stern-faced and grumbling, the big man accepted the outstretched hand of the nearest contender and wrenched himself upright. "Tough fall, Graham. Next time you will go better," the assistant said.

"There will not be a next time if I have my way," Graham whispered, then he bellowed, "Bekah, take off that damned helmet and come here."

With apparent ease, the victor drew off the helmet to reveal a cascade of blonde hair. The men cheered and chanted, "Bekah, Bekah, Bekah." As yet, I had gone unnoticed, but when my Lady trotted forward to receive her scolding from her burly brother-in-law, she caught sight of me still astride and said, "Step down, Ywain. Come meet the men you will lead." Then she turned to Graham and tried to keep from laughing.

"Oh, you bully, if you hadn't clobbered me in the backside, I never would have come after you," she said.

"You are not meant to be in the middle of this, Bekah. Mock or not, it is not a game, and I refuse to allow you to take advantage of every available situation to show off."

"Stop chastising me. I beat you fair and you know it," she said trying to take his hand in friendship.

"No, you did not. Once I realized who you were, I did nothing but defend myself. If I had fought back as I would have in real life, you would be dead, your guts spilled on the ground, your brown eyes staring vacant at the sky."

Graham's face, red with anger and embarrassment, bulged. Eyes, ears, nose, lips, everything blazed and looked ready to burst.

"Never," she said, "for I would have Ywain at my back and your opportunity for the kill would never come."

She gestured to me with an imperious wave, and I handed my reins to the nearest man and walked over.

"Graham, this is Ywain, Gordan's closest aid next to Keenan

whom you knew. He is my defender, the girls' protector, and the best swordsman and tactician you will ever meet outside yourself."

"Ywain, this is Graham, master of Lynnmer, Gwendolyn's husband, one of Gordan's closest friends, and mine for that matter if he will ever forgive for plopping him in the dirt."

I shook the man's hand, wincing as he crushed my fingers, and bowed my head as I would have done for Gordan. "I am honored." I squeezed back with what I hoped was satisfactory strength.

The men had clustered around Bekah like mud daubers to a puddle. The buzzing drone of their congratulations, their attempts to clap her on the back or receive her handshake, pushed Graham and me to the outside edge of the circle. We retreated to a pile of boulders that had been pulled from the adjoining field. Sitting, he wiped his forehead with his arm, and leaned his sword at his side.

"Do you know this woman?" Graham asked me.

"I cannot say that I do, Sir, at least, I have never known her to fight, nonetheless raise a hand to anyone. Where did she learn to handle a sword that way? Surely not just in the past few days," I said.

"She and Gwen come from a family of seven boys and their father indulged them. He allowed the girls to be part of the daily training, especially Bekah, who was more of a boy than a girl when she was young. Gwen did not take to it much, and though she knows the basic moves, she has not the strength to heft the weight and swing with any accuracy. Bekah surprised me. I had no idea how much she had learned or how much of it she had kept up with. I would not say it in front of the men—it would only encourage her—but she is not bad. It is not so much that she is skilled, for she is not. She is rusty and unfit. But she has the fierce determination that many of the men lack."

"You will not allow her to fight when the time comes," I said.

"Do you think, Ywain, that I have any power to stop her?"

"You control the lands here and in doing so, you control the men. Is that not right?"

"Not quite. I may have some control over their minds—and the biggest part of that is their fear of losing what they have—but I have no control over their hearts. Bekah is using this to her advantage. It seems clear that they would readily go to their deaths for her, but for me they would only die if they had no choice. It is a rare advantage when you take men into battle. Have you been in the field?"

"Not much, Sir. A dozen skirmishes. Two major scrapes. Whether fortunately or unfortunately, depending on perspective, Gordan insisted I be first defense at his home, to care for Bekah and the girls. It is to my eternal shame that I failed him in this, that I was not there to man a counter attack on the troops that destroyed Muirray."

"Will you tell me? I have only heard the gossip and Bekah will not speak of it."

I talked at some length, giving Graham as many details as I could remember, including the things that had been looted, what had been left behind, the number of dead, and how they were killed. Then, because it was something I needed to confess, I said, "If Bekah had not insisted that we return, I would never have gone back. I would have taken her far away, or brought her here, anything to keep her alive and safe. I believed my family dead. I believed her daughters killed or worse. I would have left them to a slow suffocating death without knowing."

"Do not blame yourself for anything, Ywain. It is done. You can only accept what has happened and then go on. We must go on, right? They leave us no choice but to fight back. I have known this for sometime, but had not really wanted to believe the inevitability of it until now. Look at her," he said. "The way she seduces them to do her bidding is sacrilege. Yet I admire her tenaciousness and passion. Our purposes are the same. Perhaps we will find a way to work together and make the best of this."

"Am I simple, confused, or just not informed? Whom do I follow? You, my lord? Or Bekah, the enchantress?" I asked.

"Follow her, Ywain. The others have decided already to do whatever it is she asks. But for your own sake, for mine and Gwen's and the children's as well, answer only to me. Somehow we must find a way to direct her incredible power."

"Your wife believes Bekah hears the Goddess and receives guidance."

"Yes, I know," Graham said, but offered no more.

I could not allow the issue to sit without discussion, so I asked, "What do you believe, Sir? It seems important for my own mind to know what yours is about."

"I both believe it and disbelieve it. I have seen my wife accomplish impossible things, and I know for certain she sees the other side and has saved us more than once from ill will and misfortune. They are sisters. They come to their power through their mother. Do I believe that Bekah hears the voice she says she hears? Of course. But is it the voice of the Goddess, or is it her own voice charged by rage and revenge? Who knows? Wars have been won and lost by men of both persuasions."

We sat in silence, Graham absently scratching his beard and fondling the haft of his sword, while I stared, mouth half open and eyes tearing as Bekah held court. The men, to a one, were struck mute and still, mesmerized not only by her beauty and her bearing, but also by what she was telling them.

"Go," Graham said. "It seems your destiny more than mine. Hear what she has to say. It is amazing how much she knows when it seems on the surface that she has lived so little."

SEA HUT

YWAIN

"Ywain," Bekah sang out as I retrieved my horse, "Come meet these men." The throng that surrounded her parted so I could move forward. She seized my hand and raised my arm upward with hers in a gesture of dominance and victory. The gathering shuffled and sniffed, cleared their throats, looked one to the other, then at us. Bekah waited until they stilled and all eyes were focused on her. The anticipation grew palpable, a sensation that crept out of the earth from the ground at our feet and rose up our legs like a tingling mist. I say "our legs" because I felt the vibration in Bekah, saw her trembling as a leaf that shivers in the evening wind. When the energy reached our waists, she pulled me into a determined embrace, nestling her head on my shoulder. A great *ah* swept through the crowd as if everyone had been holding their breaths, then released them in one perfectly timed exhalation. Upward, upward the feeling of excited bliss rose until our arms quivered around each other and when it reached our throats, she broke from me and threw her arms to the sky in an attitude of prayerful supplication.

"Ywain saved my life," she said so softly I was not sure I heard her and yet the men heard and murmured.

"Ywain rescued my children," she said and their voices hummed.

"Ywain faced the enemy with only Keenan, an old man, by

his side," she said as the muttering began to rise into a low cheer.

"And with Keenan's ingenuity and Ywain's courage, the enemy was turned back and defeated." As Bekah's voice gained in intensity and volume, so did the response of the men.

"With all of you on my right," she said gesturing to the men on one side and then the other, "and all of you on my left, and with Ywain behind me to advise and guard my back, how can we lose? We cannot be defeated because we fight for our lives, our land, our children."

The ensuing roar was unlike anything I had ever heard before. The energy that had engulfed both of us, that had spread to the men, left me as if someone had pulled the plug on a drain. My legs turned to mush and if it had not been for Bekah's hand squeezing a vise-like pain into my upper arm, I would have gone down. The rising and falling chorus beat against my eardrums like the continuous dull but threatening rumble of thunder. I braced myself for the lightning that was certain to come. As I turned to search for the source, I knew I was the mark that would be struck. Bekah's eyes speared mine and I could not look away. Within the storm-brown sea, enormous waves met and crashed, jagged bolts arced silver fire, and I saw us on the shore, naked against the rocks, our bodies drenched with the salt of sweat, the salt of the spray, and I could not tell if the screams I heard were Bekah's or mine or the gulls that whirled above us.

"Tell the men to continue their work with Graham," Bekah said, pulling the stake of her gaze away. I hesitated, then raised my arm for silence. When each voice settled, I said, "Graham is waiting for you to finish what you started."

Choreographed by their need for guidance and instruction, the men turned as one unit and walked from us to where Graham still sat on the rocks.

"Come with me," Bekah said taking me by the hand.
"Where?" I asked.
"To the sea. To the hut I now call home."

And she picked one of many trails that led down from the moor and wound its way through a copse of trees, and found its way to the shore. I retrieved my horse and followed her on foot.

It was not much more than a hut. A round room built of square slabs of stone covered with poles and thatch that had seen recent repair. A central hearth, a pallet, a makeshift table, and one stool graced the interior, which I thought would be dim, but the wide doorway was positioned so the sun stretched its rays inside for most of the day, and, on summer nights, I imagined the starlight and moonlight finding their way inside as well. A rock enclosure on the lee side of the small house provided haven for my horse, and there was a stone cistern filled with water and a pile of just-harvested grass in one corner.

"You knew I was coming," I said as I unsaddled the gelding and turned him loose within the tight but adequate confine.

"Yes, but I was not sure when. You surprised me coming now as you did. Did you meet Gwen and see the children?"

"All of them. And Pet. I left Lilith with your sister's falconer. She's more than frazzled—Lilith, not Gwen," I smiled, "and needs some quiet now and rest."

"Let us walk. Can you walk? Have your legs regained their strength?"

"I will be fine, though the sensation of what happened on the hill is new to me. Frightening in its intensity. Bekah, are you sure of what you are doing?"

"Surer than sure. I know now that this is my destiny. If I do what I am asked to do, then there is no doubt for me, or fear."

"Is that why you are here, secluding yourself, separating yourself from your family, from the comforts you are used to?"

"Ywain, I am not the woman I was."

"I see that. Gwen told me as much as well. She said you had been very ill, that she feared for your life."

"Come, let us walk while it is still warm enough. When the sun fades, the sea breeze is cold and damp."

"Will you tell me what happened? I did not see your journey as you saw mine."

"Yes, my friend," she said, taking my arm as if we were a couple who had long been intimate with each other. "I will tell you everything you want to hear and more."

Far down the beach, when we had revealed all we could of our time apart, we stopped to rest and sit in the sand at the base of a crumbling dune. Bekah did not stay away; she curled into my side the way a dog does and I draped my arm across her shoulders and pulled her closer to me. The independent, stubborn, and commanding woman who had rallied the men was gone and in her place leaned a tired child.

Reading my thoughts, Bekah said, "I am weary, Ywain, yet an energy pulses within that seldom stops even when I sleep. I have no peace."

"Is that why you have chosen to be here, to be alone?"

"That, yes. But, also, I need the quiet so I can hear. If I am surrounded by people, if the children cling to me, if I am distracted by the silly business of when to eat and what to eat and how to settle this argument or how to solve that problem, I cannot think, nonetheless be still enough to listen. Here, all I need do is close my eyes, calm my mind, open my heart, and I slip through the veil. Once there, in the Otherworld, everything is clear and uncomplicated. The Goddess speaks to me and tells me what I am to do. I have to have the sea and sand, my feet bare in the surf, my skin naked to the air, my hair blowing in the wind, then I am where I need to be for her to come to me."

I said nothing. I picked up a stick with my free hand and drew designs in the sand. Simple ones at first, then erasing those, I began with straight lines and swirls and circles and angles to create a complicated maze.

"It looks like the maze in Gwen's garden," Bekah said. "Have you seen it?"

"No, nothing but the bench in the yard, and the children playing on the grass. I have not been to the house yet."

"You will stay with Graham and Gwen and the girls and Alanna. Graham's sons will take to you like an older brother."

"Bekah, I am not staying there with them. I am staying here with you—"

"No," she began, but I kept her from ordering me to do something I would not do by interrupting.

"Yes. Even if I must sleep in the sand, or on the ground at my horse's feet, I am not leaving here tonight."

"All right, then," she said with a resigned sigh, "let us go back and find something to eat. Most days, the boy from the blacksmith shop comes and brings me what I need from the house. Since I was sick, I eat only sparingly; the rest goes to the gulls that have become close friends. There are one or two that will take scraps from my hands."

"Then I will do the same," I said as I helped her rise.

"Ywain?" she asked.

"Yes?"

"Will you always be my friend? Will you promise to stay by my side? Never leave me. I need to know you will never leave me."

The weight of her questions crushed the words of love and steadfastness rushing up from my heart. I pulled her into the circle of my arms and bent my neck to place a brotherly kiss on the top of her head. Her hair smelled of the sea and of some sweet herb that gave off tremendous fragrance when it bloomed in the autumn. I wanted to stay there, warm and content in the late sun, wrapping Bekah in conjured security and imagined bliss.

I said, "How can I make such promises to you when you have chosen a path that will put you in constant lethal danger?"

"You do not have to say anything, Ywain. The beating of your heart against my ear has already told me what I need to know."

We ate. And when the bones of the roasted birds and the crusts of bread and the pits of the dried plums had been offered to the gulls at sunset, I kindled a fire and we stretched before the flames using my cloak as a rug between us and the pounded earth floor. I swallowed the last of the wine in my cup and set it aside. Clasping my hands around my bent knees, I tried to garner the courage to say what I had needed to say all day, but had never found the right moment.

"Bekah?" I asked.

"Yes. I know you must return to Muirray, and you must go soon. I have wondered about your mother too, but I have seen her there walking among the dead with an old woman in rags and a young girl with a child. I am glad she lived."

"When I did not see my mother with the rest who were lost to us, I guessed she and Nola had not yet returned when the enemy came. They had taken the baby to the healer to get something to help him sleep because he cried and fussed without ceasing."

"Nola?" Bekah asked, though it seemed impossible that she did not know.

"My wife," I said measuring those two words with care because they hung in such a delicate balance. "The boy was six days old when Muirray was lost. We call him Wallace."

"Nola's your wife?" Bekah shoved herself away from me to stand in front of the fire with her arms crossed over her breasts. "I did not know she was your wife. Why did not you tell me you had married? Of all things you did not tell me. I do not see why you did not tell me—"

"It was no secret, Bekah. We married quietly just before the boy was born."

"And where was I that I did not know? Ywain, your mother, Maureen, worked with me in the house. She helped Alanna with the girls. And never a word. No one said a thing to me."

"Bekah, please. We did not try to hide anything from you. It was when Morgan was ill, and you were beside yourself caring for her and keeping Jenna away from her. Gordan had not come home. You were occupied with so many things, with your own family. You never said anything to me about it, and I assumed you knew."

"I did not know," she screamed and the horse outside reared, thudded down, then kicked, his hind hooves striking the wall. I heard him trying to run within his small stone cell.

I stood, then reached for the fists clenched at her sides. She struck me, the open blow to the side of my face coming so fast I had no time to move away. The next blow slammed me in the chest, shoving me back several paces.

"Bekah," I said.

"No," she ordered. "Do you think I would have begged you to love me if I had known you were married, that you had a son?

What you must think of me. What do I think of myself?"

"Do not. You did not know. We did not know Gordan would be killed. We did not know that Muirray would be lost. What happened between us was not planned. There was no deception there. You came to me in great pain, full of sorrow and despair. Can we not leave it there? Do not torture yourself as I have already tortured myself. It helps nothing."

"How could you marry her? She is a girl, barely more than a child? She is Keenan's grand-daughter."

"I married her because she was with child."

"Your child?" Bekah said with a condemnation that turned my sympathy to anger.

"Of course my child."

"No doubt of that? No way that the boy you call Wallace was fathered by someone else?" she demanded.

"No, Bekah. Wallace is my son. As you said, Nola is young, she was—"

"And you took her without being married. Without a thought to her need, to her position—"

"Stop it. Stop condemning me. I watched her grow up. We were always together because I stayed with Keenan and his wife. She was drawn to me and I was fond of her—"

"Fond? You were fond of her. So you took her and forced her—"

"I forced no one," I shouted.

"Where? In the stable with the horses? On the ground beneath the trees—"

"No. Damn you, Bekah. She came to my bed of her own accord. She offered herself, and I could not say no—"

"Could not say no. Could not say no. Why could you not say no?"

"Because I could not have you, could I?" I slammed my fist onto the table.

Pottery clattered to the floor. Regretting the words as soon as

I had screamed them, I kicked the stool and turned to grab my cloak from the floor. Bekah's feet were planted on the hem. I tugged once, then seeing her tear-streaked face set with horrible sorrow, I jerked the garment with all my strength so I could leave.

She lurched forward, a violent stumble that threw her toward me, and I caught her with one arm before she fell. One moment she was kicking and hitting me, the next she was kissing my face and neck, clutching the front of my shirt, saying, "Do not leave. Ywain, do not leave. Please do not leave. Stay. Please stay. Please, Ywain. I have no one else. I have only you. Stay. Stay."

Taking my cloak, she spread it once more on the floor. She put more peat on the fire. Then she opened her arms to me, kneeling, her face raised in supplication.

"Come to me," she said. "Love me. Tomorrow we will go together to get your mother, your wife and your son. We will bring them here where they will be safe and loved. I will help you care for them as I care for my own. But for now, Ywain, please Ywain, come to me. Not out of sorrow, or pity, or anguish, but because I need for you to love me. Because I need to love you."

She took off her heavier dress, and the thinness of her shift beneath shone with the flickering light of the fire. Her small breasts, nipples poking outward, strained the fabric. A heavy musk filled the small space and I knew the scent from before, the smell of Bekah's want, of her desire. But nothing in me stirred. I stood as a condemned man stands, with my head down, my arms hanging, my legs trembling. This time I knew I had a choice, there was no doubt in my mind, no confusion. Plain as the searing moonlight that streamed in the open door, I knew I could turn, get on my horse, and ride away. Or I could kneel and embrace the arms reaching for me, bury my face between the legs that would open for me. Either choice meant death, perhaps one sooner, one later, but with either the same ending waited for me. And so, like the doomed man who knows his fate, who relishes his final meal and savors the last things he will see and hear, I removed my shirt and knelt before her.

"I am yours," I said. "Do with me what you will."

IRRESISTIBLE ALLURE

BEKAH

There were those who would say I seduced and manipulated, that I conjured and created magic, that I was connected to the forces of evil and ill. I would say that I knew we did not have the rest of our lives, but we did have the rest of that night. Ywain came as victim to a sacrifice, and I wanted more than that for him, for myself. I wanted what all women want from men, and what all men want from women: to be desired, to be fulfilled, to be satisfied and to feel the beauty of coupling with all the force and power and majesty as when the first woman took the first man inside her to create new life. I had known no other man than my husband, and Gordan had treated me with great deference and respect. Although he was a huge bear of a man, all rough around the edges and clumsy even in his daily maneuvers, he had been tender and smooth when he made love to me. I had known pleasure from his hands and lips, from his manhood deep inside. I had blossomed with his seed and his children and cherished that part of my life. But I had never known the tumultuous cataclysm that love making could be until I ordered Ywain to take me in the circle of stones. I had never known I had such great passion or terrible suffering until he released it. Was he a better man than my husband? Far from it, but he was a different man, someone who knew the part of me I scarcely knew myself. I ordered him to take me in agony, and I released the part of myself that was destined to lead men, to forge a presence as one who would not be defeated. I knew death lay close at hand. I knew I wanted first, if possible, to protect my children and those I loved. But from there, it was only a blind, if directed, call to do what had to be done. The Goddess walked with me when I was alone. She spoke to me in the night and sometimes during waking vision when the world was quiet and still. I had learned how to walk between the worlds, and if I was not yet graceful, I was at least no longer afraid. In the stillness that followed Ywain's succumbing to my request, I heard the fire crackling, his labored breathing sounding as if he had an enormous weight on his chest, and night sounds floating in from the door and roof opening. I placed my palm against Ywain's heart and I asked the Goddess what to do. She answered me and I followed her instructions.

I undressed him and folded his trousers and set his boots to the side. Then, beginning at his feet, I kissed every inch of his skin, allowing my lips to linger each time, to taste the salt and sweat of him, to absorb his flesh into my mouth and nose. I kissed upward until I reached his loins, but he did not rise. His manhood lay limp and unresponsive, as soft and warm as a small bird cowering in a nest of dark hair. I kissed this too, not the kiss of demanding need, but the kiss of tender affection and acceptance. I kissed his gaunt belly and his sunken navel. I kissed his poking ribs and muscled chest. I kissed each finger, wrist, elbow, and armpit. I kissed his neck and throat, chin and cheeks and forehead. And, finally, I kissed his lips. I kissed him until he moaned. I kissed him until his legs moved of their own accord, and his leaden arms lightened and came around me.

When kissing him had ignited my own fires until I could not breathe, I rose on my knees and offered my breast to his lips.

Greedy as a child, he took the nipple and sucked, playing with its tautness, making the small sounds a baby makes, the expression of happiness, of satiation. When I could take the pleasure no more, when sunbursts broke behind my eyelids and my thighs jerked, I offered him the other breast. And when the inner explosion came again, louder and fiercer, I could not still the quivering in my limbs, or remain on hands and knees, so Ywain took me by the shoulders and eased me down to kiss me. From the crown of my head to the bottom of my feet, he kissed me while his fingers twirled my nipples and my hips squirmed, grinding his bunched up cloak beneath me into the earth. When I felt I could take no more, when I cried out and tried to rise, he eased me down again, and holding my breasts with his hands, he moved between my legs, pushing them open little by little with his knees. The pounding in my womb beat in my ears as well. The thick wetness seeping from me increased as Ywain nuzzled me with his bearded chin and broad lips. And then his tongue sought me and he slipped a finger inside of me, reaching in and up, sliding, moving, searching until he found the spot that mixes pleasure and pain in equal portions.

How many times did I cry out, my legs raking the air, my arms flailing? How many times did he soothe and hush me by saying, "Catch your breath and we will do it again?" How many times did I beg him to put himself inside of me and ease my aching? "Not yet," he said. "Not until I can take you no further."

There came a point when the animal sounds escaping my throat terrified me—the howling growls and whimpers, the snarling cries that bordered on singing, the long floating scream that reminded me of Lilith when she stretched her wings to fly.

"No more, Ywain," I said. "Please. No more. I am dying. If you push me over the edge once more, I will not return."

Yet still he fondled and sucked, pushed and tweaked, prodding my thighs and breasts, even my face, with his erectness until every ounce of energy I had was spent, until I could not move, not even to lift my hand to touch his face, until I was limp and drenched and shaking beneath him.

He hovered over me, the sparrow hawk above its prey, and nudged and nudged and nudged until he found my weeping opening and eased himself inside. His moan was that of a man come home again after months at war, a guttural sigh of deep contentment, of unbearable pleasure. I began to move with him, rocking together, falling apart, seeking the flesh, shying away, and our movement became the rhythmic breaking of the waves outside, our bodies glistening with firelight just as the water glistened with moonlight. The swells building and building, each one larger than the last, until, finally, the unimaginable shattering against the rocks, both of us lying beaten and broken in each other's arms, both of us sobbing because we had survived.

And above the roaring in my ears, the raucous hammering of my heart, I heard the Goddess's voice say, "That is how loving was intended to be."

TWIN SWORDS

YWAIN

The tickle of sharp iron at my throat woke me. Cold iron. Cold earth floor beneath my shivering body. Cold limbs that would not move. Cold fear lodged in the back of my skull that whispered to the cold weight of worry thudding in my chest. The warmth of Bekah's body was absent, as was the animal musk of her desire, the flood of incessant heat between us, the slippery wetness of the dreams that had soothed me after our tempestuous loving. The insistent blade turned tickle into poke. I forced my eyes to open a slit, enough to allow pearly light to reveal bare toes gripping the ground, trim ankles, thin calves, surprisingly lovely knees, fine thighs, and the hem of my shirt.

"Rise wretched wanderer," Bekah said, jabbing the sword at my shoulder. "Rise and defend yourself."

The smile that itched at my lips, the thought this was some delightful, inventive love play, disappeared when I took in her determined stance, the hard grip she had on the haft, the unyielding penetration of her stare, the wild snarls of her wet hair.

"The sun slips from the sea. I have already run the shore, swam the demanding waves, and said my morning prayers, and still you sleep. Get up." She incised a scratch below my collarbone.

The seep and smell of blood jolted me to my knees as Bekah threw me a sword that was twin to the one in her right hand. A clumsy toss, an awkward catch with my right hand and a bumbling backwards stumble to get my legs under me as I jostled the steel into my left hand to find a grip and test the weight. The cold stone of the fireplace stopped my retreat. The cold ashes on the hearth puffed beneath my feet. Behind Bekah, sun shoved through the open door and window, illuminating the room as if it were lit with countless candles. Nothing but a black silhouette, Bekah slashed, then jabbed, catching the flesh on the side of my naked hip. The sharp pain thrust my numb legs into action. I leapt forward, startling Bekah into backing up. I grabbed the cloak wadded at her feet and flung it to the ceiling. The billowing cloth and shower of dust gave me the distraction I needed to sprint to the door. If I had to fight, I wanted air and light and no obstacles to trap my back. I managed three leaping strides before I whirled to meet the fury that burst from the hut behind me. I had never raised a weapon against a woman and I tried not to think of Bekah as the lady I loved, her lips kissing me, her fingers teasing me into pleasured spasms. Still, lustful thoughts pulsed blood into my groin and I stiffened as I attempted to hold a piece of ground, fending off blow after blow as I struggled to judge her mind, her ability to injure, her capacity to kill.

"Fight back, Ywain, or I will cut that off and feed it to the gulls. I have no need for a gutless champion or a fearful lover. Fight or die, for I will make you prove you are worthy."

I parried three more slashes and gulped breaths already burning my lungs as the sun seared my back and rump. Crazy or creative I knew not, but serious determination flashed in Bekah's eyes. Not anger or upset or vengeance, just a keenly focused resolve that had me pinned like a fish on the end of a spear. I wiggled free, ran a half-dozen paces, turned and set my stance. This time, when her sword plowed into mine, I was ready to meet her and took the jarring clash and swept it to the side, throwing her off-balance as I kicked her grounded leg out from under her. Bekah fell and rolled, then bounced to her feet, but she had no time to steady herself before my blade smashed sideways in a great glowing arc that caught the sunlight and tore the weapon from her hand. The sword spiraled through the air and landed with a giant splash at the edge of the aggressive waves. I gave her no quarter, not one second to recover or retreat. If she had been a man, I would have run her through. Instead, I whipped my free hand backward, caught her on the jaw and knocked her to the ground. Jamming my foot into her chest, I rammed the sword into the loose sand on the side of her head, severing a substantial hank of hair. Her eyes never wavered from mine. Her breasts heaved beneath the sweat-stained shirt, but she did not move or struggle.

"If you had been the enemy," I said, "your blood would be staining the sea."

"If you had been a true friend," she said gasping, "you would have finished me, sealed my fate, and freed yourself."

"I will never be free of you. If you do not know that by now, your ignorance amazes me."

"Our winds blow a ferocious storm, Ywain. There is no good end to this. There is a part of me that wishes you gone, out of my life, away from my heart, so I would not have to struggle with the work we must do."

"Then you will have to do more than browbeat me or castrate me, as you threatened. You will have to kill me to force me from your side."

"I could have killed you as you slept." She arched her back to rise.

I shoved her to the sand again and with one foot pressed the full weight of my body onto her lungs. The air shushed out until her mouth gaped and eyes bulged, her arms going limp at her sides.

"Is there any reason why we cannot be allies? Are you determined to raise my wrath to the point where hate overcomes the love I bear for you? If we are fated for ill, is there nothing we can do to change the course of destiny? I am more than the slavish boy who has worshipped at your feet for years, Bekah. I am a man in my own right, with a wife and a son. Push me too far and I will not take responsibility for the consequences."

I eased my foot and allowed her to pull in enough air to speak. She did not. She took one hesitant breath, then another. The short small gasps rushed color into her fish-belly face. Still she said nothing. Nor did she move. Her eyes left mine and drifted upward. She gazed at the solemn movement of a cloud across the sun. Except for the rhythmic sigh and slap of the waves and the far-off keening of the gulls, the world went silent. We fell into shadow and my bare skin prickled with gooseflesh. Then Bekah closed her eyes.

With a gentleness that belied my last words, I moved my foot from her chest and pulled the sword from the sand to stand to the side in quiet obeisance. Time sighed by. A great weariness washed over me, pulling my eyes shut. In my mind I saw Bekah at the bottom of the stairs at Muirray. Her dress and cloak were soaked, and she shivered. The passage up was dark and cold. She did not want to climb to her tower chamber. She did not want to see what was there, though a gold light streamed in the high window where a white bird waited perched on the sill. I saw myself trying to return from some faraway place. I could see the burned out hulk of Muirray and the tall cliffs and the sea beating on the rocky shore. I heard a voice say "There is birth there, and there is death. Go see." But Bekah did not move. Deep inside the yellow light there shone an odd gold cross. The bird waited, but when

Bekah did not ascend, it raised its soft wings and flew, luminescence trailing from feet and feathers.

Only a great force of will made me open my eyes. A heaviness likened to drugged sleep seeped from my pores, and I fought the urge to collapse into the sand. Bekah stirred, pulled her knees up, then raised her head. I reached to help but she turned away, rose on her own, then walked with upright grace to her sword half-buried in a rinse of water-borne sand. She bent at the waist, and my shirt rose above her rounded rump. Lifting the weapon, she rinsed it as one would a newborn babe, then carrying it tenderly, she walked to the hut and disappeared through the dim doorway.

Though I was not close enough to hear her speak, I heard her thoughts: "If you have seen what I have seen, Ywain, then you already know what waits for us. You know that you have no choice but to fight with me. If death waits for me, as surely it does, then at least help me strengthen the skills I will need to die swinging a sword instead of cowering in the heath like a chick beneath the hawk's shadow."

No choice. No choice. No choice. The words knocked against my brain with the same slow drumming of my heart. The severed strand of Bekah's translucent hair lay drying in the sun like a snake's skin. Picking it up, I coiled it round and round my forefinger. As I approached the hut, Bekah stepped out fully clothed. She threw me my shirt and said, "Get dressed. Saddle your horse. We will meet with Graham to tell him our plans and then we ride to Muirray. The sword is yours to keep. It belonged to my father."

She strode up the hill, her weapon sheathed and swinging at her side, her tangled hair wound round her head like a haphazard wreath. The flock of gulls that had cried down the shore appeared en mass to circle her, diving and calling, rising and falling. It seemed they were determined to swoop in and carry her off, but she raised her left arm, fist clenched, and they swarmed up, lifting toward the highest cliffs, their voices retreating. A hare burst from the brush in front of Bekah, and she stopped, studied its erratic movements, then followed it.

Chagrined and ashamed, I stood like a boy unable to recite the lesson his mother had just taught him. Tears gushed down my cheeks and snot exploded from my nose. I granted myself those naked moments of frightful grief, then, when I was certain Bekah was beyond hearing me over the sound of the sea, I let loose of the pain within, a high-pitched shriek that did not cease until my throat ripped itself raw.

Leaning the sword against the low stonewall where my startled horse stood splay-legged, I draped the still wet shirt in the sun, shuffled down to the water and dove into the icy spray. The salt stung my wounds and burned my eyes. I rose for air and a rogue wave whacked me back under. Swimming beneath the furor, I went as far as my leaden arms would let me; then I turned and permitted the sea to roll me toward shore, each swell lifting and carrying me, an enchanted lightness of being. When I emerged, plodding against the undertow that tried to suck me back, I was washed clean, changed in some significant way I did not understand.

I took time to let the sun and wind towel me dry before I dressed. Then I picked the burrs from my horse's mane and tail, finger-combing the hairs until they gleamed in the daylight. Saddling with meticulous care, I mounted, rode over to the sword, hefted it, placed it across my legs, and accepted the fact that I was inextricably bound in the beautiful snare of Bekah's life. Like every man before me and every man to come, I would choose moment by moment, day by day, what and whom I would become. Over the hill, in the still peaceful setting of Lynnmer, Bekah and

Graham and Gwendolyn plotted our course. I held the sword of a man who had died of old age, yet I knew its presence in my hand would not afford me the same fate. Smacking the gelding's haunch with the flat of the blade, I galloped to meet what was mine alone to claim.

THE MAZE

BEKAH

"You look worn but radiant, Bekah. Did you sleep well? How are you feeling this morning?" Gwendolyn asked as she brushed my hair.

We sat in the center of the garden where a dozen paths through tall thick shrubs converged into a circle, a location where a spring burst from an underground source and sang against moss-covered rocks before it disappeared again. It was a place we had loved as children, the spot where we came to tell secrets, practice magic, and confess our dreams. Our mother had designed the labyrinth for her own solace and worship, but once we discovered the spot, she rarely had the sanctuary to herself. Gwendolyn perched on a stone bench, and I, cross-legged on the ground, leaned back between her knees.

"I am fine," I said. "Light. Transcendent. Liberated. I do not know how to find the right words."

Gwendolyn laughed. "Those sound like the right words to me. You smell of roses, incense and sweat. You taste of salt, fire and smoke. I hear the sea, bells, breathing and chanting. I see you held close, being carried. I feel an exquisite vibration."

Joining in our favorite girlhood game, I responded, "You have found the memory hidden behind the upper left side of my eye, the nagging smoke-like tendril that tickles my spirit. Playful, joyous, it keeps me searching because in my heart I know there is more to come. A powerful presence."

"I know it too. It is a deep and true connection. One where you think a thought and the other will taste your words before you speak. This is the one who stokes the fire in your belly," Gwendolyn said, separating my hair into three sections and pulling each taut as she began a braid at the nape of my neck.

"In the future, he will carry me close through dark woods into light. Into transcendence, purity, truth. I have to be patient. Have faith. Believe and trust."

"Odd that you said 'he,' Bekah, instead of 'she,' Gwendolyn said. "Surely you mean the Goddess."

"No, Gwen. I see him covered in blood and tears. I will give my life to save him."

"Do you know who it is?" Gwendolyn asked as she twisted a thin strip of leather around the ends of the hair to bind them together.

"Yes," I said.

Birds flitted from sunlight to shadow, playing hide and seek in the trees' upper branches. One called, chirping forth, then the notes faded just before another one answered. A black-capped chickadee lit to sip at the bubbling water, her tiny head serious as she dipped her beak, then tilted back to allow the water to run down her throat.

"You are not going to tell me, are you?" Gwendolyn patted my shoulder to signal that she had finished.

I stood and stretched. The chickadee popped off the rock and flew to my raised hand, turned circles on my palm, cocking its head, and looking at me with a canted, questioning eye before flying away.

"How did you do that?" Gwendolyn asked.

"It is not hard. They think I have something to eat and they come to see."

"More than that, Bekah. You call them. The birds and gulls. The hares and squirrels. The deer. Even the falcons and hawks. It is a part of Mother's power you inherited but I did not."

"I do not think it is power as much as communication," I said twisting at the waist to loosen my spine.

"It is the same thing, is it not? If you call and they come. If you ask and they do what you bid. It is the same with the men. There is not a thing they would not do for you. Graham has told me how you hold them in your sway."

"Gwennie, it is not because of me, or for me. It is not even about me. It is about what they must do to save the world they love. You know this. Do you not fear for yourself, for Graham, for your sons, for Lynnmer? It could easily be taken as Muirray was taken."

"I do have fears, but I also trust that what will be will be. That my power lies in prayer, in supplication, not in control, not in manipulation," Gwendolyn said.

"That was cruel. I control no one. Least of all myself."

"Not true. You control an army of men. You control Ywain."

"They are free to come and go at anytime. There are no rules regulating if they stay or leave. There is no punishment for them if they choose to go home to their families."

"And Ywain?"

"I will not speak of him."

"Yes you will. I already know he is the one you see, the one who carries you through the dark wood. You have taken hold of his heart with such a grip that he will never be free from the fate you have chosen for him."

"That is unfair. He is a grown man. He may choose for himself. If he decided to leave, I would not try to stop him."

"Why would he leave? You have seduced him and taken him until he knows no other sound than your voice, no other sensation than the feel of your skin. He lives and breathes for you, because of you. If that is not power, what is?"

"This is none of your business, Gwen. If we are together, it has no effect on you or yours. If anything, we will both serve to protect what you have."

"You are going against what is right. You have taken away his will, his personal power to make good choices for himself."

"I took nothing from him." I leaned over the spring to splash water on my burning face.

"You took his moral compass. He knows nothing else but to follow you."

"That is going too far. Gordan is dead. That tie is severed for me. There is no right or wrong here. Only what must be."

"Bekah," Gwendolyn said, "you know he has a wife and son."

"Of course I know. That is why we are returning to Muirray to find them and bring them here. Do you think I am so cold and uncaring that I would leave them to starve or be killed?"

"No, I think you have the most beautiful heart and you mean to do right by everyone. But you are on the wrong path. You cannot do what is good by taking control. Leave that to Graham. Let him take a small group to Muirray and bring back Maureen and Nola and Wallace. He has the skill and know-how to bring everyone to safety."

"And I do not. That is what you are saying, is it not? That I am only a woman and therefore could not possibly know what is right for my people?"

"Bekah, do not be angry. I am only trying to help you see clearly."

"No, you are wrong. What you are helping me see is that you are jealous. That if I control Ywain, then I can also control Graham. That the power I have to lead and persuade is power that you want for yourself. If you want this so much, then take it. Take Ywain. Take the men. "Here," I said, unsheathing the sword at my side and tossing it at the hands she clasped on her lap, "take Father's sword and do what must be done."

Gwendolyn grabbed for the weapon, but missed the haft and caught the blade. Blood bloomed from her hand.

"See," I said, "you do not even have the skill to hold the sword. You were meant for prayer. I am bent for revenge, but only to keep what is rightfully ours. Why can you not understand that?"

Laying the weapon aside, I put Gwendolyn's cut palm between my own. Heat poured up from the earth, coursing through my legs and torso and spilled through my arms into my hands. I closed my eyes to silently invoke the healing words I had learned from my mother. When the hot pulsing dimmed to warm sensation, I opened my hands and Gwen's cut was closed. Leading her to the spring, I made her kneel so I could wash the wound. The clotted blood rinsed away leaving only a puckered white line surrounded by red.

Color flushed back into Gwen's cheeks, and I helped her stand. I held her palm to my lips, and leaned over and kissed her. "I am sorry," I said. "Forgive me."

"How long have you had the ability to heal? You never told me."

"I did not know until this moment. Never thought to try before. Do not make too much of this, Gwennie. Things are coming to us that I have no power to stop. There will be many things that happen that I will not be able to heal, things much worse than a scratch on the hand."

"I am so afraid for you, Bekah." Gwen pressed her face to my breasts.

"Do not fear for me, white-browed beauty. Fear for yourself and your sons," I said.

Even as I spoke the words, I did not know what I meant. With a last kiss, I pushed her from me, picked up the sword and rinsed it in the clear water. Choosing one of the many confusing pathways, I made my way out of the sacred circle and into the world where Ywain would be waiting with the saddled horses and packed provisions.

LEAVING LYNNMER

YWAIN

Graham and I stood side by side, his massive bulk shielding me from the wind that had been growing stronger since dawn. The solitary cloud Bekah and I watched from the seashore had multiplied into dark gray formations that shimmered with gilt edges. Hidden but still blazing, the sun had nearly met its highest mark. If we were meant to go, I was anxious to leave, though I suffered a foreboding as black as the sky foreshadowing the storm.

"You should be able to stay ahead of the rain," Graham said, toying with the brooch on his cloak. "Stay off the main road. Even this far north, it will be better if no one knows you are about with Bekah. If you go back around the lake and down beyond hut to the south, you will find a cleft in the cliff face. It is a narrow, low opening and you will have to walk the horses through. Maybe a quarter-mile or so. When the tide is high, it floods. But you should be all right this time of day. Where is that woman anyway? I wish I could talk some sense into her. It would be much better if I went with you."

He fussed with the mane on Bekah's mare, trying to make all the hair fall the same direction. "Anyway," he said, "if there is water in the cut, do not enter. There is no way out except to go on. You cannot turn around. Ah, here she comes."

We watched Bekah make her way across the yard. She stopped

to speak with her daughters, Graham's sons, and Alanna. Gwendolyn appeared from one of the maze's many openings and stood a moment, her head bowed. I raised my hand in greeting, but she turned and walked toward the main dwelling. Earlier I had played with the children, tossing small stones to see which would make the mark of a bronze pot. We had laughed together and I had spun each in turn by holding them under their arms and whirling around and around. The girls had giggled and kicked until they collapsed in silly, dizzy ecstasy. The boys had been stoic, but their sparkling eyes and toothless grins belied their manly attempt not to have fun. When I said good-bye, the girls squealed and clung to me like barnacles. Alanna pried them from my legs. Now, they stood clinging to her, one on each side, the boys hiding behind them. The woman who towered before them wearing a sword, with blood on her dress and furor in her eyes, was no one they knew even if she tried to talk to them as their mother once had. When Bekah knelt and opened her arms, they refused to move. Alanna bent down and spoke to each; with reluctance they edged forward holding hands to meet their mother's embrace. They endured a quick clutching before racing back, tripping over each other, shouting in unison, "Me first, me first." The boys joined the headlong race to the house. Wringing her hands, Alanna watched them over her shoulder. When they had reached the safety of Gwendolyn's skirt, she turned back to Bekah, walked forward and knelt. Bekah touched the top of Alanna's head, lifted her to her feet and hugged her. A whimpering cry sounded from the flowered bushes and Pet emerged, crawling on his belly. Bekah moved to him, allowed her hands and face to be licked, stroked his fine head and patted his hips before she gave him the sign to stay. Leaving those she loved, she stalked toward us looking seven feet tall.

"You have your hands full, Ywain," Graham said.

"That I do, Sir," I said.

"Your knowledge is going to clash with her insight. I see a battle between the two of you that would frighten the hair off of any man. I still wish I were going with you," he said.

"It will not be easy," I said, then added, "but it will never be dull."

"It is good you have a sense of humor. You are going to need it. If you stay the trail the cleft leads you to, it will take you back to the river with the sea within hearing. Wait until the tide goes out, then you will be able to cross without complication. Look for three small cairns. They are hard to spot this time of year with the leaves fallen, but once you see them you will know for certain. They form a triangle of equal distance. That is the path that will take you back to Muirray. Much slower, and water will be harder to find, but safer. I doubt you will meet anyone going that route. I worry that Bekah will be more a hindrance to you than help. Can you not change her mind?"

"Do not underestimate her, Graham. Where she lacks strength, she has shrewdness, where she lacks skill she has determination, where she lacks common sense she has second sight. If I were not her friend, I would fear her. There is a merciless core to her heart."

"Are you so certain you are her friend?" Graham asked.

"If I am not," I said vaulting onto my gelding, "who is?"

Graham did not reply. He waited for Bekah by the mare, then cupped his hands to help her mount. She looked at me, her eyes weighted with tears. She looked at Graham, then leaning, touched his shoulder and kissed his bearded cheek.

"Take care of things here, Graham. Ready the men. We will return soon."

"Go well, both of you," he said. "When you come back, we will decide how much we can do before winter sets in."

I raised my hand in a wan salute and wheeled my horse to catch Bekah's loping mare.

THE CLEFT

YWAIN

The storm pushed us as we rode south into sunlight, all the brighter for the contrast with the formidable clouds. Bekah urged her mount, jabbing her forward into a lope whenever she slacked off to a trot. My horse flung his head, foam slipping from the bit as he fought to race ahead. I held him back, letting Bekah choose the way, crisscrossing the fields, wending through the trees, plowing through the sand. She pulled up hard at the cave-like slit, let her eyes adjust to the dimness within, then whipped her mare into the spooky maw that roared with the underbelly echo of the sea. I battled my gelding's fear at the opening, whirling with him until he knew he had no choice but to follow the mirage of the white rump now gone from view. Sand squished beneath his hooves, and the wet glimmer of water brightened the ground.

"Bekah," I shouted because I could not see her. "Stop. Graham said not to enter if the tide was high. Stop now while you can still back out."

Her voice came to me as if she spoke from the bowels of the rock. "Come on. We can make it. It is not that far. I used to play here, even swimming through the tunnel. Hurry."

Water splashed around the gelding's ankles as I goaded him. There was no way to hurry. The loose sand, many inches deep, sucked at his feet. He bent his neck to the task, sides heaving. I leaned forward to pat his chest to encourage him, and my hand came back soaked with cold sweat. Bekah had vanished. I could see nothing but sheer, sea-smoothed walls, the heavy ceiling pressing down, the glistening water rising. I strained to hear Bekah's mare or her voice calling to me, but there was only the *huh-huhhing* of the horse, the shushing of blood rushing in my veins. We plowed forward, every step like the slow motion of a dream. The sea lapped at his knees, then soaked my boots. The roof pressed against my head, shoving me lower and lower until I flattened myself alongside the gelding's neck. Why hadn't I heeded Graham's warning to dismount and walk?

The walls tore at my bent legs, and I searched for a spot wide enough to get off, then realized that the gelding was being buoyed by the deepening water, his feet only finding purchase every few strides. It would be senseless to try and lead him now. Instead, with the rock scraping my back, I slipped off behind, grasping for the sides of the saddle, for his floating tail. Stretching my neck far back, I pulled in frantic gasps while trying to speak easy to calm the floundering horse.

The open space above us shrank, then was gone. We went under, all motion ceasing, a precursor to the dream of drowning. Shoving against the weight of the water, I jammed my fist over and over into the wide haunch in front of me, holding my breath until blackness sneaked into the corners of my closed eyes.

With a sudden strangled explosion, we burst to the surface, the gelding uttering a terrified snort as sunshine bobbed into the exit ahead of us. I tightened my grip on his tail as he plunged against the waves rushing into the tunnel. Then we were free, both of us clambering into a roil of sand and surf, beating our way uphill where Bekah, fist jammed into her mouth, slumped next to her mare's hanging head.

"Are you determined to have a corpse on your hands?" I slurred as I dropped at her feet. My horse fell as well. His legs buckled beneath him, and he crashed onto the rocks, jerking, his eyes rolling back into his skull. Bekah knelt and cradled the heavy head in her lap. Rubbing his temple, she murmured the same word over and over in his twitching ear. He calmed, his body growing still bit by bit. Just as I was certain that he had breathed his last and Bekah's incantation was a death prayer, he grumbled out a gigantic breath, bolted to his feet, and shook himself with vehemence. Then, stumbling through the jumble of cobblestone to a patch of grass, he ripped and chomped the salt-graced blades. Exhausted, the mare limped after him.

"Now this." I coerced myself to sit up. "Magic to bring back the dead."

"Nonsense," Bekah said, scooting over to slump beside me. "All I did was tell him not to die, that we needed him, then I sang him the song of the Goddess."

"Which is?" I asked.

"Ywain, did it happen to you too inside the cleft? Everything went empty for me except for this beach at the other end. The sea, the cold sea, the sound of water, of the waves smashing against the rocks, those crashing heavy sounds, and the roar, like the roar you feel when you are drowning, when all else disappears except yourself and the sea. I could smell the scent of many flowers, or perhaps it was ripe fruit and the tang of the sea salt, that smell that makes your nose tingle, like heady wine, sharp and pungent, but utterly pleasant. I smelled the white musk of bodies melting together, and in my mouth I could taste a smoky flavor, rich and deep, like cured meat, and then a very heavy, dense tang mixed with a sweet darkness, like fermented berries, a good, positive, and totally sensual sensation. I felt a light vibration, a tingle, like the sense I am certain Lilith has when she lifts off to fly, soaring away from the earth, away from the body, in perfect tune, a harmonious humming, the sense of well-being and total fulfillment. Did you feel that too?"

"Where do you find strength to think like that, nonetheless talk? No, sorry to say, I felt none of that. I felt only a smashing, silent abyss. Nothing more."

"Will you let me hold you, comfort you?" she asked.

"Bekah," I said.

"No, you do not need to warn me away. This is not about loving. This is about friendship, about affection, about the deep abiding respect I have for you," she said.

I stared. She shivered in the sun. Her hair, a mass of snarls and knots, mimicked her mare's tail. Her contorted face, an odd mix of fainting white and blushing red, was anything but beautiful. Suffused with agony and indecision, she teetered on the edge of sanity, but the compassion in her eyes choked me. With the same tenderness I felt for my infant son, I pulled her into my arms and rocked her, a steady shift and sway that copied the rhythm of the waves.

"Ywain?"

"Hmm?" I said.

"When I first came to Muirray, when you were but a boy and I had no idea of the man you might be someday, I used to dream the same dream every night. For years it came to me. I saw a man coming out of the sea, running from the water where he had been swimming. He ran toward me, naked and laughing, water streaming from his body and long hair and beard. He stood over me where I sat on the sand and shook himself like a dog, the droplets flying everywhere, sparkling with the sun, for it was sunny, like today, but also very cold, the air was cold, the sea was cold.

He reached for a tartan cloak and wrapped it around himself and curled next to me on the thick blanket that covered the pebbly sand. We had already eaten, and the smell of flowers and fruit and wine and sea salt and sea air and the heat of bodies joining together was everywhere. It was not the scent of coupling alone; it was the smell of the earth and the sea and the place where we loved to walk and talk. I would wake then, trembling all over, covered in sweat, anxious and eager as a mare in heat."

I could not keep from kissing the top of her head and brushing the hair from her face. When I said nothing, she added, "It was you, was it not? The man I dreamed of? Even though we have not had our idyllic open-air meal, I saw you coming from the sea. The scent of amber and musk, of geranium and lavender, of bergamot, citrus, clove, peppermint, green apple and thyme hovers around us."

Leaning down, I touched my lips to hers, but her mouth did not open; it curled inward, dry and shriveled as a leaf. She shuddered, then buried her face against my chest. The wind gusted sharp from the north making the horses fling their heads high in anticipation. A veil of long, slender, flowing clouds wisped across the sun, casting us in filmy shadow.

"We had better go," I said. "See if we can find better shelter for the night."

"All right," she sighed. "Ywain, what good are my dreams, the visions, if the knowing is incomplete, if fate is bound to have her way regardless of what I want, what I need, what I wish for?"

Helping her to her feet, I said, "I do not know. I swear to you and to whatever power controls us that I do not know. Everything, you, me, the sea, the stars, the coming storm, what waits for us at Muirray, is beyond my ken. The only thing I know for certain is my love for you."

"Still," she said, "there is no hope for us, is there?"

"My Lady, you ask questions that have no answers. We had better lead the horses. They are spent. Shall I choose the way, or you?"

"You find it, Ywain. My ability to think is gone."

I began to climb, scrambling for footing, giving my horse every inch of rein and staying to the side so he would not step on me. Looking back, I saw Bekah holding her mare, the white-blond mystery of hair, mane, and tail whipped into whorls by the wind. She stood staring out to sea. I knew she prayed, talking to a presence I could not see or hear.

KEENAN'S REVELATION

BEKAH

As far as shelters went, the overhanging ledge was not much, but it was the best we could find as the plum-colored storm front and dusk both overtook us. After pulling the saddles and provisions from the horses' drenched backs, we pressed in against the wall, making enough space for them to shove their weary heads and shoulders in next to us. Their tails thrashed and hindquarters twitched as the bruising rush of wind and hard rain wailed down. When our legs gave out and we could no longer stand, we slid to the damp earth, knees tucked to chests, and Ywain tied the reins to our ankles.

"If we sleep," he said, fishing in a bag for dried meat, fruit, and nuts, "then they will not be driven away by the deluge."

"How can we sleep with this tumult? I cannot even hear myself think." I waved away the portion he offered me.

"Bekah, you need to eat." He opened my hand and placed several shriveled berries and walnuts on my palm.

Cursing, I flung them into the night.

"That was a childish thing to do," Ywain said. "What is the matter with you?"

"I cannot force something down my throat that will make me sick. You treated me like a child, ordering me to eat, so I reacted like a child. Now, leave me alone. I do not want to eat. I do not want to talk. I want to be left alone."

The rain ceased as if someone had shut off the sky. In the sightless space, I could hear Ywain chewing near my ear, my mare huffing near my hip. A prickly restlessness seized my outstretched legs, and they began to twist and jerk. A pain deep within magnified until I could not bear the discomfort. A whimpering mew escaped my lips, and Ywain reached out to hold me saying, "Bekah, are you all right?"

Through clenched teeth, I ground out, "Do not touch me. I am going away. Someone calls me. Stay near."

My eyes closed, my chin dropped, the great shaking stopped, and I stepped into the remnants of the squall to follow a man in a sodden cloak. We had not gone far when blinding yellow light burst from the lightning struck cavity of a hollow tree. Dazzled, unable to see, I stopped, reaching out for the gnarled limb of an oak to steady myself. When the fire died down, in the gold-red glow, a colossal eye burned. Stabbed into the blue iris, a thrown knife quivered, then fell to the ground, a slight stain of blood glinting on the blade. The man ahead of me turned, his fraying cloak spinning from his ankles and his hood falling back. The acorns in his eye sockets pulsed like the scintillation of twin stars on the coldest winter night. "Eye of the fish, eye of the roebuck, eye of your enemy" he said, "within the eye of everything you will find the answer."

"Keenan," I said. "Do not give me riddles. Give me facts. Give me the certainty of finding the path, of knowing the right way."

"There is no right way. There is only the path you choose and the way you decide to walk upon it."

"Why do you come then?"

"To let you know you are not alone. There are armed legions ahead of you, but there are uncountable masses urging you to use your courage and power to save them."

"I cannot save anyone," I said.

"Perhaps not, but you can show them the way." He drifted into the smoky mist that issued from the spent fire.

"I hate this," I said. "How can I show anyone a way I do not know myself?"

"Look for the one open-eyed and furred at birth. The swift, hoary one with divided upper lip, long hind legs, short cocked tail and long ears. She is not as timid as you may think. She will not lead you astray. Impressive, venerable, she will take you away from an early grave."

He strode into the heart of the tree whispering, "Eye of the fish, eye of the roebuck, eye of your enemy." I waited, but he did not return and the saturated silence of the night swirled around me. There was nothing more to see, no voices to hear. Only myself holding to the icy arm of the ancient tree and, cutting through the clouds at the top of the high ridge, another gold eye, the rising orb of the storm-tossed moon. I waited to watch it surround a single silhouetted tree, then when the gleaming light lifted free of the black branches, I returned to where the horses waited tied to Ywain.

I thought the same moonshine woke me, but when I pried open my eyes, it was the sun's ray that pierced me. Alone in the cave-like shelter, I stretched and yawned and cried out like a wee one wanting comfort. Ywain appeared, leading the horses whose chin whiskers dripped with the water they had drunk.

"Good morning," he said. "Are you thirsty? There is a stone basin that caught the rain a little ways ahead. Do you feel ready to go?"

"I ache all over," I said pushing myself to my knees.

"I should not be surprised, you struggled and fought and argued all night. Whom were you speaking to?" Ywain asked.

"Keenan," I said.

Ywain looked like I had struck him across the face. His cheeks above his beard blanched as his eyes sparked.

"Now you not only scold the living, you speak to the dead?"

"He is not dead, Ywain. He simply is not here anymore."

"What does that mean? I laid his breathless body in the tree. I crossed his lifeless hands on his chest."

"And you placed acorns in his empty eyes," I said.

"You cannot know that," he said. "How do you know that? I am the only one who knows that."

"I saw him last night. I went with him to the burning tree. He spoke to me," I said.

"Why would he come to you and not to me? I was his son. Closer to him than anyone save his own granddaughter." He dragged the saddles and packs from their dry confines.

"I do not know, Ywain. Maybe because you are not willing to see him or hear him. Maybe you are afraid." I tried to gather and arrange my hair that was as tangled and knotted as an old fishing net.

"Did he say anything about me? Have a message for me?"

I thought of saying no, and leaving it at that, but Keenan would not mind, would not object to a slight lie to help the day go better.

"Yes. He said to tell you that you would find your wife and son safe and in good hands. That they are waiting for you to come."

"Do you believe that, Bekah? Do you think we will find them alive and well?"

"Yes."

"Do you know where they are? Surely they did not stay at Muirray. Did Keenan tell you?"

"He did not. But I see them huddled from the storm in too tight a space, your son gurgles, his toothless mouth compelling. There is another toothless one there, but hers is the smirk of one who has lived past her time."

"That must be the healer. And Nola?" he asked.

"Your voice trembles with emotion, Ywain. Is that love I hear, or guilt?"

"You are a cruel woman, Bekah. Someday that cruelty will cut you deep."

"Cruelty counts for something in this world," I said as I checked my cinch and grunted my way into the saddle. "Your white-shouldered one is fine. She yearns for you. At night she begs the Goddess to bring you back to her. She tells Wallace how brave and strong you are, that you have not forgotten them, and that you will come in time."

"And so I will." He grabbed a handful of mane and leapt astride without touching his foot to the stirrup.

"Do not forget that I am the one who will lead you to her." I clicked my horse into a quick jog trot. "Try to keep up this time. I have no patience for someone who lags behind."

THE KISS

YWAIN

For the remainder of the day I did not speak. Not out of anger, which I had every right to claim, but out of a deep need to be alone with myself, to experience the solitary state of silence where I could investigate the sensations stinging through my head and heart. Every bit of my skin felt pierced, as if innumerable wasps had found their mark. I felt certain that I knew what Pal must have experienced at the end of his devoted life, shot through with Roman arrows. It seemed improbable that Bekah might be jealous of Nola. She was everything that Nola was not: beautiful, self-possessed, respected, powerful. Yet, females will be females, and like the older mare with several grown colts who will drive a needful filly away from the stallion, all Bekah could see was Nola's youth and innocence, the vestiges of her virginity still bright on her childish shoulders. I tried not to dwell too much on what would happen when we were all brought together. I tried only to think of my son, who, if Bekah was right, was now cooing. It seemed years instead of weeks since I had last held him close, his chubby hand clutching my beard with a death grip. If he could hold a sword as strongly when he was grown, I would not have to worry about his ability to protect and defend his mother and siblings. The notion comforted me, just as the thought that I would not live to see him grow tall troubled me.

The violence of the wind had shoved piles of leaves against the north boles of the trees, leaving a pattern of scoured ground and dumps of debris. The fury of the rain had scrubbed the sky clean of clouds, and as we rode the warmth of the sunshine weighted my eyes and made my shoulders slump. I had not slept. Bekah's restive dreams had kept me alert and on edge with one hand on my sword, the other, near her tossing head. As she had commanded, I did not dare touch her, though I longed to gather her next to me and still her body's twitching anguish. At dawn, when at last she quieted and truly slept, I had untied the horses' reins and slipped out to stretch my cramped muscles and find water. On my return from the stone catch basin, I worried that I might find her lapsed into a sleep from which she would not wake, or worse, dead. But instead, there she lay, just opening her eyes, looking for all the world as if she had spent the night in the tender embrace of a lover—her hair tousled, her cheeks flushed, her smile beatific and satisfied, her breasts pushing against the askew clothing as she stretched and yawned. No woman had the right to be that beautiful and seductive. Is it any wonder that such a sight drives men to do all that they do, including fighting for territory and killing each other?

"If you are done with your daydreams, Ywain, let us stop here a moment to rest. The mare's limping and I am hungry. If I remember correctly, the river will be only a few more miles, and we will have to wait for the tide to retreat anyway. Do you have a small, short knife, one I can use to dig in her hoof and see if there is a pebble pressuring her foot?"

I wanted to say, "You threw away your food last night, you get no more" or "If you had planned more carefully, you would have your own short knife." Instead I said, "Yes, my Lady," and jumped to the ground to assist her from her horse, but she had already dismounted, flipped her reins over a low branch, and was hunkered over the mare's left leg, the bony knee bent, and the bottom of the hoof exposed in her hands. The sight of Bekah's curved bottom poking into the air was more than I could bear. Something churlish tickled my lips, but I bit my tongue, walked around and gave her the palm sized, blunt-tipped knife.

"Careful," I said, "it has a double blade for skinning, and I honed the edges not long ago."

She puffed her breath at me as if the well-meant warning was not worth commenting on. I stayed to watch her pry mud and damp droppings from the cupped foot. There was a stone the size of a bean jammed between the soft, spongy center and the harder sole. Bekah dug, pushing hard to dislodge it, and when it finally popped free, a bit of blood bubbled from the hole.

"Hold," she said to the horse that was jerking to free her leg.

"Get a handful of those leaves behind you, the green ones just beginning to yellow," she said to me.

I did as she bid. She stuffed them into her mouth and chewed them to a pulp, then packed the slimy mass into the crevice.

"Something medicinal?" I asked.

"No, just something to pad the wound. I do not want her getting worse. We will need both mounts to get all of us back to Lynnmer."

She patted the mare's underbelly and blew on the bottom of the hoof to help the impromptu dressing dry. Setting down the foot, she reached into the pack tied to her saddle and pulled out the bag of dried meat.

"And do not tell me again that you think we should have brought extra horses. I still say that we are less conspicuous this way and leave less of a trail to follow."

"I said nothing, Bekah." I took the piece of venison she extended.

"You did not say any words, but I knew your thoughts." She squatted with her back against a gray trunk to keep from sitting on the wet ground.

I sighed and stood cock-hipped to chew the salted, smoked meat one small bite at a time.

"And if you think I am that beautiful and seductive, why do you not take me here in the mud? Better yet, straddle that log, and I will sit in your lap and ride you until you collapse. What? Ywain? Are you blushing?"

She laughed, her voice gay and carefree, the voice of a girl teasing her first love, seeing how far she could push the sensibilities of his mind until his body responded.

"You have the strangest power to either stiffen or shrivel me. Right now, that part of me that you would like to straddle is non-existent."

"I do not believe you," she said. "Come here."

There was nothing between my legs but sweat, so I strode over and stood in front of her, my groin level with her lips. As she leaned forward, her hand settled on my thigh to keep her balance. The touch, light but not unintentional, made me spring to life, the pressure swelling my pants until the bulge met her mouth.

"See," she said. "You lie."

"No," I said not moving away. "You bewitch."

"It is not enchantment, Ywain. It is denied desire."

She kissed me there, the softest and sweetest and tenderest of kisses, then stood, moaning as blood rushed into her legs and feet. Placing her hands on my shoulders, she stood tiptoe to kiss my lips that moved, still chewing the desiccated meat.

"We should go," she whispered near my ear.

"Yes. I know." I forced my arms to stay at my sides.

"I do not mean to be cruel," she said.

"I know that too," I said.

"Sometimes it is the only way I know to keep control over the horrors that rage within me."

"If only you could trust what is between us. Instead you question and demand answers. You lash out, and whoever is within reach is wounded. This is not the Lady I used to know. Where is she? Is she gone for good?"

"No. Only hidden away. Deep inside. If I do not protect her, keep her imprisoned, she will be cut down, a trembling stem slashed by the scythe."

"Why will you not trust me to protect her, keep her safe, allow the love I have for her to flourish?"

"Because when I allow her to emerge, vulnerable and open, I have no will to fight, no strength to right the wrongs or defend what is ours, what was given to us from the beginning. Not only for myself and mine, but also for you and your family, for all the people. Who would we be, Ywain, if I let you take your Lady and run away? I would be leaving my daughters, you would be leaving your wife and son and mother. How long would it be before that love began to sour into loathing and regret? I do what I do to save us all."

When I did not answer, did not move, her hand flashed up and grabbed my throat, her fingers digging into the fleshy part of the gullet. Her grip tightened, making me choke, tears springing into my eyes. I could have snapped her neck with one blow. Instead, I reached up and took her wrist and squeezed until she let go.

"If this is love," she said, "then I would rather hate you. It would be much easier."

"Bekah," I said.

"No. Do not give me kind words. Do not offer trite remarks. Just help me on my horse so we can make the river before dark. That will be gift enough."

THE CAIRNS

BEKAH

We crossed the wide water moments before the sun lay down for the night, spreading open the last of the motley-gray clouds and smearing them with unimaginable colors: salmon pink, lavender, butter gold, rosy orange-red. Compared to my earlier upstream crossing with Alanna and the girls, this was as easy as deep wading, and the horses lost their footing only once and had to swim a short way before they found purchase again on the pebbly opposite shore. The sky exploded in one last furious attempt before the rainbow palette dropped into the sea before it disappeared. Both water and air turned into sparkled silver, then deepened into midnight blue. The moon would be late. The stars would not be bright enough to find the cairns, much less the woods-hidden path, so I motioned for Ywain to stop and unsaddle while I made my way along the bank toward the sea. There I stood on a slight promontory to view the last of the day, the angles and shapes that shift and change when darkness arrives, the sounds and movements that alter when various animals are afoot. Keenan's words, which had haunted my thoughts all day, came back to me complete with their vision of the eye and the knife. I offered my prayers of thanksgiving, then asked for blessing for all whom I loved, for Gordan's departed spirit, and Keenan's, who walked with me still. I wondered but did not question why

I never saw or heard Gordan. We had been dear to each other, closer than most men and women who marry, and had been able to talk about most things, including his worries and fears. Only one thing was never spoken of, my power to see beyond the day and into the night. Gordan was too advanced in his thinking, in his view of life, to believe in the possibility of walking between the worlds. He did not forbid me to practice my power, he knew better than to cross the Goddess, but neither had he encouraged nor supported me. He did not scoff, but he did not praise. So it had been easy to keep my secrets, to succumb to the voices and visions only when I was alone, to use just the smallest ability when I worked to calm the girls or went hunting with Ywain. Had Gordan feared me? He had no need, for I loved him and would have never thought to harm him or wish him ill. Yet there was that part of me that he pushed away with quiet abhorrence, the hard gesture or subtle retort that kept me from being all I was capable of. Gordan professed not to believe in the old ways, but he lived in horror that he might be wrong. And Ywain? He neither believed nor disbelieved. Observant and open, fully aware of powers alive and operating everywhere though he could see so little of the other side. I knew he was capable of going there, but he chose to stay grounded in easy reality. Maybe the Goddess had determined this as well, that he would be the one who guarded the door so I could go without worry, a beacon to which I could find my way back. Gordan lay on a body-studded hill, a spear rammed through his heart. There had been no one left to carry off the dead or say the prayers of passage. Perhaps that is why I could not see him or hear him. Needles of memory stabbed the back of my eyes, but I warned the tears away. I had no time, nor energy to waste on crying. From a distance I heard the barking of a fox, then the answer of an owl. I felt Ywain making his way toward me through the darkness and was not surprised to feel him behind me waiting to be noticed.

"Come, Ywain. I have finished my prayers," I said.

"For whom do you pray?" he asked, drawing close enough for me to feel his breath on my hair. I knew he would not touch me without permission, so I spoke to him through silent thought, saying "Hold me, put your arms around me and cup my breasts and kiss my cheek." When he complied, I smiled and folded my arms on his. It seemed silly to stand there in the blackness, however comforting it was. The whole world had vanished, now just the two of us, joined together by affection and need.

"I prayed for all of us," I said. "But mostly for Gordan, who ghosts the place where he was slain. For our people, our families, for you."

"Why for me?" His lips grazed my ear.

"Because you have taken on the most difficult job in the world."

"And what is that?"

"Trying to read my mind and figure out who I am," I said, laughing.

"What a beautiful sound, Bekah. You used to laugh all the time."

"I know. Laughing was easy with you. Everything was easy with you. Now things are difficult and there doesn't seem to be much to be lighthearted about." I squirmed deeper into his embrace.

"There are these breasts in my hands that tell me they are glad to be touched. There is this curious prodder against your warm rump that says he is happy to be alive."

"I know the craziness of all this, Ywain. I know I tempt the fates with this passion, but—"

I stopped speaking. If I went on, I would fall into a trap I had set for myself. Ywain squeezed me tighter and buried his face against my neck.

"Would you like me to kiss you and undress you and lay our clothes on these rocks and then love you as if you were my wife?" he asked.

Laughing again, I said, "So you have been practicing. You did read my mind."

"No, my Lady, I read your heart, which in this moment is fully open and reveals the best part of who you are," he said.

"And what is that?"

"A woman first. Then a leader. It is that part of you that wants me inside of you that makes me want you more than I have ever wanted anything."

"It is our last chance, Ywain. By tomorrow Nola will be the one you hold. And I will be alone."

"You will never be alone as long as I have enough breath to be by your side. Let us not talk of last chances. Let us not talk at all," he said.

He untied my hair and ran his fingers through the snarls. Then, as if he were undressing a child for bed, he took off my garments and spread them beneath my feet and laid me down. When his body settled beside mine and his hands explored the flesh he could not see, I whispered, "My love, my husband," until the chant was lifted beyond words into the music of pounding hearts and lilting sighs. When he slid into me, pushing my back into the hard, sharp stone, he said, "Spread your legs, Bekah. Wider. Open yourself to me. Let me feel and taste that part of you that has never before been touched."

Ywain carried me to the campsite he had prepared. I heard the horses shuffle and paw, heard the lullaby of the river's current. Then there was the softness of pine boughs beneath me, a warm cloak over me. And sleep.

When I woke, a spider dangled inches from my eyes. Black with white streaks, she clung to a silk thread suspended from a twig. I watched her weave, climbing up, swinging down, connecting angles into shapes, an ethereal and intricate dance of creation. Her belly bulged. Her eight eyes gleamed like tiny black pearls in the early sun. Ywain's warmth was absent, but the horses remained tied to saplings, saddles at their feet. When I looked back, the spider waited, her long legs tucked where she curled tight in an upper corner of the sheer web. What did she wait for? Fly. Moth. I studied each fine filament, each lacy segment, until my gaze was caught in the very center where all parts came together. There, a gold eye gleamed. I blinked, but still the eye was there, staring at me. I widened my focus and saw a hare sitting in a patch of light chewing a stem of clover, her small jaws working, her divided upper lip twitching, her long ears twisting slightly to pick up any nuance of sound.

The swish of Ywain's step in the grass startled her, and she leapt into the shadowed brush. He crouched before me holding a couple of still thrashing fish. "Breakfast?" he asked. "I believe we can risk a fire."

"Good," I said not moving, my eyes riveted to the spot where the hare had been eating her morning meal.

"Did you sleep?"

"Beautifully," I said. "You?"

"Like a man who has achieved his dreams." He knocked the fish in the head with a stout stick.

"Where did you go so early?" I asked.

"Searching for the cairns. I could not find them with the leaves and the mist, but I will look again after we eat. I spotted these two lurking in a pool where they had been caught when the tide went out."

"You will not need to look for the cairns," I said.

"Why not?" he asked as he snapped small dry branches from the base of several trees.

"Because there they are," I said pointing.

"Where?" He spun around, studying the landscape.

"No," I said. "Do not look so far, or so high. Come here. Lie down next to me."

"Bekah," he said.

"No, do not scold me. This is not a trick. Come see."

He set down a pile of firewood and knelt beside me. I motioned him lower, until he lay stretched out with his head resting on his arm.

"Follow the path of my finger," I said. "See the rosehips on the bush, the dots of red inside the green and gold? To the side, through the foliage, can you see the stacked stones?"

"Goodness, Bekah, how did you ever see that? Did you dream it? Did Keenan come and show you that?"

"No," I laughed. "The hare revealed it. Go now while I can direct you from here. Take something to mark the spot."

He pulled his sword from the sheath and walked as I said, "Straight on, left, right, a few more steps, more, look for the berries, there." Raising the sword, he gave a sharp yet quiet cry and jabbed the blade into the earth. It trembled, flashing sunlight.

"They are here. Three cairns, equal distance. The path is narrow and faint, but once we are on it, it will be easy to follow."

When he walked back, I was crouched over the fish, slitting their bellies.

"Bekah," he said. "Save me from myself. Please put on your clothes."

THE RESCUE

YWAIN

We stalked into Muirray two days later, taking a circuitous route, stopping often to look and listen, searching at every crossing of the trail for tracks and sign, but all we saw were deer and fox, rabbit and squirrel, owl castings and hawk feathers. More than once Bekah commented, "I miss Lilith. I wish Pet were with us." We had heard no human sound, except for the echo of our own voices, and then we became more and more quiet as the sun rose and set, rose and set, and rose again. The silence suited me. I had many calculations to make, many mysteries to unravel, and many problems for which to propose solutions: Stay alive. Keep Bekah safe. Find my mother, Nola, and Wallace. Make a report on Muirray and any enemy movements for Graham. Get us all back to Lynnmer.

Our silence was sweet, but the silence we encountered at Muirray was oppressive. There was nothing there, no animals, no people, not even any bodies. We wondered but did not discuss anything. We moved step by step, our horses wide-eyed and prancing among the ruins, searching for anything that might give us a clue to the whereabouts of Nola and the others. The burned earth was dead. The air was still and dead. The sky hung with a dull brownish-gray pall as if permanently stained with smoke. No gulls circled overhead. No squirrels or birds graced the trees. If the place were haunted, the ghosts were not speaking.

"Bekah," I whispered, "there is no one here. We must go. It is not good to stay. The possibility of danger increases with each moment we linger."

She ignored me. Her eyes were everywhere, looking up at the tall walls, searching the face of the cliffs, studying the ground, seeking out every nook and cranny in the stonewalls. For the fourth time, she rode past the cellar from which we had pulled her daughters and Keenan and Alanna. The entrance had collapsed into an akimboed pile of beams, dirt, and rubble.

"Bekah," I said.

"Shhhh, it is here. I feel it. Go off a bit and leave me alone. Let me see what I can see."

When I refused to move from her side, she said, "Go away. I will not dismount. I cannot concentrate with you so near."

Reining my gelding around, I moved near the old gate. The moment I closed my gritty eyes for a moment of rest, I saw a pair of long delicate ears. My lids jerked open, but there was nothing but the outline of the still trees before me. Drooping shut again, I saw the same thing, the velvet-edged outline of animal ears. Bekah's jogging mare forced my eyes open again.

"Did you see?" I asked.

"Yes, the hare's ears." She scanned every piece of wood within sight.

A rush of anticipation and apprehension flew through me.

"On the fallen beam, the lintel of the old door. It was there. The hare's ears pointing this way. Here it is, another one drawn in charcoal, one pointing up, one cocked pointing west, with the crooked symbol of a trail. They are up on the mountain."

"Bekah? How can you tell? Why would they go high where it is cold and windy and there is no water? Surely they had to stay where they could find game?"

"No, it is safe there. A sacred place. No one who meant them harm could get there. It is protected by the Goddess." She motioned me to follow her as she sighted a line from the house at Muirray to Lovell Tor.

We trotted. They was no sense now of care or caution, only the idea that we were close to finding what we had come for. Breathless, when the horses could go no higher, we tethered them well. I began to untie our provisions and a bladder of water, but Bekah said, "Leave them. We must come right back."

She climbed as if a pack of wolves nipped her heels. Her breasts heaved, her face turned dark red, she stumbled and clambered up, stumbled again.

"Bekah, slow down," I said. "If they are there and they are safe, then surely it is all right for us to take our time and get there in good shape."

"No, we must hurry. A dark cloud comes. Every moment counts. We must get them off the mountain before it is too late."

The tone of her voice and her insistence on pushing to the limit drove me upward as well. Every so often, she stopped and bent at the waist, her head between her knees, fighting for breath, fighting the faint that threatened us both in the thinning air. At every fork in the trail, eyes closed, she would turn a circle, hands raised, as if she could feel which direction was right. Then, like she had been clubbed dead in her tracks, she dropped, her face to the dirt, sucking in great gasps of air.

"Around this bend," she groaned, "there is a giant tree with three arms that reach upward from an odd angle. They are there in a shelter built of branches. It will be hard to see. She has used her skill and magic to conceal the place. Call out for them at a safe distance first. Go on now. Leave me here to rest. But hurry. Do not linger. We must go down and get away."

I jogged, searching for the tree. When I saw it, I stopped and whistled. One note at first. Then two. If they were there, they could not help but hear. Then I called for Nola, imitating the cadence of the notes. I held my breath and waited, hoping to hear a reply. I heard nothing but the wind howling high in the branches, screeching around the stones, harassing the brush. Then I saw her running toward me, her arms outstretched, her clothes filthy, her hair a flaming rat's nest. Behind her, an old woman in rags held Wallace against her shoulder.

Nola leapt onto my chest, throwing her arms around my neck and winding her legs around my waist. I spun her round and round, laughing, trying to catch my breath, trying to calm her cries. I carried her to the woman, set her down, and reached for my son.

"Rowena," Nola said, "this is Ywain. Wallace's father."

The old one held the infant close and stared at me. She did not move to hand me my child. Instead, she reached out for Nola and pulled her close.

"Where is the other one?" she asked me. "The one who talks to me when I sleep."

"Just around the bend. Back down the trail. She says we must hurry. Is there anything you need? Anything I can carry?"

"We have nothing," she said.

"Hurry then," I said. "Where is mother? Where is Maureen? Nola, where is Maureen?"

"With the rest. When she saw what had happened at Muirray, when she found no one alive, she died. Simple as that, a great keening wail, then she fell and I could not rouse her. I did not know what to do, so I went back to Rowena's hut. She took care of Wallace and me. She is the one who said we must drag the dead and lay them in the cellar. For days we worked in the night, with

Wallace on my back, until all were put to rest. Maureen went last, Ywain. I hated to put her in that dark place, but it seemed better than leaving her for the wolves and birds. Rowena said the prayers. She and I pulled and jerked and hammered on the beams until the doorway caved in with a great thunder of dirt and stone. Then we came here. Rowena said you would find us. Who does she speak of? Who is back on the trail?"

"Bekah," I said. Seeing her confused panic, I said, "our Lady. Gordan's wife. Hurry now. I will tell of it later. Rowena?"

"I know the trail," she said. "He is safest with me. Take Nola."

Grabbing Nola's hand, I pulled her behind me, half dragging her as she looked back repeatedly for the old woman and her child. Bekah was waiting where I had left her, staring down from the high place, her nose sniffing the air like a hound.

"Good," she said as she started trotting down the steep hill. "We have no time to waste. Ywain, put the women between us. Bring up the rear. Do not stop for anything."

Nola planted her feet like a balky horse, staring at Bekah as if she saw a specter.

"Go on." I gave her a gentle shove and ushered Rowena into line. "I will be right behind."

"Maureen?" Bekah called back.

"Gone," I said.

Then we had no time to talk. All our energy was expended on keeping our feet on the slipping stones, of measuring our breath to keep going. When she reached the horses, Bekah untied them, cupped her hands and asked Rowena, "Can you ride?"

"Yes, though it has been many years." Rowena handed Wallace to Nola and grappled her way into the mare's saddle. I took Wallace long enough to cuddle him for a second before shoving him into Bekah's hands and boosting Nola on behind. Bekah handed the boy up to Nola and said, "Tie him to your breast with your shawl. Hold on very tight to Rowena."

I vaulted onto the gelding and reached out an arm to Bekah. She grabbed my forearm and I swung her on behind as I nudged the mare ahead of me down the trail. "No matter what happens, keep going. Rowena, you know the way out of Muirray on the trail past your hut. Follow it north and east. If we must stop to fight, go on. Take them to my sister at Lynnmer. Ask anyone and they will tell you the way. If you encounter the enemy, admit nothing, know nothing."

When we reached the flats, Bekah lashed the mare's rump and she burst into a gallop. Rowena bent low over her neck. Nola clutched the old woman's thin back as Wallace screamed. I kicked the gelding until we were in an all-out race for the stretch of sand beneath the cliffs and the main trail away from Muirray headed north. Bekah grabbed the front of my shirt with her left hand and sucked her body into my back, tucking her cheek into my shoulder. With her right hand, she pulled her sword. Then I heard what she had been hearing all along: the pounding of hooves that separated from the pounding of the waves against the rocks. The sound gained in strength. I dared not look back. I kept low, my heels gouging the horse's heaving flanks. Rowena and Nola were ten lengths ahead on Bekah's faster mare.

"Ywain," Bekah screamed close to my ear. "Do not stop. I beg of you. Get them to safety. If you love me, get them to Lynnmer."

I hollered back. "There is no way—"

But she cut me off. "I will live," she shouted. "I see myself at Lynnmer. Save yourself. Save your son."

I wrenched my head around. Through streaming eyes, I saw the force of men gaining on us. Like me, Bekah knew that my horse could not make it carrying two. She jabbed me in the side, shoving the hilt of her sword into my hand. As I grabbed for it, she cried, "Keep going," and then was gone, her body slipping away from mine.

THE ENEMY

BEKAH

Did I fall off or let go? I do not know. I hit the rocks and sand with a resounding smash, my right shoulder crumpling under my full weight, the pain of dislocation sending me into vague milky blackness. Though I could not see, I still heard the horses coming. I tried to roll and rise, but my body refused to move. I wanted to run, but I could not even stand. Then there were hooves milling all around me, the stamping and clashing of men and beasts, shouts and curses, though I did not understand the words. I prayed they would take me and allow the rest to escape. In my mind I saw Ywain catch up to the mare, wrestle the reins from Rowena and gallop on, pulling the women and child behind him.

"Gordan," I said over and over. One of the men lifted me, shaking me by the shoulders. I knew his words were asking me who I was.

"Rebekah," I mumbled. "Wife of Gordan. Gordan. Gordan." He heaved me onto his shoulder, then threw me over a horse's back. My head flopped forward, bashing into the stirrup. My shoulder screamed, and I allowed myself the blessing of darkness.

Four rough hands helped me stand and led me down a long corridor into a room lit with many torches. They shoved me in front of a man whose dress and bearing said he was important. I fell to my knees, not from obedience, but from pain and fatigue. He stood over me. He reached down and grabbed me by my hair and pulled me to my feet. I stood swaying, trying to focus on his wavering odd-colored eyes. He said something, demanding an answer. I did not know the words. Someone spoke behind him, saying in my language, "Who are you?"

"Rebekah, wife of Gordan," I said.

He sneered. Stamped his foot. Spun around and slapped me to the ground. This time I did not stay down. I shoved myself upright and forced strength into my legs. He came close once more and started to speak, the other man saying his words in my language.

I spat at him and shouted, "I do not care who you are. You are scum. You are filth. You are nothing. You are no one. To me you have no name. You are evil."

When the man behind him repeated my words to him in a whisper, he raised his hand to strike me again. I did not flinch. I stared him down. He lowered his hand. He spoke, his words clipped and hard. Then there was silence broken only by the flaring and crackling of the fires. He said more words, slammed his fist into the palm of his other hand and stomped from the room.

The man who had stood behind him said, "He said to tell you his orders. 'Take her and scourge her, but do not kill her. Take her back to Muirray where you found her on the beach and dump her. Let the wolves have her.'"

A death sentence with hope. Perhaps the cruelest kind.

"What did he say at the last?" I asked.

The man shuffled his feet and cleared his throat.

"You speak my language. You know my fate. If you tell me, I

will forgive you for your part in this," I said.

He came out of the shadows, the flickering light casting shifting shapes that moved and danced with abandonment. From inside the darkness of his hood, his eyes gleamed like polished acorns. He stretched out a hand to me and as I reached for it, he said, "His final words were: Rape her. Do it now."

I dropped my arm. He stood quiet.

"Keenan," I said, "How? Why are you— You must—"

"I have no power with him. He does not know the Goddess or believe in the Otherworld." He faded back into the dim recesses of the room.

"Keenan," I said. "Save me."

"No, you must save yourself. Vision yourself alive," he said, "and you will survive."

ROWENA

YWAIN

Wallace would not stop crying. His screams had softened to mewls and whimper, but still he whined in his mother's arms. My horse's ears flicked back and forth in furious confusion as he tried to figure out the sound behind him. Though the mare kept pace with the gelding, her nose often nudged his rump as we trotted, and my arm ached from holding her reins. I looked forward to scout the trail, then I glanced back, hoping by some miracle to see Bekah jogging up. Rowena slumped in the saddle, both hands gripping the horn. She had sliced off her hair, what little of it she had, and the spiked gray ends stuck up at awkward angles like a crown of thorns. Over her back, Nola's white face mirrored shock and surprise, joy and sorrow, life and death. She kept trying to catch my eye, to mouth words to me, but I did not have time to focus on her. When we had been pushing hard long enough for the sun to dip toward the horizon and I heard no one following us, I allowed the sweat-stained horses to slow to a plodding walk.

"Ywain," Nola said. "May we stop? I need the bushes."

Rowena raised her head and nodded at me. I took this to mean that we were safe. Her permission bolstered my resolve. For miles I had been beating myself for following Bekah's command to leave her. I tried to keep the sight of her flat on the sand surrounded by armored men and horses from my mind. Instead,

I made myself remember her words, "I will live. I see myself at Lynnmer."

Choosing a thicket where dried berries hung thick on the bushes, I wound our way deep within, glancing back to make certain the horses left no droppings. When the sky disappeared from view, I knew no one could see us from the trail. I took Wallace and helped Nola slide from the mare's back. Rowena plopped off by herself, her knees buckling as she grabbed for the stirrup leather to maintain her balance. She nodded to tell me she was all right. She gathered the mare's reins, then the gelding's, and led them a short way, to the sparse grass that grew in the thick shade. She turned her back on us, a gesture of respect and privacy.

Pulling Nola into the circle of my arms, I kissed the top of Wallace's head and shushed him.

"Go ahead, Nola. When you return, nurse Wallace. Then we will go."

"I cannot nurse him," she said as she walked away. "I have no milk."

I held my son close, his shriveled face screwed up to howl again. I bounced him and murmured love words. Rowena came carrying the sack of dried meat, the bladder of water, and my horn cup.

"Pound a little of this. Add a bit of water. I will get a few berries." She took Wallace from me and shuffled off.

Finding a nearly flat rock and a smaller stone to hold in my hand, I beat a thin strip of the roebuck into powder, pinched it into the cup, and dribbled in some water. Rowena returned, chewing a mouthful of red fruit. When she had it ground to a paste, she spat it into the cup, added more water and swirled the mix. As I held the horn, she dipped her finger into the mix and tucked it into Wallace's toothless mouth. To my surprise, he quieted and sucked.

"Once Nola is safe and calm and she has enough to eat, her milk will return. Do not worry for your son. He will be fine. He will grow strong."

She had the gravelly voice of one who does not speak often, and though she met my eyes for seconds at a time, she never really looked at me for long. Nola returned, and seeing Wallace content, she lowered herself to the ground near our feet and rested her head against my leg.

Rowena began to chant in a whisper, the singsong melody meant, I thought, to soothe Wallace into sleep. But Nola jerked her head up and listened intently. Though there were some words I recognized, most of the song seemed garbled and unintelligible. Nola began to translate, glancing from Rowena to me and back again:

> At Muirray the white swan swims alone
> And in her nest the shattered skull and jawbones
> Of the last warrior who journeyed that far north
> To be the black swan swimming close beside her.
> What turn of sun and star bids her to come forth,
> The bride of the Golden Hair, to stalk and lure
> A lover-soldier to his accepted demise,
> His own sanity forsaken in order to be wise.
> What she sees when looking in the darkened glass
> Causes the earth's common men to flee in mass,
> But the warrior sees beyond the hag that kills,
> He sees the gift of love lurking in wild eyes,
> He sees the face of the Bride of the White Hills
> And hears the swan's piteous calls nightly cried.
> In life the warrior blindly follows his fate;
> In death, he succumbs to love that will not wait.

*There comes a time when each season surely ends
But lovers parted will find no way to mend
The broken circle of the long forgotten trees.
The warrior goes on seeking to know the story
Hidden in the wind-swept tale of autumn leaves
And of the swan who swims in splendid glory,
Circling alone, feathering her empty nest,
Waiting, waiting, waiting for renewal and for rest.*

Wallace slept as Rowena swayed with him in her arms. I looked at her, but she gazed up at the birds in the thick canopy of nearly bare branches. Nola dropped her head in her hands, her shoulders shaking.

"What?" I knelt beside her. "What is it, Nola? What does it mean?"

"It means she will kill you."

"Who will kill me?"

"Rebekah. Wife of Gordan."

"That is ridiculous. Rowena?" I turned to the old woman. "Here, take your son. Take your wife. Go on to Lynnmer. It is what you are meant to do."

She placed Wallace in my arms and stooped to kiss Nola on the top of her head. She took a couple sips of water from the bladder. She picked several strips of meat from the bag and shuffled away.

"Rowena, wait," I said. "Where are you going?"

"She calls for me. I am going back," she said, but did not stop walking.

"Nola, what is going on? How did you know what she was talking about?"

"It was the language of the old ones. It was the way my grandparents spoke," she said as I helped her to her feet.

"What? In riddles and rhyme?"

"Ywain, tell me what happened. Tell me everything you can."

"About Gordan? About Bekah?"

"About everyone, but especially about Bekah." She tugged Wallace from me and moved to the horses.

"Why about Bekah?" I asked.

"Because those of us who did not know her well, but watched her from afar had another name for her."

"What does that mean?" I asked.

"We called her *White Swan*."

THE WOLVES

BEKAH

The howling song woke me. Far off yodels of agony and pleasure, the uneven notes rising and falling, then rising again, the pitch quavering as it faded into silence. Then it would begin again, as if some seer directed the chanting rhythm. My mouth, filled with sand and blood, hung open, and it seemed the howls bubbled up from deep inside my own chest, my agony stressed by every strip of tattered flesh hanging on my back, my pleasure the evidence that if I could hear the wolves then I was still alive. Insects glued to my drying wounds signaled with twitch and quiver that my struggle was not over. The birds had come to peck and investigate, but when my bound hands were cut free and I was shoved from the saddleless horse, I had landed face down, my eyes protected. My dislocated shoulder no longer screamed; it whimpered. But my right hand, clawed into the sandy rock, cried, "Bring me a sword."

I could smell the musty rust of seaweed, a hint of rotting fish, the throat-restricting clench of gull droppings, and somewhere, drifting on the night air, a wisp of bergamot and citrus. Broken shell and sharp stone stabbed my breasts and hips. Was I clothed or naked? I could not tell. My eyes would not open. My legs and arms would not move.

The padding of many feet. Sniffs. Growls. Snapping jaws. Circling, circling, packing the sand around me. Whining. I heard Keenan's words again. I visioned myself alive and well. I made some part of me struggle into a groveling crawl, my words croaking out as harsh as a raven's. "Live. Live." I collapsed, rolling onto my back, needles of sand stabbing into the raw welts, my belly and eyes exposed. I tried to curl into a ball but could not. I tried to open my eyes and the lashes ripped apart in slow motion. The brilliant pricks of a sea of random stars floated above me. Then the earth began to move below me. Or I began to move over the earth as something dragged me by the hair away from the sound of the waves.

The song of lapping woke me. Tongues lolling. The slurp of saliva and smacking of water against mouths. The ground under me, wet and damp, sucked at the fever burning in my back. My head ached as if every hair had been plucked from my scalp. My throat worked against a gargle of blood and spit. The smell of water tortured me. I could feel the cool rushing inches away. The wolves whined and settled. I heard their heavy bodies hit the earth, felt their hot panting at my feet and hands and shoulders. Sun seeped through the trees, tickling my eyelids. They fluttered open, and I saw a hare crouched on the other side of the stream, hidden in the bracken, her colors camouflaged by leaf and shadow, her eyes laid back against her neck and shoulders. Perfectly still, with no wind to stir her scent, she was safe as long as she did not move. One of the wolves, dark-tipped hair shimmering in the sun, rose, stretched with forepaws extended and rump high in the air. He yawned, shook his head, and stood, ears up. I felt for a pebble beneath my left hand and gave an awkward half-hearted toss toward the hare. Startled, she burst from the brush and dashed right beneath the wolf's belly. He sprang upward, all four feet leaving the earth at once, and when he landed, he was in full pursuit, the other wolves charging after his black tail. The earth sighed. I sighed. The water sang in the mossy streambed.

The song of humming woke me. Rowena sat on the side of the water where the hare had hunkered. She had carved a small pit in the ground and lined it with leaves. In this she mixed something thick and gooey, on occasion reaching for a finger-scoop of mud from the rill and stirring it in. I groaned out her name, a garbled mess of unrelated syllables.

"Awake? Good. You look a mess. I see they did everything but kill you."

My first tears pooled and spilled.

"The tears are good. They will cleanse the inside where I cannot reach. Cry. The time will come when you have no tears left."

As I choked and spluttered, forcing my thick tongue against the sludge in my mouth, Rowena leapt the stream in a graceless arc, then knelt by my side. Bracing herself against my shoulder and hip, she rolled me once, twice, a third time, the pain of movement oozing out in a long, thin lament. The next shove landed me in the water face down, and the next flipped me over onto my back. Rowena pulled a moss-covered rock from the bank and slipped it beneath my neck to keep my head out of the flow, then with light but determined strokes she scrubbed my skin, ripping away what was left of my clothes and letting the pieces drift downstream. She scooped the debris from my mouth, tipped my face to the side to let the ripples rinse my lips and teeth and tongue; then she cupped sips in her palms and let the water trickle down my throat. The wavelets beneath nudged the sand and sucked the caked blood from the swollen wheals crisscrossing my shoulders and back and buttocks. When she reached my inner thighs, she pried my clasped legs apart and rubbed her fingers through the clotted hair, swishing away the filth of stiffened male seed, gently probing into my opening to release the festering within. The water pulsed against me, and all the while Rowena hummed a lullaby melody as if she were rocking a child to sleep.

The song of grunting woke me. My scalp crackled with fire, my neck trying to break off, so my head could tear away. Rowena tugged at my hair and left arm, inching me up the grassy bank to her medicinal pit.

I sputtered, "Did you drag me here, or did the wolves?"

"Does it matter?" She grabbed my feet and lined up my hips with my shoulders. She walked back to my head, bent over and grabbed my useless right arm. Taking the hand in both of hers, she said, "Hold on," and reared back with a quick jerk, popping the joint back into the socket. My scream made her laugh.

"It will feel better in a minute." She scooped a handful of the ripe, resinous-smelling mixture she had made. "So will the rest of you once I get this smeared on. Then, you will sleep and I will go find us something to eat."

"Rowena," I said. "You are the one I met up on the mountain some months ago. You are the one who came to tend Morgan when she was ill?"

"Yes," she said.

"Why did you never stay? Why did you keep yourself away, alone, when we would have welcomed you to the fire, as healer, as friend?"

"You know the answer to that." She rubbed the cool mud and pitch in small circles into my skin.

"I do not," I said.

"No man is my friend," she said. "No woman either. I have the beasts of the hills and sea. They know me. It is enough."

"Is it fear or sickness that keeps you away?" I asked.

"Both," she said. "The fear of being too close. A sickness of the soul."

"But you healed Morgan. You helped Wallace and Nola and Maureen. You came back for me."

"I am bound to help and heal those in need." She rolled me over onto my stomach.

"Because?" I asked.

"Because I am unable to heal myself." She plopped the soft unguent from her fingers and dabbed it into the burning sore of my back.

"Rowena," I asked. "Are you all right? You must be very tired."

"I am tired of dragging bodies." She wiped her hands on her half-bare thighs as she crouched by my face. "Lie still. Sleep if you can. I will return."

"The wolves?" I whispered.

"The two leaders feasted. They and the rest will shade up and wait. Before the sun sinks too low, I will be back."

"Ywain?" I asked.

"Headed for Lynnmer as you directed." She walked away.

"Rowena," I said.

"Do not thank me," she said. "Thank the hare who gave her life for you."

YWAIN'S CHOICE

YWAIN

We stood with the horses in the yard, their heads hanging to the ground as they snuffled the dry earth, wanting water. Lynnmer shimmered, a green tapestry woven with gold and brown threads. The lake sparkled with a multitude of sunspots. I stepped down at the same time Angus stepped from behind the rock wall of the falcon's keep. When he saw me, I raised my hand in salute and he dashed for the house, his feet slapping up puffs of dust. I took Wallace from Nola's arms and helped her down from Bekah's mare. Graham and Gwendolyn, the boys, Alanna and the girls, and Pet with a cascade of other dogs poured down, all talking and barking at once. Gwendolyn pulled Nola into her arms, then reached for Wallace and I handed him over.

"Your mother?" she asked.

"Gone," I said. "Nola buried her with the rest."

"Bekah?" Her eyes searched the yard and the road beyond.

I could not answer. I handed Bekah's sword to Graham, then pulled my own, the one Bekah had given me, and handed that to him also.

"You left her," Gwendolyn said, pulling her sons to her side. "I have seen her surrounded by wolves."

Morgan and Jenna rushed to grab my legs and I settled my hands on their tousled heads as they cried. Alanna shushed the dogs, and Pet belly-crawled over to me. I squatted to rub his ears and gathered the girls in my arms.

"The one who once wore the white skirt went back for her," Nola said.

I could not look at Gwendolyn, so I forced myself to study Graham's set face.

"Who?" he asked.

"Rowena. A woman of the woods who helped Nola and Wallace. She—"

"You let a woman go back for my sister?" Gwendolyn asked.

"She ordered me—"

"Ywain, that is ridiculous. You sacrificed—"

"Gwen!" Graham shifted the hilts of both swords against his thigh and raised his arm to silence her. "Go on, Ywain."

"Bekah told me to save the women. Save my son. She said she knew she would live."

"And you believed her—"

"Gwendolyn, go to the house," Graham said. "Take Nola and her child. Take the children. Alanna, help her."

When no one moved, he shouted, "Now," and I pushed the girls away from me as the dogs slunk off in mass, all except for Pet, who stayed shivering at my feet. As the group ascended the slight hill to the dwelling, Graham handed me my sword, swung Bekah's sword onto his shoulder, and motioned me toward the falcons' keep. We stood in the cool shadow of the wall and watched the birds turn their heads at the sound of our approach. Haughty, Lilith sat on the highest perch and preened her wings.

"Tell me," he said.

When I had said all I could think to say, he asked, "You know what they will do to her?"

"Yes," I said. "It feels a grievous dishonor to be here. To be alive. I do not expect you to grant sanctuary to me or my family."

"That is nonsense." Graham said pulled on his beard. "You did as Bekah asked. I understand why, even if Gwendolyn does not. If you sacrificed one, you saved three. Bekah knew that as well. What of Rowena?"

"I do not fear for her. She is like the deer and fox. They will never find her, or if they do, they will fear harming her. Even in their own odd beliefs, they will know she is one who was chosen. They are smart enough, I think, to recognize her powers and leave her be."

"Is it possible that Bekah is alive?" Graham asked.

"I like to think so. I cannot think of the harm they will have inflicted on her, but I see her alive in my mind. I see her stretched out naked by a stream, covered with mud and herbs, her eyes closed, her hair drying in the sun," I said.

When I saw the grin on Graham's face, I added, "Forgive me."

He laughed and said, "It is no time for laughter but, Ywain, it is a sight I do not mind holding in my own mind. What do you want to do? It is for you to decide, not me."

"I want to go back, but I think the chance of finding her is slim. I would have to search every mile of forest from here to Muirray. That could take weeks."

"I will go with you. And the answer I think lies in not finding her, but in letting her know we are there. Then she will find us."

"The men?" I asked.

"Ready as they will ever be. We will need a few skirmishes, more than one close encounter before we will know if they can hold and fight, or if they will flee. When we tell them about Bekah, I believe it will incense them, fire them into the purpose of gaining back Gordan's territory. Before, they felt all they needed to do was hold the line at the river and keep the enemy from coming farther north."

"And you are certain this is the right thing to do? Move forward before the winter?"

"It is that or hold off until spring. They will need to return to their families soon to hunt and prepare for the cold to come. I doubt we can regather them again in four or five months and still have this kind of dedicated resolve."

"How soon can we move?" I asked.

"Two days, maybe three. Finding enough horses and stocking provisions will take a little time. Other than that, they are as trained as possible," he said.

"Do you want me to ride with you?" I asked.

"Of course. What good would you be to me here? Or elsewhere?" Graham waved to Angus who waited nearby.

"Take the horses to water and turn them loose. Bring me the big bays; saddle one with Ywain's gear," he said.

"I am unworthy." I sheathed my sword.

"Why? Because you followed Bekah's orders? Because you saved your wife and son? Leave it be. The rest will unfold as it will," Graham said.

"Nola and the boy will be no trouble?" I asked.

"Certainly not. I saw Gwendolyn's eyes light up when you handed Wallace to her. She'll be glad to have another baby around. I will leave Trevor and fifty men here with orders to take everyone north if we fail. Will that suit you?"

"More than I can say."

"Ywain, do not beat on yourself over this. If I chastised myself every time I obeyed Gwendolyn's command, I would be nothing but a whipped and sorry pup. You do what you think is right in the moment, then live with it."

"It is as Keenan told me before he died. It is hard to be so young and want so much."

"It is far harder to be old and want so little. Let us see where tomorrow takes us," he said.

Tossing Bekah's sword to Angus when he brought the horses, Graham swung onto a gigantic bay with black stockings. I levered myself onto its twin. The boy approached to hand Graham the sword, but he waved it back to me. I took the tarnished hilt and nodded. Longing swelled in the boy's inexperienced eyes like a storm cloud. He wanted to ride with us, to swing a sword, to become a man. I wanted to sit him on my knee and tell him it was not what each of us thought it would be. It was far less and far worse. Far more horrifying than any grandfather, father or uncle or brother could tell us. It was the path all boys must travel, but each was forced by circumstances beyond his control as to the time and place. For some it came far too soon. For some much too late. I wanted to hold him a moment and brush the hair out of his eyes, tell him to go run in the grass, splash in the stream, chase butterflies and daydreams.

"Whose boy are you?" I asked.

"Trevor's, Sir," he said, his gray eyes clearing.

"Tell him he has a fine son. Tell him to keep you safe." And I trotted after Graham, and Pet trotted after me.

THE WHITE SKIRT

BEKAH

I want to return to the sea. I go there, but everything is burned. Inside Muirray, a charred wooden statue waits. A chalice is there, and a sword and helmet. A voice tells me to pick up the sword and cleave the statue in two, to open it. There is a man inside. Surrounded by light, strong and determined, I pick up the sword. I walk toward the statue carved like a man with the sword blazing over my head, ready to strike the wood and release what is inside. But I cannot do it. The voice argues with itself saying, "Strike now before you die" and "Put down the sword, it no longer matters."

I am in a stone hole, enclosed where I cannot move. There is a sword above my breast, a wide sword as large as the span of my hand. It is not straight, but curved. I can see the angled edges and it is sharp on the bottom. I must push the sword up and out so I can be released, but how can I push something so sharp. It is not only driven through the stone, it is driven through something light and transparent. Still, it must be removed so I can be free. I am waiting for someone to come and pull the sword by its hilt to release me. I see a Roman arrow fletched in black feathers, like the ones that killed Pal. The arrow will sever the sword. Who will come with the arrow to release me? What is the sword? What is the arrow? Who will come? Betrayal imprisons me inside the dark place. Scorn keeps away the one I once loved. But he holds the arrow, the arrow of truth, the truth of what happened to me, to us. I need to ask his forgiveness for sending him to his death, for killing the child that was of his making. He needs to tell me the truth. He needs to tell me the truth.

"Bekah. Bekah. Can you sit up?"

I cannot return. I do not want to come back. I want to stay by the sea and wait. My arms are so heavy. I hear Rowena speaking, but I cannot move. I know I must get up and compose myself. We must leave. But it is hard. I do not want to come back to this day, this time and place. I want to be by the sea where I can wait. I am so tired. My arms so heavy. My eyes burn. My head hurts. I am rising in a mist.

"Bekah, open your eyes," Rowena said.

I do. I feel half in this world, half in the other. My eyes are so heavy. They close again. But Rowena wakes me.

"Open your eyes, Bekah. Open your eyes."

When I open them, it is evening and the light is strange, tinged with aquamarine and salmon pink. Rowena hovers over me. From afar I watch myself. I watch her. She floats in the air full of white light, shaped like a man, yet not a man. Lavender light fills the white light. I am not afraid, but cautious, pierced by the intensity of trying to see what is going to happen. My eyes squint painfully. I squeeze them shut, hard, so as not to see, but I do see. The images do not come to me in understandable order. They are disjointed but entwined. I cannot understand it all. I keep asking, "What does it mean." I cannot stop the images from coming back to me. I am in the maze at Lynnmer. There are colors everywhere, not flowers, just the evening colors of light spilled along the tops of the hedges. I do not want to see what I am bound to see. I am in the maze.

"Bekah, come back," Rowena said.

I feel her hand on my forehead, then on my shoulder as she pulls me upright. I am crying.

"I do not want to see," I said. "I do not want to see."

"All right then. Keep your eyes open. Here, drink this." Rowena handed me a chalice.

It is the chalice from the dream, the one I saw at Muirray near the wooden statue and the sword and helmet. I strike at it, at her, my arms flailing.

"Keep it away. Keep it away."

"Bekah, they are coming. We must go. If you drink this, it will help you with the pain. It will give you strength to walk. I cannot carry you and I cannot drag you any farther."

"The wolves?" I ask.

"No. The men. From both ways. From north and south. Men on horses. Destined to meet. We must be ready."

"Where will you take me?" I fought to get my legs beneath me.

"To the hovel. There are things there you must have. Here, drink this." She placed the chalice against my hand.

"Rowena, where did you get this?" I asked staring into the milky liquid.

"The cup? At Muirray. I found it on the floor beneath a cloak I took for Nola. Do you call me a thief?" she asked.

"No. It was Gordan's. I am glad you have it."

I placed the rim of the cup to my lips, shaking so hard the elixir sloshed from side to side.

"Do not be afraid. It is from the roots of the tree that grows in the high place. It will help you."

Tipping back my head, I poured the liquid into my mouth

and gulped twice. The sweetness surprised me. The coolness that soothed my throat turned to a warm burning in my chest and stomach. Within moments, my arms and legs tingled, the aching pain that had pounded through me eased to a gentle thrumming. The startling colors I had seen disappeared and in their place hung a fabric of misty gray with pinpricks of starry light. Enough to show the way.

Rowena took my hand and led me a few steps. I walked on sponge and dross. I walked with no feeling in my legs or feet.

"All you need to do," Rowena said, "is follow me. I will keep a slow but steady pace. The way is difficult, but possible."

"How will you know where to go?" I asked, my words slurring together.

"I will follow them," she said, pointing.

I leveled my eyes along the length of her arm, adjusting them to the dimming light, blinking to help me focus. Six pairs of small red-gold spheres gleamed from the surrounding thickets. Rowena patted my shoulder.

"They see better in the dark then even I do," she said.

She clucked her tongue and the wolf eyes moved together, then disappeared. Rowena followed them and I followed her.

The shadows of morning shrunk until we cast no shadow at all. Then our shadows came out of the sky and snuck behind us, minute dark spots just beneath our feet. They lengthened and grew longer. If I stepped with precision, I could walk on Rowena's head. The game made me smile and helped me think of something else besides the pain that had returned ten-fold.

The wolves were gone. Sometime near dawn, I had heard them

singing together. Then, one last mournful howl before Rowena and I were left with the other smaller night sounds. The scurry of mice. The soft twitter of birds perched in the trees. Once the startled snort of a buck. I thought I could hear the echo of the sea, but perhaps that was only my mind playing tricks on me. I longed to immerse myself in the waves.

"Give me more of the drink," I said to Rowena.

"There is no more," she said still walking.

"Get some more," I said.

"If that is an order, then there is no way I can obey. There is only one source and it is far away in the opposite direction."

"Why did you not bring enough of the root to make more?" I stumbled over my own feet as I trudged to keep up with her.

"Because, Bekah, we only take what we need in the moment. You do not know this yet, but you are past the point of needing the root's power. You still hurt, but your healing will come quickly now and you will have more strength than you have ever had. The enemy meant to demean and humiliate you. They succeeded only in increasing your determination and resolve."

"Ro— I cannot go on." I fell to my knees.

"Yes, you can. Get up. There is nothing stopping you except self-pity. Tomorrow the outside pain will be gone. The inside pain will remain to drive you to your purpose."

"And what—what is that?"

"To inspire and lead. Now, get up. I did not go to all this trouble to save you to have you quit on me."

Rowena walked back to where I knelt naked in the leaves, my hands covering my face. Her step said she was going to kick me up. Instead, she placed her hand on the top of my head. Heat flowed through my scalp and down into my skull. A stinging prickle crept out of the earth and crawled up my legs. I stood. I straightened. I walked in Rowena's shadow.

"How did you do that?" I asked.

"I did not do anything," she said. "You did. Someday you will come to know your own ability to draw power from many sources. Someday you will not need me as a go-between."

"What must I do?" I pushed myself into a shuffling jog to keep up with her trot.

"Trust," she said. "And ask."

"Is that all?"

"That is all. So simple that most believe it impossible."

Rowena pulled aside a woven brush door and invited me into a dwelling that was part hut, part cave. The front portion, flooded with the unnatural light of day going to dusk, made the interior seem dark and forbidding. Several smooth-top stumps served as seats and table. She motioned for me to sit and went into the darkness. She returned with a finely woven cloak and gestured that I should put it on. Then she kindled a fire in a stone pit and brought water to boil. She scooped herbs from a sack to make tea and set out bark plates and horn spoons. I dozed, then woke to the overpowering aroma of meat and vegetables steaming before me. Rowena mimed the action of eating and when I lifted the first bite to my mouth, she walked out into the approaching night.

An owl called. Another answered. The high-pitched death squeal of a hare startled me into standing. Rowena appeared holding the animal by its ears, its legs limp, its belly ripped and devoid of heart and intestines, its eyes glazed and already drying. A smear of blood graced Rowena's forehead and each cheek. She nodded at me and made signs that indicated I should lie down and sleep. She pointed into the cave. I did as she bid.

Inside the darkness my feet found the stiff hair of deer hides. I knelt and felt until my hands found a pallet covered in furs. The space smelled like the lair of a beast mixed with the scent of berries, flowers, and herbs. I kept the clean cloak wrapped around me and squirmed into the warm nest. Rowena added wood to the fire and the flames leapt shooting light into the place where I lay staring at a ceiling of crystals hung with dried plants and bird wings. In the corner stood a bulging chest overhanging with clothing, yet Rowena wore rags. I heard her humming as she worked. My nose told me she was concocting something bitter and sweet. I fell asleep with the pungent odor, the tickling taste of it on my tongue.

Rowena's vow of silence lasted through the morning. I did not ask her why she refused to speak. I did not ask her why she insisted I eat the plate of hare meat and drink the chilled broth, but had nothing for herself. I did not question her when she searched through the trunk, shaking out garment after garment, folding them and setting them aside. I did not inquire where she had gotten the long, wide, white skirt she helped me put on, cinching it around my waist with a heavy belt woven from strips of leather and decorated with dried hare's feet. She found soft grass sandals for my feet and over these placed short boots of deerskin decorated with symbols burned into the hide. Then she led me into the sun, sat me on the ground, and worked the knots from my hair. She took her time pulling a bone comb through the strands, separating and fluffing until an aura of whitegold burst from my head and fell to my knees. Last, she took a small pot full of red, viscous fluid and began to paint my face and breasts. Though she said nothing, I knew it was the blood of the hare she had killed the night before while the owls were crying to each other. When she had finished with me, she tidied up the hovel, made certain the fire was out, closed the brush door, and walked into the day waving for me to follow her. In her rags and bare feet, with her butchered gray hair and stooped shoulders, she seemed as sad and powerless as a pauper.

THE ENCOUNTER

YWAIN

"Do you hear them?" I asked.

"I hear nothing, Ywain, but these men and their horses. A hint of wind. The sea of course," Graham said. "Do you?"

"Yes. At least I think I do. Perhaps it is only something I sense. My gut tells me they are twice our number."

"It shouldn't matter if we have surprise on our side. I do not think they can know we are coming, unless, like you, they have someone among them who knows without knowing. I have never had the ability, despite my long time with Gwendolyn. You?"

"Only a recent sensation. I think it came from being with Keenan and from knowing Bekah."

"Has knowing her in that way been what it seems it might be?" Graham asked as the bays jogged side-by-side at the head of the long columns of armed men.

"They say if you speak of it, it will be taken from you," I said.

"Then do not speak of it." Graham stood in his stirrups to search for the scouts who ranged in front of us.

"I will say this much. It is more than you can imagine. More sweet and horrible, more beautiful and bitter than anything I ever thought possible."

"I guessed as much. Do you fear her as I do? That is not something I would usually ask or admit, but the times are strange."

"Fear. Yes. But an apprehension mixed with lust and love. Wanting her takes me to a place where I lose the man I am and become only a thing that begs to please her. It is a sorry state, Graham. Do not wish it for yourself. All men wish for this, and then, like me, have no idea how to handle it."

"Do you feel a sense of loss or of victory?" he asked.

"Odd with the situation against us, the numbers against us. But I feel this will be a good day. That things will fall in place. That triumph will be ours."

"I feel that too—what in the—"

Both our horses reared at the same time, sending the mounted men behind us into a stomping, crashing standstill. Rowena stood in the road in front of us, her hand outstretched. The scouts whirled around and raced back, swords drawn. I motioned to Graham, and he raised his arm to stop them. Their horses skidded to a stop raising a cloud of pale gray dust.

"The one who wore the white skirt," I said to Graham.

"Give me her sword." Rowena walked forward and took hold of the cheek band on my horse's bridle.

I did not hesitate. I pulled the polished metal from the dual scabbard at my side and handed it to her haft first. She took the blade, and using it like a cane, she shuffled away.

"She lives?" I called after her.

"She lives," Rowena called back. "Look for her in the high place."

Then she was gone. One of the scouts kneed his horse after her, but Graham ordered him back.

"Let her go," he said. "Ywain?"

"I do not know," I said, "but relief floods through me. I guess we wait and see. We ride into whatever waits for us at Muirray."

A soft murmur rushed through the afternoon, moving from

man to man away from us. "She lives," they whispered, and the words served to spur us forward and became a mystical incantation that matched the sound of the horses' hooves punishing the ground.

THE WAIT

BEKAH

I sat in the lee of a stone slab to keep away from the wind that was scouring every surface with sand. Far below, the remains of Muirray accepted the kissing swish of the waves. I tried to remember what it had been like to live there with Gordan and the girls, the mornings of hunting with Lilith and Ywain, the afternoons of doing simple things the household required, the evenings of playing with Morgan and Jenna with Alanna looking on as she wove cloth or worked her needle. Comfort, security, peace, joy, all faded into nothing but memory. A sea eagle soared up from the lower cliffs, her wings catching the thermal. The shadow she cast molded itself to the shape of rock and bush, as fluid as black water, as contained as spirit within body. I knew there was a way to become shadow, to ease myself over all the obstacles of the earth without injury, without leaving a mark. If I concentrated long enough, focused on the wind and lightness, I knew I could glide and dive.

A butterfly flitted from dried leaf to shriveled berry searching for a flower. How odd that she should have survived the cooling nights, the absence of nectar? Why hadn't she flown on with her kind when the days grew shorter? Her white wings, transparent in the sunlight, held the marine-blue shape of twin eyes that fluttered open, then closed. She settled with graceful precision in each spot, her tongue reaching out to touch and to investigate.

Then she lifted off, a short smooth poof before she flew an erratic dancing pattern. Like me, she had chosen this place out of the wind to rest.

Drawn by color or scent, the butterfly spun toward me and when I did not move, lit on my blood-painted breast. The tickle of her feet and antenna stiffened the nipple, cracking the dried rust red with a sunburst of white skin hidden beneath. The ecstasy was unimaginable. Desire pulsed through both breasts and shot downward, the hot explosion between my thighs turning to molten wetness. I closed my eyes. Bliss engulfed me and I imagined Ywain kissing me, his broad fingers swirling the warm wetness over swollen lips, the small bud of deepest pleasure swelling. I lay down and pulled the skirt to my waist, spread my legs and opened myself to the sun and wind, allowing the power of the earth and sky to enter me. When I stopped shaking and opened my eyes, Rowena was leaning against the slab of stone with my sword by her side. Heat hotter than the sun flushed into my face.

"Do not feel shame." She set the blade aside and came to sit near me. "I was once the same way. There is nothing more fulfilling than beckoning the gods to take you. Not every woman has the ability to permit the deepest power to seduce her. It is a gift."

"I did not think I would ever feel pleasure again after what they did to me." I pulled down the skirt and sat cross-legged.

"It is a good sign. It means you are healing. Though they hurt you terribly, they did not destroy you. I brought your sword."

"I see. So you saw Ywain? Graham?"

"Yes. For a moment. The men who ride with them speak your name. When they encounter the enemy tomorrow, they will be ready to give everything."

"Rowena, what does it mean? The white skirt? These boots. The cloak worn only by people of great wealth. Can you tell me?"

"It is a long story, but I will tell you what I can. Most of it has faded far away into the memories of another time." She pulled pieces of dried fruit from the pouch at her side and handed them to me.

"I think it will help me to know." I sucked on the shriveled apple to soften it so I could chew.

"It always helps us to know the stories. It is how we learn to become what we must become."

She stopped and stared out over the expanse of land and sea before us. I sensed her mind searching for a beginning, a place to start. I squirmed closer to her, and she placed her withered hand on my knee and sighed.

"I was once a woman of great power, high born into a family, born late to a woman who sat on her hand-carved chair with weariness, dressed all in black, her thin arms heavy on the thick arms of the chair, her hands so weighted she could not raise them to hold me. She was weary of life, weary of wielding power. She had no time or energy for me. A woman of the woods who was my mother's handmaiden raised me. So I learned the ways of the wild ones as well as the ways of the greedy ones, the men and women who sought my mother's blessing and protection, the ones who hungered after her power like wolves in winter. I knew that I would have to someday choose whether I would follow on the path of my mother's clan or on the path of the deer and the hare. Either way power would be mine, but each choice wielded a different kind of mastery and authority."

Rowena sighed, pulling air from far down in her lungs and exhaling her past. I reached out and held her hand and she smiled at me, her torn teeth and cracked lips making it hard for me to believe that she was once young.

"The weather was stormy with clouds and heavy mist all around.

The woman of the woods took me to her other home, the hovel with the ceiling of stars. We put our things there and then walked up Lovell Tor, passing the herd of horses along the way. She spoke to them in their language and they came to her, each shuffling and pushing for the right to feel her hand on their head. There was storm and lightning and thunder and rain all around us, but we had only a few sprinkles as we walked and talked, stopping to hug the oldest of the trees. 'Grandfather,' she said, or 'Grandmother, it is I, Sacred Circle Woman, come back to embrace you.' At the tallest spot, spent and sweating, she offered her prayers, teaching me the chanted words. On our way down the mountain, the moon began to rise, an orange crescent just above the dark blue, heavy nebulous horizon. A huge orange globe glowed, spectral in the sky, before it disappeared behind the clouds. To this day, I see that moon and she guides me."

She shivered and shook her head. Her hand clenched on mine like Lilith's talons, then she sighed once more and leaned back against the stone. Her face softened as her eyes closed.

"By the time we got back to the hovel, it had begun to rain. We put on the water to heat for tea and ate apple slices, cheese, and cakes. We talked. At dark we set up our pallets in the brush arbor. I went out to clean my teeth in the rain and then farther out to relieve myself, with the tall wet grass brushing my hips. I turned my face to the sky and loved the rain on my skin. We curled under our hides and furs with the rain hard and heavy on the leafed roof, and the lightning put on a show while the thunder rumbled. The woman took out a drum and drummed a spirit-calling song. It soothed me, and all the tension of my young life oozed out of me, and I fell into a wonderful sleep. I woke several times to see the moon climbing in the southwest in scattered clouds and the aftermath of the storm. Before dawn I lay a long time thinking about many things, then rose and put on my boots and cloak and went out. I walked into the setting moon with the rising sun at my back. I walked a long time in the damp cool day traveling up to the top of the Tor to pray. When I returned, the woman and I ate the stale cakes and curdled milk and nuts and seeds and fruit. A horrible pain seized me, doubling me over until I felt that I would throw my heart onto the earth. Then a piece of the grand puzzle slipped into place for me. I knew what I must do. I would choose the pathway of the deer and hare. I would wear the white skirt the woman had woven for me.

"I asked the woman to drum for me. I lay on the damp ground and she drummed for a long time, singing a song the old ones sang to call the giant fish from the sea. It was beautiful. I could see the great ones leaping from the water. I rose and took off my clothes. I put on the white skirt and danced to the chant. The woman gave me a small bag on a string that hung between my breasts. She painted my face, shoulders and breasts with blue clay and I danced again. I danced and danced until I could no longer stand."

Rowena had finished. It seemed she had nothing else to say.

"And?" I asked.

She hesitated, then went on.

"When I woke from a long sleep, the woman was gone, but all her things remained. The birds came and the squirrels. The hare and fox. The deer and wolves. The owls and hawks. They all came. I was not lonely. I had everything I needed."

"You never went back," I said.

"No, I never went back," she said.

"Your mother?" I asked. "Your family? Your people?"

"Died. All of them. In the great sickness that swept the land clean."

"But you never even saw her again?" I asked.

"No. Well, only in my dreams, only with the second sight."

"The woman of the woods. The one who gave you the white skirt?"

"She came once more, bringing me the chest of my mother's things pulled on a travois behind an old shaggy pony. She did not speak to me. She only tugged the heavy casket to the ground, took the water I offered, and left."

"You have never seen her again?"

"No. But she speaks to me through the hare. She guided me when I did not know what to do. All these years I have felt her close to me."

"Rowena, how long ago was this? Who were your people?"

"Much too long ago for you to know. My people are gone. They do not matter now."

"What does matter then? Why do you give the white skirt to me? Why do you ask me to embrace the power of the hare? The Goddess works through you, and now you show me the way for her to work through me. Why?"

"Because your people live. They matter. If you do not fight for them, with them, who will? If nothing is done, they too will be gone from the earth. Her ways slip from us. You are chosen. The one who can bring back health and wholeness."

"You have greater power than I. You know everything about the right way. Why not you?"

"Because I am old. Because I am ugly. Men will not follow me. They will not lay down their lives for me. It is beauty that draws men to do her will. Beauty and the force nestled between your legs. Use it, Bekah. It is why it was given to you."

She pulled her hand from my grasp and patted my head as she would a dog's. She stretched and paced in the narrow space between stone and bushes. She lifted her arms above her head and tipped back to face to the sun. I knew she was praying, though I did not know what she asked. I wanted her to sing, to find a drum and beat the rhythm so I could dance.

When she finished, she gestured for me to be quiet and still as she curled on the ground, making herself small and round. I watched her as a child watches a magician. The day softened toward evening, the heat of the sun giving way to the chill the sea breeze brought to the shore. Slight movement in the brush caught my eye, and I stared until the shape of a hare appeared. She hopped, then nibbled, her ears going back and forth, her lips twitching. Bit by bit she drew nearer Rowena's rock-like body. When she capered close enough, Rowena reached out and touched her on the back. The hare did not leap away. She stilled and laid her ears along her back. Rowena picked her up and brought her to me. I cradled the trembling beast like a kitten or puppy, feeling her wild heart throbbing beneath my fingers.

Cutting a long, twisted fringe from my leather belt, Rowena made a noose and slipped it over the hare's head.

"Tie her to your ankle," she said. "She'll come to know your scent and learn that no harm will come to her. For now, we rest. When the moon rises, we will go the place where we must wait. Tomorrow, when the time is right, you will release the hare and she will tell you which direction you will send the men. She will divine the outcome of the conflict."

"We will fight tomorrow?"

"Yes." Rowena settled herself against the sun-warmed stone.

"When?" I asked.

"I do not know."

"Will victory be ours?"

"I do not know," she repeated.

"Why do you know some things, but not others? Why is your knowledge not complete?"

"Why do you ask so many questions?

I tethered the leather thong to my right ankle and set the hare on the ground. I worried that she would run and choke, but she hopped a hesitant foot, then turned and hopped back and crouched under the shelter my skirt made. Her whiskers brushed the skin of my shin.

"One more, Rowena. Please?"

She nodded at me, her eyes already closed, her hands clasped under her chin as she lay like a worn crescent of wood.

"What happened to cause your sickness? The thing you cannot heal. That which keeps you away from any clan?"

I thought she had fallen asleep. The rhythm of her breathing matched the snuffling breath of the hare. The sun burst open, spraying the sky with bloody color, then sank into the sea. The first stars appeared, winking like innumerable silver eyes.

"My mother called to me, but I did not go to her. I heard her for many nights, begging and pleading for me to return, but I did not go," Rowena whispered.

I teetered on the verge of asking her "why?" when she said, "Because I did not love her. She was nothing to me but a reflection of what I never wanted to become."

"Ah," I said to encourage her.

"Bekah, remember this. When some one asks you to come, beseeches you to help, you are bound by the beautiful workings of the Goddess to respond, to give whatever it is that you have to give. Do not turn a blind eye. Do not cover your ears to be deaf. Never assume it will not matter. You are here to serve, and you serve her best by loving and caring."

The hare's heartbeat slowed and if she did not sleep, she at least had calmed enough to rest. A pressing weariness pushed me to the earth, and I took care to place my legs in a way that would shelter the small creature as I slept.

"Bekah?"

"Hmm?" I sighed.

"Be grateful your daughters love you," Rowena said.

"I fear I am far from them now. Will I ever see them again? Will I see them grown with babies of their own?" I asked.

"You will see them again," Rowena said. "Now sleep."

THE BATTLE

YWAIN

By sunrise, the scouts had returned with word that the enemy had moved into the large fields surrounding the south side of Muirray. Mounted and armed, they brought wagonloads of goods and supplies as if they intended to fortify the place and remain through the winter, thus holding their northernmost territory. We had all dozed sitting at the feet of our saddled horses, snatching whatever moments of rest we could find between the thoughts of those we had left behind and those we were destined to meet in the morning. Graham had given the order of "no fires," so we tried to content ourselves with the dried rations each man packed. "No noise," either. So there was no sharpening of knives or swords, no fiddling with gear, no conversation. Trail weary, our horses stood three-legged, heads low. Only the squeak of leather and the sweet jingle of chomped bits competed with the music of the night. Within a hard stone's throw, the sea galloped onto shore, each wave building a sigh as it crested, groaned as it crashed, then shushed back into itself. So far off that the sound might have been my imagination, a wolf wailed. I tried not to think of Bekah. I worked to keep my mind on the men and formulate the plan that Graham and I had worked between us as we rode. But her visage kept returning; her face enveloped in blazing auric flames. Throughout the hours, I burned with want of her and did not sleep. When the first film of ashen light sifted through the trees, I forced my stiffened legs to stand and leaned against my horse, quivering with exhaustion and anticipation.

"Ready?" Graham whispered leading his bay alongside mine.

"Yes. I thought Bekah would have joined us by now. One of the falconers leads her horse."

"How can we know the ways of women?" Graham struggled to get his foot into the stirrup. "I suspect we will see her soon enough, so whatever plans we made might be for naught. Are you prepared to let go of what we have decided? You know when the men see her, they will turn to her and forget their allegiance to us."

"I think I am ready for anything. But Bekah has stunned me more times than I care to admit. I both long and fear to see her again."

"I, too." Graham raised his arm in the silent signal to move out.

We kept a tight rein on the horses that were tossing their heads and trying to prance. Our tightly-wired energy seeped through reins and saddle skirts, telling them something would soon happen. We heard the muffled murmuring of the men, but Graham turned back once and his glare shut off the sound. Coming out of the trees into a widening glen, the horses quit their columned ranks and milled, pushing together and separating. We had a major choice to make: take the lower finger down to the sea and approach along the beach below the cliffs, or take the upper finger around the heights, skirting Lovell Tor to sneak in from behind their camp. Either way, the element of early morning and surprise sat on our side. I slouched as Graham studied the lay of the land. The sun inched out of the sea, slathering the dawn chill with a taste of warmth and color.

A commotion at the rear of the mass spun us around. The

head falconer clung with one hand to his rearing horse as Bekah's mare whirled away. Losing his grip, he slipped backwards and smashed onto the ground, releasing Lilith into the air. She screamed, a crazed note that split the morning silence, and rose, her sharp wings slicing the air. All eyes followed her up, up, up, and there, ignited on the bald top of a knoll stood a cloaked figure surrounded by a burning cloud of wind-stirred hair. The men gasped, tugging their horses to a standstill. Graham and I trotted forward. The female shape stabbed the sword she held into the earth and pulled a limp hare from her cape. She held the creature by its neck fur to her chest, then set it on the ground. For a breathless moment the beast did not move. Then it ran toward the trees, slid to a stop, and turned to race back toward the sea. Three times it repeated its erratic dance, then dashed under the woman's white skirt. She threw off her mantle, and the sun caught the red mounds of her painted breasts. She flung her arms wide, each hand pointing in the opposite direction. The men bellowed in one voice, a stupendous roar that ripped through their ranks, dividing them into a blistering charge.

"Go low," Graham yelled. "I will take the high road."

And he was gone, spurring his horse to catch the men bolting back through the trees. Gouging the bay, I pulled my sword and fought to turn him toward the group dropping headlong onto the beach, their horses already tearing up the sand in a furious cloud. I glanced back for one last look and saw Bekah standing in the same spot, her arms raised, Lilith with lashing wings on one hand, her sword clasped in the other.

How long does it take an agitated horse to tire? For a fevered man's furious rush into battle to turn to fear? Those two thoughts grappled for answers as I churned toward Muirray, my mount's stumbling strides trying to overtake the horse in front of it. The bay ate the ground, his heated chase overcoming the others until he lagged two lengths behind the trio of leaders. We spilled into the compound, four horses abreast sailing over the rock walls, the speed of some carrying them over the next wall and into the field beyond where men were just rising from their sleep. I wrenched hard on the reins and the bay buckled in the middle, falling back on his rump as I kicked free and landed upright. Dashing out of the line of leaping horses, I spun right into a tight cluster of men wielding clubs against a body hanging from its feet from the gate's arch. Rowena, bloody and beaten. All thought stopped and I knew nothing but the weight of my sword as it sought each target and the slow motion sound of blood gushing. Men with swords replaced men with clubs. When they fell, more appeared in their place; the churning clamor and suffocating dust overwhelmed my eyes and ears.

Then she appeared. Her white mare burst over the wall, her sword swinging, and the enemy fell back, tripped and scrambled away from the bloodstained wraith, wailing, "She lives!" Our men took up the cry, moving south of Muirray, taking down everything in our path, galloping after those who had run in retreat. In the middle of the great field, the white mare wheeled in circles as Bekah searched the fallen and the slain. She caught sight of me crawling through the gate, then Rowena's body twirling on its rope axis. A horrible sob erupted from her throat. Every hair on my body fought to be free of my skin, and I collapsed. She started toward me, then spun her horse by bringing the flat of her sword down on the haunch to goad the foaming mare after the disappearing fray.

TRIUMPH

YWAIN

T he world had taken on an unbearable silence, as if every man and animal had vanished from the earth. I thought I could hear the distant sounds of the battle still raging, of the sea seeking to calm the shore, but mostly I heard the emptiness of being entirely consumed. The slow step of dragging hooves approached. A man grunted from his horse and clomped to my side. He grasped my sword arm and rolled me over. My eyes sought the sun in the sky and found Graham wavering above me.

"Ywain, I am glad you live," he said.

Because I could not speak, I blinked, ashamed of the tears that escaped my eyes. He took the sword still gripped in my hand and led me to a spot of shade against the wall. We hunkered there, our sweat drying in the light mating of breezes that blundered down from the cliffs and up from the sea.

"Rowena?" he asked nodding at the grisly corpse twisting and turning of its own accord.

I blinked again and looked away. He stood, wrenched my arms and legs around, and probed a slash that had opened my shoulder, as well as another that had ripped my thigh.

"Nothing broken or life threatening. A club to the head?" He did not wait for an answer. He limped over to his horse, mounted, and kneed the bay to the swinging body. One swipe of his sword and she fell; the echo of her weight hitting the ground blasted open my ears. Graham rode away, his head hanging, his chin touching his chest, his back round with the jaded weight of victory.

In small groups of two or three, the men began to return. They gathered in clusters, dismounted and stood holding their horses. A few began the rounds of examining the fallen, finishing off the enemy who lived, and helped their own wounded to rise or carrying them to the untromped earth outside the wall and laying them in the shadow of the stacked stones. Someone saw me sitting there and brought me water. Slowly, as if I were waking from a dream, my hearing returned to take in the low murmuring, the moaning and cries, Lilith's scream as she circled Muirray's tower. Sensation itched into the bottom of my feet and tingled back into my hands. When I could rise and hold onto the wall for support, I tottered toward the gate, motioning to one of the men to come with me.

"Take the rope from her feet," I said, "and lay her out along the wall. Bring me something to cover her."

The man's nostrils flared, his eyes widened. He took a step forward, then stopped and stared at me.

"Go on. Do not fear her power. They have beaten it from her. Whatever might be left can wield no harm."

He cut the braided jute cord from the burned ankles and dragged Rowena's corpse by her bare feet, the featureless face staring upward into the vacant air. I pointed to the bay I had ridden where he quivered in a corner, his nose in the dirt. The man walked over, untied my cloak from the saddle, and brought it to me. I unfurled the cloth and let the thick wool sweep down over Rowena. She had buried Muirray's dead. She had saved my wife and son. She had brought Bekah back to life. Apparently, she had walked into the camp of the enemy with nothing but her rags and her wisdom for protection. Remorse burned behind my eyes and scalded my throat. I had never thanked her.

"You can thank her now," Bekah said behind me. "She will hear you. Though she would say no thanks are needed. When she left me last night, she said if I would do the Goddess's bidding, if I did my part and she did hers, then victory would be ours. I had no idea what she intended to do, that using her for sport would distract the guards and give us a strong advantage."

I turned. Speckled with blood and mud, the white mare still flung her head and fought the bit. Red rivulets ran from Bekah's breasts to her waist and stained the white skirt hiked above her knees. Plastered to her head and back, her hair had turned from white gold to red gold. Her lower lip, bitten through, bled a thin steady stream down her chin. I reached up to help her down.

"No," she said, her eyes crazed with fiery light. "Let me find Graham first."

"Bekah," I said as she turned her horse away.

"No, Ywain, we will not speak of it. I will not bear your pity on top of my wrath. I want to find Graham and have him order the men to strip anything of value from these bodies and burn them. I want Muirray cleansed of their evil and ill will. Can you organize things here? Get a group to bring wood and water, fix a stockade for the horses, take care of the wounded, dig a pit for our dead?"

Before I could reply, she sheathed her sword, gathered the wet hair off her neck, spun it in a coil to hang over her shoulder, and trotted away. Flickering sunlight caught the crusted red whip marks on her back and turned them into a mass of writhing snakes. She heard Lilith's scream and lifted her head, eyes searching the sky above the cliff top. The falcon stooped, wind keening through her wings, and sought Bekah's raised fist.

THE SEA

YWAIN

"Go now," Graham said to Bekah, "There is nothing else you can do." He turned to me and added, "See if you can get her to settle down and sleep. She's on the edge of swooning."

"I have never swooned, Graham, and do not plan to do so." Bekah handed Lilith over to the falconer.

The man trembled as he reached for the great bird, his eyes riveted to Bekah's blood-and-sweat stained breasts. When she did not release the leather straps that held Lilith to her hand, his eyes traveled up to find her eyes as feral and fierce and commanding as the hawk's. He ducked his head in apology and stood mute while Bekah settled Lilith on his fist and stroked her breast feathers with grimy fingers. Graham handed her a blousy over-shirt and she took it but did not put it on. She dismissed the falconer, then repeated to Graham, "I have never swooned."

"All right, then," Graham said. "Let Ywain take you to get some rest. If you cannot admit to being done in, I can. The guards are posted; the horses secure in the yard; the men are eating. Do the same. I will see you in the morning."

He gripped my shoulder and said close to my ear, "Watch her."

When he was out of hearing, Bekah asked, "What did he say?"

"He asked me to watch over you." I took the shirt and held it out for her to slip on.

"Do you think I need watching?" She shoved my hands away.

"Everyone is watching you, Bekah. Hundreds of eyes are trying not to stare, but are intensely curious about what will happen next."

"I am going to walk down to the sea and bathe. Alone," she said stepping away from me.

I followed at a discreet distance, carrying the shirt and her sword that tapped against mine hung at my waist. She turned once to scowl at me, but I did not scowl back. I gave her a small salute and a brief smile and kept on following. She walked through the encamped men, stopping to say a word or two, often squatting to touch the face or arm of one too weak or wounded to rise at her approach. She stopped at Rowena's body, the only corpse we had not buried, and knelt and placed her hands on my blood-mottled cloak that served as shroud. When she rose, she waved me forward and said, "Tomorrow, early, we will carry her to the top of the Tor."

We walked together through the throng of horses crammed into the yard. They shoved and jostled to come close, each of them reaching out a supple nose to sniff her hand, some nuzzling her palms and arms and licking the salt that had crusted on her skin. It made her laugh and the dulcet sound rippled outward on the evening air like a blessing. Her mare came with laid-back ears and shouldered her way through the herd. The others parted and moved aside, not one of them nipping or kicking or challenging her in any way. Bekah stroked her fine face, cradled the big head, and kissed her eyes. The beast heaved a heavy sigh, her lips twitching as Bekah fondled her ears with one hand and scratched her chest with the other. A wound on her shoulder ran, and Bekah reached out to trace the outline with her finger.

"Remind me in the morning and I will search for the salve Keenan used to put on the horses. It may still be in the shelter behind his house."

"Bekah—"

"Please, Ywain, do not talk to me about it. I cannot. It is better forgotten."

"How can I forget when I— when your back—"

"There is nothing you can do." She took her sword and climbed over a makeshift gate where the wall had been breached.

"Let me hold you," I said, but she was gone and my words were wasted.

I followed as far as a crowd of large rocks that had tumbled from the cliff face, and there I perched to watch her. She sat where sand met stone and slipped off her boots and belt and skirt. She rolled the white cloth and set her sword over the bundle as if to keep the wind from stealing it. She made her way to the waves, picking a path that would be easiest on her bare feet. I heard her gasp as the cold water met her hips, then a yelp as the salt met her wounds. She dove and disappeared. I stood and searched the dim light that still sparkled on the surface and far out I saw her bobbing between the swells. A great fish leapt next to her, the weight of its return plunge sending a white-capped shower to engulf her. She dove once more, and reappeared crawling on the shore, struggling to get her feet beneath her to stand. I wanted to run to her to help, but made myself sit again and wait.

"Ywain," she called, plopping down next to her clothes, "come here. Give me your sword. I will stand guard so you can swim."

She held out her hands and I helped her rise, then slipped the shirt over her shivering shoulders.

"Go on. The water will revive you as it did me. It will sting your wounds, help you heal."

I unbuckled my sword and laid it next to hers, then stood as embarrassed as a boy as I removed my clothes. Darkness had overtaken the beach, and I stumbled my way down to the waves and waded out. I did not go far for fear my injured arm could not bring me back again. Instead, I ducked under to wash the filth from my hair and bounced on the bottom until my legs wearied.

When I scrambled back to the berm, Bekah had gone and Graham waited in her place.

"She asked me to tell you she was going to her old rooms and did not want to be disturbed." He handed me my shirt and trousers.

I shook my head to rid my hair and beard of water and swiped the moisture from my face.

"All well?" I asked.

"Yes. Word from the men is that few of the enemy, if any, escaped. Tomorrow, when the wind picks up to take away the smell, we will finish burning the carnage. The supplies they had brought in are enough to rebuild and refortify. I am thinking about spending the winter here. Holding the line with the men who are able to stay with me. It will serve as a buffer, a defensive position to keep them from getting to Lynnmer or beyond. We can talk about it more in the morning."

"Graham—"

"I know," he said walking with me back to the compound. "She has a mind of her own. Do not worry about it. Would you mind staying in the house with her? Maybe near the stairs so you can hear her if she comes down again. I will post other men at the doors so you will not have to be on guard."

"She doesn't seem to want me around," I said.

"I doubt it's personal. She doesn't want to be around anyone. Just keep her safe if you can."

"I will do my best, but she scares me. I do not mean fear. I mean unnerve. I never know what she is going to do next."

"I doubt you ever will." He handed me a pack of provisions and blankets. "I had them fill the cauldrons outside the door with fresh water. Do you need anything else?"

"Sleep, if possible," I said.

"Well, I hope you at least get some rest," he said. "Send the guard if you need me in the night."

Then he was gone, winding his way through the small fires in the field.

THE DREAMS

YWAIN

Her crying woke me. That and the guard from the front door who nudged my foot. I sat up, surprised that I had fallen asleep. The man stood in a patch of moonlight, his face twisting with panic as he stared at the top of the stairs where Bekah's screams and moans puddled, then flowed down to us.

"It is nothing," I said, rising. "She dreams."

I gestured him back to his post. Then I wrapped one blanket around me and carried the other up the stairs, my hand against the dark wall to guide me. I went slowly, trying to assess whether she was crying out in her sleep or if she was awake and calling for help.

She sat curled on her pallet in a close corner of the looted room where the wind stealing through the windows in sudden gusts would not reach her. Naked and quivering, she held her face in her hands. The moaning screams turned to sobbing.

"Bekah," I said from the doorway. "Bekah."

She raised her head and reached for me, still crying. I approached with care and when I could tell that she was fully awake, I knelt and gathered her into my arms. She cringed when the blanket touched her back, so I held her loosely, urging her head into the cradle between my head and shoulder.

"I saw a bird, a large bird, hawk like, red, all red. Perched on a branch and flexing its wings, with the face of the sea eagle, the eyes of a hawk, piercing me. It was too young to fly. It was finding its strength, trying out its wings.

"I was in a dark place, cold, where it was all white with blue light. Only ice and cold. A frozen sea, white and cold. I was alone. I had been there alone a long time. I was not afraid. Only tired of waiting. A bear came. A great white bear, one with acorns for his eyes. There were no people. Only the bear. There was no fire, only a cave where it was cold and I was alone. There was a hole in the ice with black water, and the bear told me to go into the water and dive down, but I did not want to go. It insisted. I was not afraid. I just did not want to go. There was a great fish, a silver fish, like the one tonight when I was swimming. It leapt from the water with sprays behind it and golden light. Joyful. Exuberant. It made me laugh. The bear kept pushing me toward the hole in the ice where the fish leapt, and where a heron waited standing on the ice. Then I was in the water staring up at a golden light above me, going down deeper and deeper into the sea, not swimming but sinking, and there, half-buried in the sand, was a glint of gold, a bright reflection of a cup on the sea floor.

"I saw a sheep skull against a red background that looked like a cliff. I saw a woman walking and I knew it was me. I was on the banks of a river, walking where the grass was tall, very tall, and the river was running calm and peaceful and quiet. I was walking upstream in the grass alone. Then there was something behind me. Frightening. I began to run. Terrified. I ran and ran until I could not breathe. I was so afraid and I fell hard, shaking, my body curling inward, trying to be small. There were men on horseback, galloping over me, and the thundering of hooves. I was hidden by the tall grass, breathing so hard, gasping, so afraid they would find me. It grew dark and I grew cold. The bear came and sniffed all around me, then lay down beside me and kept me warm. I saw people leaving, walking away, going away, in a long line down a road. They were leaving me behind; leaving me alone. They were very sad, walking a long way and leaving me alone, grieving.

"I did not know where to go. My people were gone. I followed the bear and he went north, his brown coat turning white. He stopped to tear open a log, and his paw was white with grubs. He licked some of them off and offered me the rest. The sight sickened me. I did not want to eat grubs, though I was cold and hungry. There were a few berries, dried and shriveled and I ate those. The land became colder and colder with snow and ice. The bear crawled into a cave, and I followed. The days grew short and there was only darkness. Then the heron came to stand at the open hole of black water on the edge of the ice. She opened her wings and flapped slowly, gracefully, then lifted off into the sky.

"Through the heron's eyes, I saw the people in a circle around a fire, tired, beaten, blankets around stooped shoulders. There was no drumming; no singing; no talking. I circled and landed. They told me it was better for me to be there in the cold land, the ice and the darkness, than to be where they were which was a horrible place. Everything they knew was gone. The land. The animals. Everything taken from them, and they knew they would die. But they had not forgotten me, and how I once tried to save them.

"There was a high mountain with a peak glowing with intense green light that pulsated. It filled the dark sky. I was in the cold and snow again where the light was blue and white. The white bear was gone, and I was alone again. I was very old; my hair white. Yet, I felt strong. I did not feel old. I wore the skin of the bear outside. Then I took it off, and like a seal, I slid into the hole in the ice and went deep into the sea. The heron stayed behind to guard the opening's shimmering light. The great silver fish was there, leaping and diving and guiding me. Bubbles of air escaped, going back up toward the light while I went farther into the darkness. The cup was there. It had been there a long, long time, gleaming gold in the sand. Like a seal, I swam to it. I nudged it with my nose, pushing it in the sand. I wanted to bring it to the surface, but I had no hands. Then I could not breathe and I was out of air, so I pushed to the surface and my hands returned to grasp the edge of the ice where the heron stood. Leave it there, she told me. It is not yet time. Leave it where it is safe. It has great power, power that would be abused and misused. It is for you, but it is not yet time to bring it into back into the light. I crawled from the icy water and put on the skin of the bear and lumbered back to the cave to wait."

She stopped speaking and sobbing at the same time. Her breath huffed out in short gasps as if she could not breathe. I rubbed her arm and kissed the top of her head.

"Just a dream," I said. "Only a dream."

"No, Ywain. More than that, but I do not know what it means. How am I to know what I am to do if I do not know what it all means?"

"Will it help if I say I believe the bear is Keenan and the heron is Rowena?"

"Yes, but what of the sea eagle, and the cup and the people? What does it mean?"

"I think it means nothing; only that you are tired and worried and the best thing you can do is sleep. With time, perhaps, the meaning will be made clear to you," I said.

Her body melted into mine, the shaking slowing to a dull pulsing, her flesh like thawing ice.

"Let me stay and hold you, keep you warm so you can sleep."

"No. Yes. I mean, I do not care. Do what you want, Ywain. It matters not to me." She slid down on her side, curling into herself.

Cupping my body around hers and being careful not to brush her back, I brought the blankets over us. I placed my head on my bent left arm, my fingers finding the loose strands of her sea-washed hair. I set my right hand on her hip and pulled her frozen rump into my warm groin. When I closed my eyes, the face of a snarling wolf appeared, its eyes glowing red-gold. It slobbered and snapped at a huge hawk surrounded by red-orange light as it flapped its wings and tried to fly.

LOVELL TOR

BEKAH

"Two men is all I need, Graham," I said, shoving my foot into the stirrup and clamping my hand to the saddle to keep my seat as my mare spun, half rearing. "Ywain and I can lead their horses while they carry Rowena's litter. Then we will go on to Lynnmer. There's no sense in coming this far south again only to turn north. That is, unless you need to see us once more before we go. Ywain, pick out two men you know and trust; one who can handle Lilith would be good."

"Bekah, if they catch you out on the track, you will have no chance," Graham said.

"We would have no chance with ten or fifty either. This way will be quieter, easier to stay hidden. Do not worry. I see us reaching Lynnmer. I will give Trevor your instructions and tell Gwen what your plans are. Perhaps it would be wise for Trevor to come bide the winter here with the men and you to return. Whatever you decide, send a messenger. Ywain and I will work to rally more support."

"Tell the boys—

"Yes. Yes. I will tell them what a dashing and heroic father they have. Do not look so grim. I am not teasing. I am saying what is true. And thank you. We could not have regained Muirray without you." I leaned over to squeeze his shoulder and kiss his furred cheek.

While Ywain directed the men loading the bundle that was once Rowena onto a makeshift litter of poles and boughs, I walked the mare through the men. They did not speak, but they reached up to grasp my outstretched hand or touch my white skirt as I said thank you over and over again. I said I would talk to their families. I asked them to take care. I told them I would return. I made promises I did not know how to keep. I accepted their gaping adoration because shunning it would be rude. But the weight of worship sat heavy on my shoulders. The power they believed I had was nothing. Nothing. I looked to the pit that had been filled and knew there were wives and sons and daughters whose lives had been changed forever because of me. I looked at the burning pile of bodies and knew that all I had done was enrage the enemy. I saw the sad procession of Ywain riding and leading twin horses and two men carrying a woman who could have been a queen. We were going to bear her up the trail to a resting place worthy of her life and her dying. Trying to think of some prayer to say for all of us, something that might encompass the magnitude of the choices made, the lives changed, I began to understand why Rowena had decided to follow the path of the hare and the deer, and why she had turned her back on the ways of men. How in giving up one kind of power, she succeeded in obtaining power far greater than most ever know: the power of loving and healing, the power of sacrifice. I tried to justify her last choice by believing that in giving up her own life she had saved many. But the pyre of charred stinking flesh mocked me.

"Send the men back down to wait by the horses," I said to Ywain, "then come help me. We will place her in the brush hut she built near the sacred tree."

When I looked for the pointed-eared squirrel who first showed me the place of power, I saw nothing but dried needles and leaves, the damp ground swirling with mist. I searched for some sign that Rowena lived beyond the veil of the bundle of smashed bones and broken flesh at my feet. Uncertain of my role, unwilling to admit even to myself that I did not know how to help her move on to the next world, I reached out for the branches of the tree that had first brought me portent and vision beyond the daydreams and vague knowing I had known as a child. The gnarled bark bit into my hands. A string of flames twisted and wove together, connected like a web, blue blinking flames on a dark background, and then a river of darkness and light flowing together, undulating, spilling into rivulets that covered the land and sent the azure twinkling fire blasting into the sky, turning them into stars. A sun appeared, boiling out of the sea, and the earth ran with animals of every kind. I felt a hand on my shoulder, but did not turn. I heard the voice of someone I once knew and he said, "We will remake her and she will be born anew." I released the tree and turned into the arms of the man with acorns for eyes. He held me, rocked me, sang in my ear. He took my hand and we walked back to the corpse. We knelt and I watched his hands and made mine follow his movements.

He started at Rowena's feet and began to mold and shape the body under the blanket, gently pushing back and forth, moving to a different area, up her calves, past her knees, to her thighs, softly pushing and kneading. He worked around her groin, above her hips, focusing on the navel, then stopped with his hands over her heart. I felt warmth pulse beneath my hands, pleasant and enjoyable, but strange. We moved our hands to her head and held all four palms around her face and felt her ears return, her cheekbones piece together, her eyes open, her mouth move. Keenan stood back. I did the same. I saw nothing except that the cloak and blanket covering Rowena's remains had expanded, as if she had taken a great breath, and then they fell in, collapsing under their own weight until they were flat on the litter, the ropes that bound them loose and hanging. I watched as Keenan held out his hand, not to me but to some other being hovering in the sky; white light, shaped like a man and yet not a man. Lavender light filled the white light and when I looked back, Keenan was gone.

Hearing Ywain return, I rolled the blankets and cloak together and took them into the brush hut that had been partly torn away by the wind. When I stepped back outside, he was there by the empty litter looking around, looking lost and uncertain. I opened my arms to him and said, "Ywain," and he came to me, his eyes full of tears.

"How did you—"

"Keenan came and helped me," I said. "Is he here? Show me. Keenan," he called searching the swirling mist.

"He's gone, Ywain. Rowena's gone with him. We have done all we can here." I took his hand and drew him away from the hut and the tree.

"Keenan," he called again. "Keenan."

"Ywain, come away now."

"Why will he not come to see me?" he said. "Keenan."

"I do not know. Perhaps the Goddess bids him stay away."

Ywain fell to his knees, choking to keep a terrible cry from ripping out his throat. I held him while grief ravaged the world inside him.

Our muteness on the trip back to Lynnmer silenced the men who rode with us. They whispered to each other, and at night they settled some distance away, within sight but out of hearing, so they could talk without disturbing the quietude that Ywain and I had between ourselves. Lilith rode calmly, making the rounds of our varied arms as the hours wore on, never needing to be hooded as she took in the journey with her placid eyes. The time of her molt was upon her, and she was content to be carried and not fly, content to eat the bits of meat we offered from our fingers when we shared an evening meal. On the last day, at dusk, with the lake still far off but within view, I stopped our caravan and handed the falcon over to the oldest of the men.

"Take her in. Find Trevor and tell him all that has happened. Tell him we will be there in the morning. Thank you for all you have done," I said.

The men looked to Ywain. He shrugged, then nodded.

"Do as she bids," he said. "I will as well. We will follow in the dawn."

I dismounted and held my mare's head. She pawed the ground and neighed, wanting to follow the other horses, anxious to be back at Lynnmer where she could roll in the dust and graze and laze in the sun. Handing the reins to Ywain, I said, "Tie them well and unsaddle, then come to me. Bring the blankets and food pack."

I did not go far. I made my way through the trees until I found a small clearing where the fall-dried grass would make a softer bed. In the last light, I tromped a circle, beginning at the center and working my way out, around and around, pressing down the knee-high stems. Then I lay my cloak down and undressed, folding and stacking my clothes with my boots underneath to keep them from the dew. When Ywain appeared, I sat cross-legged, pulling my fingers through my knotted hair.

"Come," I said. "Be with me. It is our last chance before you return to your family."

"Bekah." He stood at the edge of the circle. "I am afraid to touch you, to hurt you."

I crawled to him on my hands and knees and took the things from his arms. I unbuckled his sword and unlaced the tie holding his trousers. Nestling my face into the limp warmth of his loins, I breathed and kissed and squeezed his buttocks with my cold fingers until he rose, his blood rushing to meet my lips. When his knees gave way, I helped him lower his body to the ground.

"Bekah." He took my hair and pulled back my head.

"No, Ywain. It is all right. I cannot take you inside me where the pain is still great, but I can take you this way. Let me feel you. Let me please you. For my own sake, let me love you."

The rising moon blessed us with her light. There were no night sounds, not even the breath of wind in the trees or stirring the seed heads on the grasses where we lay. There were only our sounds, the sounds lovers make when they have survived something horrible and lived to love once more. I kissed my way down Ywain's chest and belly. I wet his stiffness with my tongue and took him into my mouth.

NO MAN'S WHORE

BEKAH

I stayed only long enough to watch Ywain leap from his horse and run to scoop Nola and Wallace into his arms. My girls and Alanna, Gwendolyn and her boys, circled the trio, all hugging and kissing and clinging and talking at once. Swelling with tenderness, pushing against the bones of my chest, my heart ached for all of them. I longed to be in the center of that celebration, to let down my guard and fling myself into the joyousness of safe return, but I could not. The sea hut called me. Days without interruption. Nights alone. The power of the water and sky, the rock and wind, to scour me clean, and break me down into an element of pure revenge. I could not allow myself the pleasure of gentle exchange for it would destroy my resolve, melt me back into being an ordinary woman who wanted nothing but the arms of a husband and the playful interaction of her children. The Goddess called and I had no choice but to go.

Trevor's son came to take the horses, and I handed him the reins of Ywain's mount and waved him away from the mare. He nodded, his handsome face glowing with the delight of being in service. Wheeling away, I glanced back to see my girls racing toward me, their arms outstretched, crying "Mother, Mother." I spurred ahead, setting the mare into a gallop and leaning low as she gathered her long legs, then sailed over the remains of an old wall. Looking back once more, I saw Jenna and Morgan on their knees, clutching each other, as Gwendolyn and Alanna approached to comfort them. As much as I loved them, as much as I knew they loved me, they would be better off now not to be too close to the woman I had become. They still needed their childhood games and dreams and a safe place where the world of war could not scar their hearts.

At dusk, I visited the mare dozing in her stone enclosure. I had spent the afternoon cutting dried grass for her, building a series of shocks in the field to keep the wind from blowing the fodder away, and I hauled water from the hillside spring for both of us. When we finished our nose-to-hand and nose-to-nose snuffling conversation, I walked down to the sea to wash the last vestiges of the battle from my body, though they stayed imprinted in my mind. I scaled the face of a short cliff wall and stood above the waves crashing into the rocks. The sun, dying in radiant splendor, cast stripes of colored light over the land and water. I began to shake, not only from the colder air of coming night, but also from the power that bristled out of the pockmarked face of the stone beneath my feet. Words clashed and fought inside my head, then welled from my throat:

"Do you think I would not kill all of Rome if I could? It becomes an easy thing—the mind steeled with vengeance, the heart turned to stone by sorrow. Anger, fury, rage, hatred, all fuel for the driving force that says, *kill or be killed*. Only a fool would stand aside, head bent, eyes down, hands turned palm up, weaponless, saying to the invaders—*Here take me, scourge me, misuse me, turn me into a slave, or worse yet, a conspirator, an accomplice*.

"I am no man's whore! I kneel to no one. Bow to nothing but the Goddess who gave me the ability to see beyond the veil, the second seeing of knowledge gleaned beneath the ordinary surface of things. She alone gives me power to prevail. She alone forgives the taste of blood in my mouth, the feel of blood on my hands, the sound of spilled blood beating in my ears. Do not seek to control my thoughts with accusations of guilt and shame. I do not know those words. I know not the blasphemy of blame. I know only this. If the enemy treads too close to the edge of my sword, they will die. Guiltless. Shameless. Without fear. I will take their lives and be grateful for the day I was given the strength to swing a sword.

"This is not idle threat or agony's simple anger. This is a solemn vow. I will never surrender shield or sword. I will never lie down. Not in a fur-lined bed. Not in a field of stones. If Rome did not hear me, I will say it again. I am no man's whore. I kneel to no one."

When the last shouted syllable echoed off the rock and was absorbed by the sea, my strength left me and I sank to the sand-and-wind ravaged granite. I did not feel the darkness come to cover me. I did not see the stars and moon appear to comfort me. I did not know anything until the sun returned and kissed me awake.

WINTER

BEKAH

The winter months wore past, with raucous storms interspersed by days so calm and clear and soft that they seemed like spring. I never went to Lynnmer, and I never allowed anyone to come to me at the sea hut except for Trevor's son, Angus, who brought me food, helped me harvest more feed for the mare, and brought tidbits for Lilith who had joined me after her molt. She kept me company in the small space, going in and out whenever I opened the coverings on the window or sometimes following me in through the door. She seemed content to exercise her wings nearby, riding the thermals, harassing the gulls, often perching on the small cliff to sun herself or study the view. We talked. I offered her my thoughts, and she chirruped in reply. A family of hares decided to make their home nearby, and we spent a great deal of time watching them hop and bounce, cavorting through grass and rock before they disappeared down an opening in the earth, into their mysterious world where we could not go. Lilith eyed them from my arm, but I asked her to leave them be, and she did. She allowed herself the occasional kill of a small bird to stay in practice or nibbled on the remains of some fish washed up onto the shore. I rode the mare bareback, often going long distances to tone my legs and back and to re-explore places in the area that I had known as a girl. I ran on the beach or swam in the waves to increase the capacity of my lungs and engage my heart. I practiced with the sword and knife, with my spear, attacking the same cloth sack stuffed with straw over and over again, imagining it as enemy. I spent the evening sewing up the rents and wounds in the feather-light corpse. Many days, when the weather raged outside, I sat by the fire thinking and planning, feeding the rage within. I slept for long periods, hibernating like a bear, allowing the dreams and visions to guide me.

Some days when Angus came, we sat in the sun and talked, or, rather, he talked and I listened. He told me Ywain and Nola and the baby stayed on at Lynnmer. Gwendolyn and Alanna had their hands full with the children, and Gwendolyn was wasting away with worry for Graham. Ywain had taken Trevor and a small group of men to Muirray and they had returned with the news that all was well there. The men who had chosen to stay with Graham constructed thatched huts for shelter, and they were busy rebuilding the walls and stone enclosures. They were vigilant and kept guards posted day and night, but no one had seen any sign of the enemy. It was as if the men they had fought and killed had come from nowhere. They spent every other day or so hunting, and some of the ones skilled in blacksmithing or leatherwork set up a new shop to forge swords and repair saddles. When he spoke of the men in the winter camp, Angus' eyes lit up like a just-kindled fire. He said many times with great conviction, "My father says I may go with him in the spring, that I can ride with him all the way to Muirray."

He said the girls asked about me constantly, and he plied them with stories, most of them made up, about me and the mare and Lilith. He suggested that I allow him to bring them to see me, but for a long while I refused. Then the weeks of aloneness became more weight than joyous retreat, and I agreed. I did not want them to come where I was. I did not want them to know the place where I stayed for fear they would try to find me on their own, so I agreed to meet them halfway. Angus brought them on horseback, Alanna and Pet as well, along with food to share and games to play. After that we made it a habit to gather at every quarter of the moon when the weather was pleasant enough to be outdoors. The girls chattered with me, telling me the things they did, why they hated Gwendolyn's sons, that they wished they could have horses of their own or one of the new puppies that played in the yard by the falconer's keep. But when they had an argument or grew tired and cranky, they turned to Alanna for comfort and advice. I knew it was for the best and did not try to regain their close affection or serve as confidant. The day might come when I never came home, and it might be easier for them to bear if they had Alanna for their mother. I forbade myself to ask any specifics about Ywain or his family, partly because I did not want to intrude, but also because I would not allow myself to feed the fantasy of being with him. When Angus repeatedly said that Ywain had asked him to seek my permission to come, I told him that it was my wish for Ywain to stay away, that I needed stillness and solitude for the work I was doing. Once he said, "What work is that, my Lady?" And when I did not answer, he blushed as only a boy can blush and stared at his feet.

"I am sorry," he said. "It is not for me to know what it is that you do when I am not here to talk your arms and legs off."

I had ruffled his hair and kissed his cheek and sent him on his way. There were days when I walked some distance from the hut and hid myself in the rocks or brush and watched while he approached, calling out for me. When I did not reply, he would search the shore and the sky as if he might see me swimming as a great fish, or soaring above the water as a giant bird. Then, looking sad and dismayed, he would leave the food and supplies near the hut's door and ride away. He was a wise boy; he knew never to enter the place where I slept.

The days grew longer than the nights and the air lost its harsh bite; birds began to return, the bushes bore tender green buds, and small flowers opened to the sun's rays. I put my hut in order, packed the few things I had, saddled the mare, secured Lilith on my arm, and rode into Lynnmer. Winter, and the months of resting and preparing, disappeared. The future of us all depended on the decisions I had fought for, the plans I had struggled to formulate. I knew Graham and Ywain had done the same. I wondered if we would be in agreement about the course we plotted, or if we would bristle and snarl like wolves over who got the privilege of the first bite after the kill.

THE GARDEN

BEKAH

Gwendolyn and I worked through the maze giggling, each of us taking a separate way, shouting from time to time, "Here," just as we had as girls, racing to see who would reach the garden with its purling fountain-like spring first. We met and embraced, laughing again, and playfully shoved each other, loving the kinship between us. We sat beneath a tree with its new leaves, next to the high hedge, me on a bench and Gwen on the grassy ground at my feet. I unpinned and brushed her curly hair, which was just a shade lighter than it had been when she was a child. The day was warm, bordering on hot, and we wore lightweight dresses for the first time. It felt wonderful to shed the heavier clothing of winter and to discard the self that had kept me separate from everyone for so long. I felt carefree and full of love for Gwen—sister, friend, even mother and daughter, for her few years of age above my own made her seem serious and proper. The world, full of sadness and longing and despair and danger, whirled around us, but we were sheltered and happy in that small safe place. We talked about the children, the latest news that Trevor brought from Graham and the men at Muirray, and finally Gwen mentioned Ywain and Nola and Wallace.

"He is a beautiful boy, like his father, but with his mother's calm. Already he crawls and tries to speak. Your girls and my boys love helping to care for him. Alanna, Nola, and I never have to worry for a minute about his happiness or his safety."

"He is well?" I asked.

She hesitated because she knew I was not asking about Wallace. Then she replied, "He is fine, Bekah. We talk often and he seems to have come to terms with his situation. He is an honorable man and dedicated to Nola and the boy. Can you leave him be?"

When I did not answer, she struggled to her feet and took me by the hand.

"Come and look," she said. "There is something here you must see if you are to know what to do."

She led me to the bubbling spring, and we watched for some time before she eased me to the place where the water pooled and stilled before it ran over a stone lip and channeled away through the brushy maze.

"If you calm your mind, you will see what I have seen. Prepare yourself," she said, and then moved away from me.

What I saw in the mirrored-surface of the water was a female specter of pure power, totally domineering, nothing beautiful or good or light, but only darkness filled with force and unnatural control. Inside of her, writhing and twisting, was a man in agony, tortured and in terrible pain. The pain was not hers, but his. Hers was an intense joy and incredible satisfaction at his suffering. His hurting healed her, his pain made her whole, fed her need for power, unleashed the vortex of her spirit and fulfilled the essence of who she was.

I hated the image and feared what I saw; yet I loved the image more than anything imaginable because of its rare wholeness, even though the completeness came only through the destruction of the man. So this was why men would not look me directly in the eye for longer than a moment. Why women shied away from being my friend. Why I had disguised my own likeness when I was young, why being quiet and alone kept me sheltered. Because to let myself blaze in the full power inherent in my being would be to destroy another and be glad of the deed. It was why I wanted, when I was grounded and centered and calm, to tell Ywain to stay away. I knew I was dangerous, too capable of darkness and cruelty, too prone to consume and gorge myself with wicked intent.

This I also knew: if Ywain kept allowing me to touch him, undress him, revealing him, strip him bare of his own disguises, I would destroy him. I had found the path through infatuation, burned through the fog of romance, made my way through the smoke, and what remained between us, the only thing separating us, was a fragile skin that I could scorch until I had the hard shell of his being in my hand. This I would chip and cut and gnaw and grind until I found his still beating heart, and that I would slice thin and eat raw, nourished by his strength.

Ywain had helped me unleash the she-wolf inside of me. Now, on the loose, I was unstoppable, delighting in the full force of motion that could not be slowed or turned away. I realized that I was no longer afraid for myself—I was afraid for him. I heard myself saying to him "Run, run now and do not look back." Yet, I knew I would coerce and plead. I would ask him to stay. If he could endure the dying at my hands, I could promise him rebirth and renewal. What I broke, I would mend. What I stripped bare, I would clothe with kisses. Where I inflicted pain, I would instill pleasure. What I destroyed, I would replace with unimaginable beauty. What I burned to ashes, I would breathe new life into and recreate in an ever more glorious guise.

What I saw in the mirrored surface of the magic spring was an incarnation of the Goddess. What I saw was the key to the rest of my life.

Shaking, I turned and walked back to where Gwen sat on the bench twisting the hem of her dress in her hands. My face looked awful; what I had seen had ripped my beauty from me and replaced it with agony.

"Did you see, Bekah? Do you understand why I ask you to leave him be?"

"Yes," I said forcing my lips and tongue to work in unison.

"Can you let him leave? He could take Nola and the boy and go farther north to our cousins."

"He would never go. He would never leave me."

"He would if you told him to, if you ordered him to go."

"I cannot do that." I paced the stone walkway.

"Why not? Why can you not release him and let him live a happy life?" she asked.

"Because he does not deserve a happy life. Not without me."

"Bekah. That is selfish. Why not? Why not save him if you cannot save yourself?"

"Because Gwen. Because. Because I carry his child." I stared her down.

"Oh," she said, a soft exhalation like a sigh. She walked over to me and took hold of my quivering shoulders.

I refused to cry, refused to allow her to see even the slightest hint that I might crave sympathy or compassionate outpouring. But her eyes did not soften; they hardened, gleaming in the sun. Her fingers dug into my flesh as if she meant to hold me, to keep me from escaping her grasp.

"How do you know the child is his?" she said. "I know, everyone knows, what happened to you."

I slapped her hard, hard enough to cause her to stumble backwards and fall. I had to force my legs not to move, to control the horrible desire I had to kick her.

"Never speak of that again," I said standing over her. "If you say one word about this to Ywain, I will kill you. Gwendolyn, I will kill you."

I left her there, clutching the grass with both hands, her face hidden from me. I had just severed the tie that bound us to each other as sisters, and as women. I would never trust her again. Not for anything.

THE MEETING

Ywain

I watched Bekah burst from the maze, her fists clenched at her sides. She looked like she wanted to kill someone. It was the look of unrestrained fury I had seen on her face during the battle at Muirray, the same determination I first glimpsed that long ago morning by the spring near the circle of stones where I had first joined my body and heart with hers. The air pulsated around her, shimmering with sparkling streaks of colors that ran together, exploded, then faded. Angus reached out and grabbed my hand. Despite his outward growth into becoming a man, he still retained a boy's fear and wonder. He tugged my fingers, and I tore my gaze from Bekah's back to look down at him. Tears glittered in his eyes.

"Sir, I have never seen her so mad. Is it something I have done? Something I did not do? I try to make sure I follow all her requests right away," he asked.

"No, it is nothing you have done or have not done. Let me go see if I can find out. Can you finish this here? After you clean the leather, set the saddle in the sun, and when it warms, rub this oil into it. All of it, even under the stirrups and the skirt."

"I can do that," he said and released my hand.

I squeezed his shoulder to reassure him and followed the direction Bekah had gone. As I passed by the maze, Gwendolyn emerged wild-eyed and pale, her step stumbling and uncertain.

I stopped to grab her arm and steady her.

"Gwen, are you all right? What happened? Did she harm you in some way?" I asked.

She shook her head no and patted my work-blackened hand on her white forearm.

"What happened?"

"Nothing," she said.

"Nothing?" I lifted her chin and forced her to look me in the eye.

"Nothing but the squabble of sisters," she said and looked away.

"You do not want me to know. You even turn your face away so I cannot see the truth in your eyes."

"It is not for you to know because there is nothing you can do. With time we will forget our anger and mend the breach. Until then, we will keep our distance."

I hugged her with the light intent of a brother and began to walk away.

"Ywain," she said. "Be careful. Listen to your head, not your heart."

Nodding, I waved and went on. I found Bekah standing hip-cocked on an open knoll behind the house. The rigidity of her body had been replaced with a relaxed slump and her arms hung at her sides. Before I was close enough for her to hear my steps on the pebbled grass, she turned to watch me approach.

The months without her disappeared, and it seemed like I had seen her the night before, her mouth warm and wet, her willingness to please me suffusing my body, my hands tangled in her hair, my legs raised to wrap around her back and pull her closer to me. All the tender, affectionate friendship I had enjoyed with Nola washed away as I strode into Bekah's presence. I forgot I had a wife and a young son. I forgot the vow I had made to keep myself aloof and distant, to remind myself that I would serve Bekah as warrior to leader, but I would not allow myself the magnificent, destructive euphoria of her touch.

"Do you wish to leave here and take your wife and child farther north?" she asked when I was within hearing.

I waited until I was close enough to touch her before I said, "No. Why would I want to do that?"

"So you will all be safe. So you can raise your son and love your wife and find some measure of happiness again," she said.

"Bekah, there would be no measure of happiness for me or any of us, if I walked away from this. Graham is depending on me to bring the relief men by the next new moon. He wants Trevor and me to replace him at Muirray so he can return home for awhile."

"And what of me?" she asked.

"We have been waiting to hear what you had to say. Graham asks with each messenger if we have spoken to you, if we know what you are thinking. I have had to tell him that I have not seen you, because you secluded yourself at the sea hut and would see no one," I said.

"Are you angry with me, Ywain?" she asked.

"Of course not," I said. "I feel uneasy because I do not know what has happened to you or what your thoughts are. You have kept me away for reasons I do not understand, but I have tried to honor your request. I am on the edge of—"

I stopped because I did not want to give away my heart. I heard Gwen's warning in my ear. I saw her panicked face and remembered Bekah's slashing power to wound.

We stood toe to toe, our faces only a hand-span apart, and stared at each other. Our thoughts tangled and teased, twisted together and ripped apart, spun evasive circles then clung tight. My knees weakened, and Bekah's body began to gradually dissolve, softening like something frozen left in the sun. I reached out to catch her before she fell and lowered us to the grass. We ran together like water and earth, mixing into a warm mud that soothed and healed. I ached to kiss her, but when I lowered my lips to her closed eyes, she said, "Please do not," and I satisfied myself with the feel of her in my arms.

"Do you love her?" she asked.

"Yes. Without doubt. I would not hurt you, Bekah, but neither would I lie to you. You already know my heart better than I know it myself. Trying to disguise what I feel for Nola would never work with you. Right?"

"Yes. I needed to hear you say it. I need that stern knowledge to keep me from you. Gwen says I must leave you be."

"Gwen thinks she knows everything, but she does not understand what happens to us when we are together."

"She said the two of you talk. Have you grown close to her while I have been away? Does Nola know?"

"We have all become close these past months. Gwen drew me in. She listens easily and well. I think she loves you deeply, and she has come to care for Nola and me and the baby as if we were her own family. She wants no harm to come to any of us, yet she sees the complicated web woven around us."

"Ywain, what would you do if you were free of the duty you feel toward Graham and me and the lurking menace of the enemy working its way north? Would you leave?"

"No. If I had my choice, if I could make the world the way I want it to be, I would entrust my wife and son to Gwen's care, trust Alanna to keep your daughters, and then I would take you away. I would take us some place where there would be nothing but knowing you, days of watching you delight in life and nights of loving you until you begged me to stop. It would fulfill me to make a baby with you, to see him suckle at your breast and grow up beside us. I would die a happy man if I could just have you with me all the time."

"You should not have told me that," she said.

"I know. But it is what you wanted to hear, was it not? That what I feel for you is deeper than any other bond I have. That I will never leave you. That I will never stop loving you."

"I had rather you hate and despise me," she said.

"Bekah."

"No, it is true. If you did not love me, all of this would be easy. I would not have to worry about you or your family. I could simply ignite my rage and anger and release the vengeance that burns inside me. If you did not love me, I would be content to die in battle, to let the last great power ooze with my blood into the earth. Everything would be so uncomplicated if you did not love me," she said.

I knew not to ask, but the words whispered from my mouth before I could stop them.

"Do you love me?" I asked.

Bekah was silent for so long that I thought she had fallen asleep. Then she sighed and said, "You have been honest with me, Ywain. Now I will try to be honest with you. Yes, I love you. I love you for who you are, for the man I have seen grow up, for the man who has helped me rear my daughters and who has allowed me the freedom to be who I am. Mostly, though, I love the way you love me. The way you look at me, touch me, the way you make me feel when you are deep inside me, and the otherworldly places you take me when we are joined. It is that bliss that makes me love you."

"And if we cannot have that?" I asked.

"I do not know." She shifted her weight away from me as if to rise.

I stood and helped her to her feet. She looked young and

vulnerable, standing with the wind ravaging her hair, her eyes troubled and stormy, her lips quivering. Her face had filled out over the winter, her cheeks rounder and more flushed, and her hips felt broader under my hands, her breasts pushing against the cloth of her dress. Ripe and fully alive, her beauty was heightened by the changes her time alone had wrought within her. I drew her close and held her against my chest to feel her heartbeat.

"What will we do, Bekah?" I asked.

"I do not know. I see many things. But I cannot see us. It is a tight and narrow trail we walk, and the fall on either side means our death. We cannot walk side by side. One of us must lead, the other follow. Which shall it be?" she asked.

"You lead, Bekah. I will follow, just as I always have. I know no other way."

"All right. We will allow each day to unfold as it will and trust that somehow the answers will be revealed to us. Are you ready to ride to Muirray? Is Trevor set as well?" she asked.

"Yes to both. Will you come with us?"

"Certainly. We must meet with Graham and decide whether we will maintain a defense at Muirray or mount an offensive against them."

"You are thinking of going into the territory they hold to the south?"

"Yes." She twisted so she could see the far view.

I left my arms around her, letting my forearms snuggle beneath her breasts, letting my chin drop onto the top of her head.

"That is a dangerous move, Bekah. You will infuriate them even more."

"Yes. It is a risky choice, but if we succeed then perhaps we will have peace again. If we fail, it is only the fate they have planned for us anyway. Annihilation."

"Can you talk about it now? Can you tell me about the one you met—the one who ordered your scourging, misuse, and death?"

"Does the violation change the way you feel about me?" she asked.

"No. The fact that you lived and you survived to seek vengeance is all that matters to me. If you can tell me about what you saw and heard, it might help us determine the best way to move against them."

"All right," she said. "I will tell you what I remember and you can tell Graham. I do not want to talk to Graham or anyone else about this."

"I understand," I said.

"Keenan was there," she said.

"Keenan?" I asked. "That seems improbable."

"I know. It troubles me. He stood in the shadows and translated the words I did not understand. He warned me of my fate so I could prepare myself. He said he had no power to alter the course of what would happen."

"And you believe that?"

"Yes."

"Why would he allow something like that to happen to you? He must have power if he returns from the Otherworld to consort with the enemy. Why could he not save you?"

"I do not know. But he gave me the key to survive, to vision myself alive, and it worked. Even Rowena was surprised that I lived."

"Do you still see him? Speak to him? Can he help us, now?"

"I have seen neither of them since he came to take Rowena away. I have called for them, but they have not come. It seems they come only when the Goddess wants them to appear."

"Can you tell me all you know?" I asked.

"Yes. But first, will you go and get something for us to eat and drink? I do not feel well. When you return, I will tell you everything I can."

I left her there, standing alone on the knoll. Angus waited in the yard at a spot where he could see us in the distance. He did not mind that I saw him watching. He smiled at me and opened his hands and shrugged.

"How can I help you, Sir? How can I help my Lady?"

I laughed and tousled his hair and told him to bring us some wine and cheese, some bread and fruit. I asked him to tell Gwen where we were. Then I returned to Bekah taking with me the hide of the hare that Alanna had given me, the one Bekah had killed so they could eat on their first trip to Lynnmer, the one that I had hand-tanned over the winter. It seemed a foolish gift when I would rather have given her a jeweled brooch for her cloak or a necklace or a ring. But she wore no gems or metals. Her only adornments were her white skin, her fair hair, and her rare dark eyes.

ON THE EDGE

BEKAH

Three days later, I waited for Ywain near the garden. I expected him. I had told him to come. I had been unkind to him later on that night after we had talked, when I had told him everything I knew, both of the real world with its wars and of the other world with its visions and dreams. Then he had said something to displease me and I exploded. But I loved him with a passion I scarce understood. I would give my life for him. Surely he knew that. Surely he knew that his silly comment, his slight flirtatious remark about Gwen, was an offense I would overlook once I got over my initial fury. I had sent him away, told him to leave, banished him from my presence and my heart. Or so I thought. I could not bear his absence any longer. I sent for him so we could finish our plans to leave for Muirray. I sent word through Angus to meet me in the garden, where we could be hidden and safe, where we could have a loving moment alone, where I could ask his forgiveness. I waited, but he did not come. It was evening and the light was odd and unsettling, a bruised mauve and bloody pink.

I held the hare's hide in my hands, stroked the smooth soft fur, remembered the times the creature had given its life so we could live. Without its presence I felt off-kilter, out-of-balance, and without guidance. Soon, I would have to go to the place where the hares ran and snare one and tie her to my ankle. I would use her wily mind and quick legs to help me divine what we should do next.

From afar I studied myself being watched by a figure made of light. It observed me on the inside edge of the garden. It told me to go into the maze, but I was afraid even though I had run those pathways as a child. The tall hedges worked themselves into the gloomy labyrinth. In the center, the fountain pool provided a still source of seeing, a place where two swans, one black and one white, mated for life, swam in harmony. But I did not want to go into the maze alone. I was waiting for Ywain, for the one I loved to meet me so he could go with me.

"No," the being of light said to me, "you must go alone."

"I cannot."

"You must."

Miffed and feeling imperious, I asked, "Who are you to interfere?"

"Who I am does not matter. It is none of your business. You must go into the maze."

I argued, our thoughts battling. I waited for Ywain. I wanted him. I needed him, but he did not come. Sadness and fear tugged at me, overcame my hesitation, and goaded me forward.

I found myself within the maze and the being of light disappeared. The last light of sunset colored each branch, every new leaf with an auric glow. It was beautiful and frightening. I did not want to see or hear. But voices came to me first. Whispers. Tender words. I crept forward wanting to call out, to warn of my approach, but I could not. I walked with stealth and I stayed silent, even my footfall had no sound. Through the smoky green fuzz of spring growth I saw Ywain holding a woman, her hair wound round her head in braids. They thought no one could see them, but I saw. I saw him lift her chin and kiss her. I saw him pull her close to his chest and cradle her. I thought the woman was Nola, but then she turned and the light caught her profile. I knew then what they had done to me. The word "betrayal" exploded and burned in my mind, turning the real unreal and the unreal real.

The swans no long swam placid on their quiet pool. The water rushed away, and they paddled frantically trying to escape together but they could not. The black swan disappeared. The white swan swam in circles looking for and calling out to her mate who was gone.

YWAIN AND GWENDOLYN

YWAIN

"Did you hear that Ywain?" Gwen asked me.

"I heard nothing," I said, then patted her shoulder. "You said Bekah asked you to meet her here?"

"Yes," I said.

"She was angry. Do not take her fury personally. I can hardly imagine what it must be like for her to try and live a normal life anymore. There is nothing normal for her to focus on."

"I did not take it personally, but she ordered me away. What choice did I have?"

"None," she said, laughing. "What choice do any of us have? I know she is sorry for the hurt she has caused you, me, the girls, Alanna. It is not something she does on purpose."

"I understand that. She told Angus to tell me 'at the gloaming.' It is near full dark now. I wonder where she is?"

"She will come. You stay and wait. I am glad you found me here so we could talk. I do worry about her. I fear for her mind and her heart."

"You disapprove of us, do you not, Gwen?"

"I do not know if disapprove is the right word. I know the choices you have made have caused great pain. I cannot be glad for that."

"I am not certain that Bekah and I chose to love each other. It seems more a force that infused us without our even knowing."

Gwendolyn shook her head and reached out her hand to me. I took it. Her flesh was warm, her palm pulsing with power.

"I know there is nothing I can do," she said. "I wish there were. I wish I could change everything back to the way it was when Bekah and I laughed here and played here as children. We knew nothing of love, nothing of war, nothing but the joy of being alive in the moment. Will you do your best to care for her, Ywain? She needs you. I can no longer help her."

"I will do whatever she asks of me," I said.

Again Gwen shook her head. I lifted her chin and kissed her, then gathered her into my arms and held her, rocking her the way I would rock Wallace when he cried.

"Wait for her," she said. "I hope you both will find some succor. Truly, Ywain, I wish you happiness, but all I see is darkness and storm and death."

"What will be will be. I do not know how else to go about it. Will you tell Nola where I am? Tell her I will be coming in later."

"I will. And I will kiss Wallace for you and tell him a story."

"Thank you, Gwen. You have been a good friend to me, to all of us," I said.

"You will wait," she said walking away.

"Yes. I will wait until moonrise," I said, but I did not know if she heard me. I sat and waited and listened, but Bekah never came. The moon rose, its reflection in the pool spectral and uneven, creating light and dark patterns that looked like swans swimming. I waited alone until the far off wailing of the wolves and the penetrating cold drove me inside to my bed.

THE ORDER

BEKAH

The horses blew and stomped, raising white dust. Everyone gathered in the yard as Trevor, Ywain, many new men, and I swung into our saddles. I had spent the night with my girls and Alanna, all of us cuddled together in one large mass like puppies against their mother. They stood waving, smiles on their faces, small feet dancing up and down. We had said our good-byes at breakfast. Angus held my mare's head and I touched his shoulder and he released her.

"Care for those here," I told him. "Graham will be home within a handful of sunsets. Any last questions?"

"No, my Lady," he said and nodded to me.

He walked over to receive the handshake of his father, and of Ywain, and then he strode away to stand with Gwen and her boys. I would not look at Gwen. I had not spoken to her and I would not. Sensing my unease, the mare reared, striking out at the air. I settled her, leaning over her neck to whisper in her ear. Ywain rode up beside me.

"Where were you last night?" he asked. "I waited for you long past moon rise."

"Really?" I said. "That is too bad. You look as if you want me to apologize for inconveniencing you."

"No, Bekah, I only—"

"I do not apologize. I give orders. And here is yours. You will leave us now and go south on your own to where the enemy plots. Two things: find out what they plan to do, and find a way to go to the place where Gordan was slain and bring back the spear that killed him."

A great milling and muffled objections sounded among the men. Trevor pulled his black gelding close, and Gwendolyn motioned her family back with her hand as she trotted over.

"Bekah! You cannot do that. You order him to his death."

"I order him to do what he must do. He is the only one who has reason to go, the only one with the courage and the ability to do what I ask. We cannot succeed without this knowledge or without the spear that set us on our current path. Ywain?"

"You are right," he said, his teeth grinding, the muscle in his lower jaw clenching. "I am the only man who has a private stake in avenging what happened to Gordan and what happened to you. I will go though both of us know the outcome."

"Keenan will walk with you. He told me so in vision last night. That is why I do not fear to send you. Will you go?" I asked.

"I will go." He grabbed the lead rope of a packhorse and spurred out of the yard.

"No," Nola screamed running after him.

"No," Gwendolyn whispered clutching my ankle. "Bekah, call him back. Call him back before it is too late."

I watched him leave, saying nothing. Then I turned to Gwendolyn and said, "You waste your tears. He goes to meet his destiny. I go to meet mine. And what of you? See? You have no reply. Stay home and tend the children. Wait. I do not mock you or demean you. I tell you that we all do what we must do. Take care of my daughters for me, will you Gwendolyn? Give them what I cannot. I will send Graham home to you now. The rest remains to be seen. Pray if you can. Otherwise, if things go bad, take everyone north."

She hung her head and pressed it against the calf of my leg. I reached out to touch her hair, but pulled my hand back. Gesturing to Angus, I said, "Come here. Take her away."

I nodded to Trevor and he nodded back, raised his arm to move the men forward, and they followed me, the horses filing into one long train of trotting hooves and clanking metal. I did not look back. I looked forward, into the morning, into the days to come.

ACORN EYES

YWAIN

He came to me the way Bekah said he had come to her before. One moment I was trotting the horses through the dim woods on a scant-used trail, and the next moment they were rearing and tried to bolt. A hooded figure stood in our path. When I demanded, "What do you want?" he faded into the shadows. By the time the sun sat high overhead, the encounter had happened three times. On the fourth occurrence, I swung off my mount, drew my sword, and hollered into the thick brush, "Show yourself, coward and fool."

The horses stood on tiptoe, poised to run. I saw nothing, but in my mind I heard a soft familiar voice say, "When you are done being upset and angry, I will come forth."

For the remainder of the day, I concentrated on picking my way through the landscape, staying inland and working south. I also skirmished with Bekah in silence: she was wrong, she was right, she was cruel, she was determined, she loved me, she loved only herself and her mission. I had a right to be upset and angry. But those emotions did nothing but cloud my perception and harden my heart. As the sun traced an arc lower and lower, the arguments raged on, until thoroughly spent in body and mind, I searched for a secluded place to tether the horses and curl to sleep.

Deep within a thicket of brambles, I found a jumble of rocks with a mossy lip that spouted enough water to keep the horses and me happy. They fidgeted in the small space I stomped down for them, but once I had unsaddled and let them drink, they contented themselves by nipping the slender strands of grass that competed for the sun. I settled myself with the packs to lean against and stretched out my legs to gnaw on dried meat and berries as the final light faded. Nothing could make me keep my eyes open, not even the strained conversation of owls close by.

"Ywain? Are you ready now?"

"Yes," I said. "I have argued it until I am sick of the reasons on either side."

"Then I will walk with you, if you wish."

"Are you dream or vision? Spirit or man? How am I to know how to be with you?" I asked.

"I am all those things. All you need to do is believe I can help you and I will."

"You did not help Bekah and she believed in you," I said.

"Not true. I did help her. What happened was her choice."

"How foolish is that. No one would choose what happened to her."

"She did."

"What was her other choice? To die?"

"Yes. Each person chooses in each moment. Those of us who walk between the worlds can only guide and allow. We cannot interfere."

"Keenan, why are you here? If you come only to confuse and irritate me, perhaps I would be better off alone, with only my own stupidity to guide me."

"Fine. If that is what you wish."

"Wait," I shouted and my eyes jerked open.

I expected to see nothing, but he stood with his back to me, one hand on the shoulder of my horse, the other held out to the pack animal that snuffled his palm with loud snorts.

"Stay. Walk with me. Help me figure out what it is that I must do. You know what Bekah has required of me?"

"I know." He turned back and stepped to where I sat.

I began to rise to meet him, but he gestured me to stay. He knelt and grasped my forearm, and I clasped his. With one hand, I reached up and pulled back his hood. The acorns that served as his eyes smoldered, caught fire and blazed as I blinked into them, died down into embers, then black ash. When I let go of his arm, he looked at me through orbs that were human and unafraid.

"Hello again, Ywain."

"Are you here to stay? Can I trust that you will not go away again? I thought you dead. I grieved your loss. I do not think I can let you go another time."

"I will be with you as long as I am needed, then I will go once more. It is as simple and complicated as that," he said. "You need to sleep. I will stand guard for you and watch the horses. We will talk in the morning."

"Will you not sleep as well? I am certain we are safe here." I settled back into my makeshift bed and pulled my cloak over my shoulders.

"You are safe from men. They will not find you here. But there are other forces alive in the night. The owls speak of it. Sleep now. I will watch," he said placing his hand on my knee as he used to do when I was a boy.

"Keenan, are you not weary?" I asked.

"I am past weariness or fatigue. I no longer need sleep."

Is there anything you need?" I asked, allowing my eyes to droop, then shut.

"I need to see you into the rest of your life," he said.

The barking chatter of foxes was answered by the fierce squawk of a night heron. They went at it with determined abandon, old enemies, each looking for an advantage.

FINDING THE ENEMY

YWAIN

I fully expected Keenan to be gone when I awoke, but I rolled over in a gray mist and he was standing there staring at a place in the bracken where the horses had plowed through the night before. It was nothing they could see or hear or smell, for they stood with their heads down, dozing.

"What is it?" I asked.

"Nothing." He turned toward me with a smile, his hand outstretched to pull me up.

"If it is nothing, then why do you stare as if something were there?" I asked taking his offer to stand.

"Nothing to see or hear, taste or smell. Only image and knowledge. He is closer than you think. We will not have days of hard riding to meet him. He travels with a light guard to scout Muirray and decide what needs to be done. All winter he has held his men off, waiting to see if Graham would pull back or stay. The reinforcement he asked for from the mainland is en route. Many more are coming. He knows his is the greater force and all he needs to do is choose when to attack and drive north."

"When?"

"I do not know. Soon, but not so soon that you cannot do what you have come to do."

"Then it is inevitable. I feel my end as surely as I felt yours as I held you in the oak grove and watched you take your last breath."

Keenan laughed. "An end is only an end if you perceive it as such. I see an end for you, but it is a long way off, Ywain."

"So I will live through this?" I asked as I saddled the horses.

"If you choose to. If you choose otherwise, then—"

"You know, all of this choosing and not choosing, decisions and options, living and dying, it is beginning to make me crazy. Are you saying that Gordan chose to die? That the people of Muirray chose to be slaughtered? That my mother and Rowena chose their fates?"

"Yes, in some way or another. Why do you sound so angry, Ywain? It is only—"

"And Bekah. What of her? Tell me if she lives. Do you see her end a long way off as well?" I asked as I heaved the packs in place.

"Wait," he said. "Take them down. Let us go through and take only what we need. We will both need to ride so we can travel light and fast."

Together we opened the gear, stacked and sorted, keeping weapons and food, rewrapping the excess and stashing it. I cupped a hand for Keenan to use as stirrup and boosted him onto the stump-legged dappled gray. He looked like a beggar in his holey cloak and battered boots, but his eyes shone bright and he smiled.

"It feels good to be astride again." He leaned forward to pat the gray's thick neck.

"You did not answer my question, Keenan, and we are not going ahead until you do. And do not say, 'what question?'"

"The answer," he said, kneeing his mount through the broken bracken, "is that I do not know. I cannot see what she does not want me to see. All things about her are closed to me now. I know no more than you about this."

"Keenan," I said.

"I have no reason to lie or withhold anything I know, Ywain. If I knew I would tell you. Quit. You have another goal now. You must begin to focus on what is ahead of you in the immediate moment. The future will take care of itself and seek its own path. There is nothing you can do for Bekah."

"Then tell me what you do know. When do we meet this invader? The one who has caused us more pain and distress than we can bear." I followed Keenan back onto the ghost of a path that wound through the trees.

"Tonight. We will ride into his camp," he said.

"Just like that?" I asked.

"Yes. Just like that. He is expecting us," he said.

Prickles itched all over my skin. Bekah had said that Keenan had interpreted for her when she met the enemy, when the rogue had sentenced her. She said it troubled her. Something black flapped over my head and I reined my horse sharply to watch a raven settle on a branch in front of me. It croaked out a greeting. Or was it a warning?

Keenan stopped his dappled gray and looked back at me.

"Coming?" he asked.

"How am I to know if going with you is the right thing to do?" I asked.

"Well," he said, moving on, "you either go with me or you go alone."

"How will I know what to do once we get there?" I gigged my horse to catch up with him.

"I advise you to tell the truth," Keenan said.

He reached into his pocket, brought out a dried crust and held it aloft. The big bird burst into the air behind me and I felt the sky above me part and rush back together after his wings had passed. It swooped, grabbed the bit of bread in its burnished beak, rolled once, then lifted away calling out "Rock, rock."

"A friend?" I asked.

"He is the one who told me where to find your enemy," Keenan said.

FIRE AND WONDER

YWAIN

The pace Keenan set was made for men tougher than me. The horses suffered even though he stopped often enough for them to drink and snatch a few mouthfuls of feed so that they were able to keep going. How could I question the focused frenzy of getting to the place where I had no desire to be? What I wanted was to be back at Lynnmer, close by the fire with the women chattering and the children laughing, the dogs rolling and growling and biting in mock play. What kind of man was I that I preferred the calm of peace and safety to the raw roil of war? "A normal one," I heard Keenan say in my head, though he spoke no words aloud. His ability to know my thoughts unnerved me until I realized I could read his as well. There were not many. Fleeting glimpses of his enjoyment of the day, his observations of the plants and animals. Old memories of his life at Muirray, back when I was growing up, when Keenan was at the height of his power and ability. So that was what old men think about. Then there was nothing in his mind but blank space, an airy darkness, flashes of light that went nowhere. I could no longer tell what he was thinking. We had long since lost the daylight, and I imagined Keenan was following whatever trail there was by mere instinct. I heard, rather than saw, him raise his hand, and I stopped.

"Not long now," he said. "Are you ready?"

"I do not know how to be ready," I said. "Any suggestions?"

"Be yourself. Trust your head and heart."

I did not mean to laugh, but I did. Keenan shushed me, and I felt the scald of being scolded rush into my face. We rounded a natural wall of stone, and there before us was a roaring fire and a cluster of men I could count on my fingers. They had been talking, but when one of them gestured for silence, they quieted and turned our way. I studied their leather and metal armor, the way they had their hair tied, the gleaming helmets and shields stacked to the side, their booted feet and sheathed swords. None of them reached for a weapon, though one of them walked to where the horses were tied to a long line and stood guard. The meat, roasting on a spit to the side of the fire where coals had been raked into a pile, smelled like venison. Bloody juices spat and hissed as they hit the flames.

Keenan reined in close to the firelight and dismounted. He motioned for me to do the same. I had not had time to draw a knife or unsheathe a sword. Keenan was unarmed. He walked forward and clasped the hand of the man who stood foremost among them and bowed his head, not much, just a dip of the chin and a nod. The man gripped Keenan's shoulder, the gesture signaling a close friendship. I felt my guts twist and squeeze, my head and heart alternating a pounding beat like a skin drum hit with two stout sticks.

"This is the one you told me of?" the man asked.

"Yes. Ywain of Muirray. Guardian in Gordan's place," Keenan said. "He has come on his own. No force was needed."

"So," the man said to me in my own tongue, the words difficult in his mouth as if he had just learned to speak. "You have come to ask me what I plan to do?"

"Yes." The one word hung dry as ash on my lips.

"I admire your bravery. You are the one who led the battle to reclaim Muirray. I admire that too."

When I said nothing, he walked over to me. I kept my hands at my sides, the reins of my horse easy in my right hand. He clenched my shoulder as he had Keenan's and attempted a smile. I nodded as Keenan had done, but I did not dip my face in submission.

"I plan to regain Muirray and head north. Scouts have told me that the opposition is small but fierce. Is that correct?"

"That is true," I said.

"You will not be able to stop me. It would be better for all of you to submit. A simple laying down of arms and giving over would prevent a great deal of bloodshed."

"And for all of us?" I asked.

"Life much as before. Except that we will oversee and command. Will you agree?"

"It is not for me to decide," I said.

"So I have heard. The fury in white leads you. Men tethered to the tit are no men at all," he said turning away. "I admire her ability to survive, but she must know that if we catch her again, her fate is sealed."

"She knows. As I do." I allowed one of the men to take my horse as he had taken Keenan's. "She is not apt to surrender."

"And you?" he asked again.

"I have come to find out your plans. I have come to ask you to direct me to the place where Gordan fell," I said.

"You come here to my camp to ask a favor?" He sliced off a hunk of the still dripping meat and brought it to me.

I took it and bit and chewed and swallowed, then said, "Yes. That and no more. I have no plans beyond going to seek my father's bones."

"Your father?" he asked with surprise.

He handed Keenan a chunk of burnt-edged venison and Keenan squatted by the fire. One of the other men handed him a flask, and he took that as well though he neither ate nor drank.

"Near as could be. He replaced the man who gave me life and later died. Gordan raised me as his own."

"Then you have cause to hate me." He wiped his knife on the leg of his pants.

"I have many reasons to hate you."

"Do you know where she is? Where she rides?" he asked, coming back to meet me nose to nose, the knife held loosely in his left hand.

"I do not. The last I saw of her, she was leaving Lynnmer."

"And she did not tell you her plans?"

"No. She asked me to find you and learn your plans. They are much as we thought. There will be no surprise to her there," I said meeting his gaze.

"I could kill you now," he said. "And I would have one less thing to worry about."

Keenan turned his head and raised his eyes to mine. He spoke without speaking, urging me to stay calm.

"I know." I reached out and took the rogue's knife from him. I walked over to the roasting haunch.

The men moved back. Several of them put their hands on the hilts of their swords, but I saw the leader raised his hand to hold them. I cut off another piece of meat and held it on the tip of the blade until it cooled, then I shoved it into my mouth and handed his knife back to him. When I finished chewing and swallowing, I said, "But you will not."

He laughed. It was not a sinister sound, rather, the chortle of a man who liked a good argument, a fun sparring.

"Then what will I do?" he asked.

"You will let me seek the bones of the man I loved more than any other. You will tell me where to find him and you will allow me safe passage."

"Why would I do that?" he asked sheathing his knife.

"Because you may be an enemy and you may be an invader, but you are not a barbarian. I have come without ill intent, and you will honor that as you know I would do for you if our positions were reversed."

"And when you find Gordan. *If* you find him, after months of scavengers and weather?"

"I will do what I have to do to ease my heart. Then I will return. Then I will kill you," I said. "Unless, of course, you are already dead."

I stooped beside Keenan and touched his arm. He looked up at me, nodded and rose. We walked over to where our horses were tied and loosened the reins from the rope. My horse squealed and lashed out at a blaze-face sorrel that he had been sniffing noses with a moment before.

"Here," I said. "Stop that."

Slipping my foot into the stirrup, I paused a moment to see what Keenan would do. He stood by the dappled gray playing with the thick forelock that hung over its half-closed eyes. Keenan cleared his throat and said, "I will take him to the coast and tell him the way. Then he will be on his own."

"Fair enough," the man said. "Will you return?"

"I do not know," Keenan said. "I have no way of knowing what the days and nights will bring. Will you forgive my indecision?"

"Of course," the man said. "You have already given me more than I had hoped for. Knowledge of this place and its people. The language you taught me over the winter. These are the things I will need when they are subdued and brought to heel. You may go, but only if you know that if you join forces with them—"

"I understand." Keenan vaulted onto his horse as if he had the strength of a young man. We rode out side-by-side, going the same way we had come. I strained my ears to hear if anyone followed or if they planned some furtive attack once we were out of the circle of firelight and wonderment. But there was no sound except the slow plodding of our own horses' hooves and the breath that sighed in and out of my lungs like a lullaby that had been sung many times over.

THE WOLF

YWAIN

We rode until the horses stumbled blindly along the trail and my chin dropped to my chest, waking me when my neck snapped. The landscape of thick timber and impenetrable undergrowth had thinned into scattered trees, rolling hills, and sandier soil. Dawn boiled bright colors along the horizon, promising a brilliant day.

"Keenan?" I said.

"We will stop in a moment," he said. "I am searching for the right place, one where we will be hidden and have some protection."

"So, you do not trust him either." I rubbed the crust of dozing in the saddle from my eyes.

"I do not distrust him. I respect him and honor his passage," Keenan said, signaling that we should turn off the path and head toward an outcropping of rounded rocks.

"Why? Keenan, why would you aid the enemy? Teach him to speak our language? Help him destroy that which gave you life? I do not understand your motives. Were you not the man who planned that striking attack against him and his men last fall?"

"I am man no more." He slid off his gray in a graceful dismount.

Keenan grabbed a handful of long grass and rubbed the dappled hide from withers to rump, taking time to scrub at the crusted sweat and matted hair. He looked up at me as I slumped in my saddle, my shoulders nearly to my horse's neck. Ground-tying his mount, he reached up to help me, making me smile.

"You still care for me as if I were a boy," I said, accepting his assistance.

"You are a boy. I suppose you always will be one to me." He unsaddled my tall gelding.

"This is what you need to know, Ywain. The world has changed. Doyle follows orders from his superior across the sea. He is no better or no worse than you or I. He is doing what he must do. I can see no victory for our people. Doyle's forces outnumber ours greatly. We can fight until only a remnant remains, or we can surrender and hope for a better future. One way or the other, it means we lose our sovereignty and our right to be who we have always been. Which will you choose?"

"That is a stupid question. Fight, of course. Why else did you and Gordan train me as a warrior?"

"Hmmm," Keenan sighed as he rustled in the packs for something to eat. He handed me dried meat and hard bread. We sat close together on the lee side of the rocks, the horses within easy reach.

"So, the rogue is called Doyle. The dark stranger?"

"That is what I call him. I have no idea what his real name is. Nor do I care."

"Yet you cared enough to befriend him. Interpret for him with Bekah. Why did you go there? To him?"

"I did not go because I wanted to, Ywain. The Goddess called on me and I obeyed. There is so much you do not know. So much I cannot explain to you. Everything is different on the other side. There is no right or wrong, no good or evil, no day or night, no love or hate, there is just—"

A wolf appeared in front of us, only his ears and eyes and

the black glistening tip of his nose visible in the underbrush. I stared. It did not blink or move. I turned to glance at Keenan. His eyes were closed, his brow furrowed. I looked back at the wolf. It opened its large maw and yawned, exposing sharp teeth and a long black tongue. Keenan took the piece of meat from my hand and tossed it toward the beast. The wolf waited a moment, then burst forward. He grabbed the tidbit and disappeared.

"Did I just see—"

"Yes," Keenan said. "It is time for me to go. Do you mind if I take the gray?"

"Keenan, you cannot leave me. How will I know—"

"Go back to the trail we were on. Follow it south and east to the sea. You cannot get lost. The sun, scent and sound will guide you. When you reach the water, look farther south for a peninsula that juts out into the open ocean. There you will find the place where Gordan died. Your horse is weary. It may take you a day or more. Good luck to you, Ywain. May the Goddess guide you."

He had already led his horse to a low boulder. By the time I stood, he had mounted. The gray's head drooped, resigned to its fate of traveling on.

"Will I see you again? Keenan, do not just—"

"I must go. The Goddess calls. Bekah is in need. I may already be too late. Do not despair. Do what you must do. Trust your head, but listen to your heart. You cannot go wrong."

"What is wrong? What has the Goddess told you about Bekah? Keenan, please—"

He did not hear my questions. He had already turned away, headed north. My horse whinnied after his, a forlorn and drawn-out come back plea. I stood there like an idiot with a piece of hard bread clasped in my sweating hand. Furious and afraid, I hurled it against the rocks where it shattered into small pieces.

"A lot of good that will do you," I heard Keenan say in my head. "Tie your horse well. Sleep. When you wake, things will become clear to you."

THE VISAGE

YWAIN

A moaning, night wind woke me. My horse stood humped up against the stone, a dark spot against the paler rocks that were cloaked in blackness. I lay listening, trying to remember where I was and where I was going. Stiff and cold, wound into myself like a child in the womb, I tried to stretch my legs, only to have the calves assaulted by stabbing cramps. Stifling my screams, I rolled onto my back and tossed wildly. A hint of a quarter moon filtered through roiling clouds, and the wind's whine picked up in force and pitch. Startled by the sudden movement, my gelding leapt against his brush-knotted reins and snorted. "Steady," I said. A bluish-gray veil whipped from the moon's face, exposing a silver crescent that spilled argent beams over everything. Something white and glowing moved where the wolf had been. I struggled to my knees and stared. A form took shape, billowing streamers of light from its edges. I could not move or speak. Not knowing what it was or if it bode good or ill, I held my breath and waited, praying for Keenan to come back.

"Ywain," the shape whispered.

I nodded and swallowed but did not speak.

"Ywain, forgive me for what I am about to do," I heard Bekah's voice say.

"Bekah. Bekah!" I called, but already the apparition had vanished. The sparkling image winked out like a falling star as new clouds whirled in to disguise the moon.

"Bekah, Bekah," I cried into my hands as I fell forward, my forehead hitting something sharp in the matted grass. I felt the warm seep of blood oozing from split skin, but I did not care. My chest muscles wrenched, squeezing my lungs until I could not breathe. Blackness darker than the night sucked me down against the earth, but still I could see the shimmering figure behind my closed eyes, and hear her haunting words.

THE CROSS

YWAIN

Consciousness returned with bird song and my horse pawing the ground, signaling a thirst that matched mine. I tried to open my eyes, but they were sealed shut. I remembered the wind, the moon, the visage, and the sharp object that had pierced my forehead. With caution, I felt my face. The wound had scabbed over, but the dry crust of blood was tacky beneath. With slow deliberation I began to peel the mask away from my eyes. A world transformed by storm greeted me. How had I slept through a maelstrom that had torn shrubs from the ground, moved rocks, and uprooted a gigantic tree to the east? A vicious wind had cut a clear swathe before me. If this were meant to be a sign, then I would trust and follow it. Trust in what? Ghosts with acorn eyes. Ravens and wolves that came with messages. A man like Doyle who would eliminate us from the earth. A spirit woman begging for forgiveness. What had happened to the real world, the one I had known and loved?

Small rodents had stolen the bits of bread from the ground, but one large crust remained stuck in a crevice of the rock where I had hurtled it. I tucked it in my mouth and hoped it would ease my thirst. Stroking my gelding's nose, I murmured love words to him and accepted his nuzzling of my chest as the only affection I would have for some time to come. As I led him forward for the saddle, he jerked a front foot up and stumbled sideways.

I looked down. There, gleaming in the bloodied grass, was the sharp object that had cut my head. As I reached down for the gold shape, a great roaring like a wind twisting in on itself filled my ears. I hesitated and the sound died. I moved again and the wail returned. Finally, I shoved the thing with the toe of my boot, tilting it sideways in the earth. An elongated cross, it bore arms that were not squared off but drawn into points. A beautiful piece of craftsmanship, but foreign, unlike anything I had ever seen. A red jewel bled at its center.

"Take it," I heard Keenan say in my mind. "Wear it. It will protect you where you are going. But beware of its power. It harbors a future you will not understand."

My hand shook as I pulled the piece from the ground and wiped off the damp dirt on my leg. The hand-sized cross hung from a heavy chain, one long enough to wear around the neck. I turned it over and rubbed at the obscure designs marked on the back. There were lines and angles in rows from top to bottom and across the arms. My horse stretched out his neck to smell the metal, then jerked his nose away. Whatever it was and whomever it had belonged to, the cross had not been there long. Aside from the moist sandy clay that soiled the edges, the gold still shone bright. Heeding Keenan's instructions, I slipped the chain over my head. The ornament settled in the middle of my chest, and my heart thumped against its weight. If nothing else, I would take the jeweled piece back to Bekah as a gift. If she were still living. Horrified, I shunned the thought. Of course she lived. She had to live. I was on this journey because she lived, because she had ordered me away. Why had she ordered me away? Why had I not been allowed to stay by her side and protect her? Why was I in the middle of an unknown landscape in search of a spear I did not know how to find?

My gelding did not answer my questions. He pawed the ground once more as if to say, "Let us be on the way. I am restless. And thirsty." I saddled him and set out, following the ripped open way the spinning wind had made.

THE GAUNTLET

YWAIN

The swathe led to a trail, the trail led to the sea. The horse and I stopped only three times. Once for us to drink from a seep. Once for him to graze away his hunger. And once for me to dash for a sheltered place so my bowels could unloose and splash a wretched, foul-smelling mess between my boots, which left me weak and trembling, panting for fresh air. It made me wonder if the meat I had eaten at Doyle's camp had been poisoned. Or if the Goddess punished me for wearing an adornment not of her choosing. How was a man supposed to know the right thing to do? Trust my head, Keenan had said, but listen to my heart. My head ached, a welter of confusing thoughts and condemnations. My heart felt like a piece of shriveled fruit, too dry and closed to say anything.

I stood at the sea's edge, letting the crash of waves, the sound of the eternal surf soothe me. As I knelt at a tidal pool, the water reflected back the blue sky, a few meandering clouds, my bloodstained face and the glimmering gold of the cross. If I swam and bathed, it would refresh me and give me strength to go on. I slipped my horse's reins under a rock and began to undress. Keenan's voice called to me from among the cries of the circling gulls: "You have no time. Ride on. Your own blood paints you as a warrior. Wear it. Take care, Ywain. Beware. Beware."

Pulling my boots back on, I watched the water's endless surge and swell, felt the way the ridges split, then gave way, spilling onto the sand to disperse the pebbles and shells and seaweed with no obvious plan. "No time," Keenan had said. Why should I hurry toward a fate that needed a face painted for war? What enemy could be here along a deserted stand of beach where the gulls spun and screamed in dizzying flight?

The peninsula appeared to be nothing but jagged black rock pounded by foaming water. The roar sounded like warfare, the thunder of hooves, the clashing of sword on sword, the screams of men and horses, a deafening morass of unstoppable sounds spinning inside of other sounds. I shook my head to clear my ears, but still the roar remained. My gelding pranced in a tight circle even though I held a loose rein. He chomped his bit and tossed his head, his ears thrown forward. With caution, I eased him toward the wall of rock that looked like a buttressed fortress. High overhead, impenetrable, its glossy surface was scarred by eons of blowing sand and decorated with the dull-white splash of gull droppings. The noise of the sea and its underworld continued as I urged my horse forward step by slow step, my sword drawn and flashing back the brilliant sun.

A cleft in the cliff's face opened into a sandy swale from which the cacophony poured. I pushed the horse inside, keeping close to the stone's shade. Grasses swayed atop rippled waves of sand. All around, the land swept upward in gentle undulations to a high plateau. I kneed the gelding forward, and we stepped out of the shadows into full sun.

Riderless horses appeared on top of the rise and plunged down. Caught in the turmoil, my gelding reared, dumping me. I grabbed for the reins, but missed, and he disappeared into the milling herd. The reverberation of panicked hooves gave way to the grunts and cries of engaged men. Sword still in hand, I ran for the ridge, slipping in the sand, sliding backwards, clawing my way forward. When I reached the top, breathless on my belly, I gasped and ducked as a man and horse leapt over me. On all sides, silhouetted against a setting sun, men and horses clashed, then separated. I could not tell friend from foe, kin from enemy. The battle raged full-blown, the suffocating smell of blood and offal pressing down on me as I searched the fray for some sign of what to do. If I stood, I would be slashed down. If I crawled, I might make my way—

I spotted Gordan on a small rise, his tawny hair and beard blowing in the wind as he stood in a circle of slain men, swinging his sword and crashing his spiked club into victim after victim. I studied the distance between us for a way to get to his side. Behind him, his gutted horse thrashed. The din quieted and I heard his thoughts: "In a moment. In a moment. If these curs would give me a bit of peace, I will put you out of your misery." He raised his sword, his arm extended against the sunset's crimson color, and a spear sliced through him. He arched his back, his head thrown skyward, then he fell face forward.

I sprang and ran, yelling, "Gordan!" Swords and spears, knives and clubs, gashed and stabbed as I dashed ahead, dodging, ducking, feinting my way through the fray.

A fly's buzz bothered my left ear. I tried to raise my hand to brush it away, but the weight of my sword held it down. I concentrated my energy on lifting my arm, and when it rose, I held a long bone in my grip. Throwing it down, I scrambled up, then fell to my knees. Skeletons surrounded me. The wolves and ravens had done their work, along with the rain and the wind. As far as I could see, there was nothing but the glaring white and deadening gray of bones with bits of clinging flesh. The awful odor that had assaulted me had been replaced by with the sharp, stinging scent of salt air. Wildflowers grew out of eye sockets and open mouths. The waving grasses made the skeletons look like they were trying to reassemble, rise and dance. I was as weak as if I had been in the battle and lain alongside the dead for many months. I could not comprehend what had happened to me. Had I really seen Gordan's death?

As I stood, I heard only the rhythmic washing of waves against the rock, saw a couple of foxes pouncing on mice, tasted the metallic deadness of my dry tongue. I closed my eyes and saw again the scene of battling men, saw the spot where Gordan had stood before the dying sun. I made my way in that direction, scanning the gnawed and pecked corpses as I passed, looking for anything that might be important. A weight bounced against my chest, and I looked down to see the gold cross with its red eye winking in the sunlight. I placed my hand on it and felt my heart banging against my ribs. Wending my way through the field of the slain, I reached the spot where a spear stuck up into the air at an awkward angle, the faded cloth streamers tied to its shaft still fluttering in the breeze.

The bodies had been pulled apart by scavengers. There was no way to tell whose skull was whose, but the spear held a ribcage to the earth. Thrown from close range, the long lance had entered the back, slid between ribs both rear and front and embedded itself in the ground when the man fell. The point had probably pierced his heart. Few weapons lay amid the bones. The victors had taken most of them, but this spear remained. I grabbed hold of the shaft and pulled. It did not move. Prying back and forth, wrestling with the earth that held it tight, I managed to loosen it enough to try again. Straddling the bones of the upper body, I reared backward and the ground released its grip. With the kind of tenderness I had known only while rocking Wallace to sleep or holding Bekah, I eased the spearhead from its prison of ribs. A great cry erupted from my chest, but it lodged in my throat and stayed there.

Something sparkled from the chewed saddle still on the horse skeleton that formed a crescent around the man's bones. I knelt and found a clasp half-hidden in the remnants of wool tied behind the cantle. It was the brooch that had held Gordan's cloak together. Unhooking the circle of bronze, I said a few words to serve as a prayer. Then I added, "Father, I will take these things to your wife."

Blindly stumbling, I left the open-air graveyard. At the lip of the ridge, a glint of sun revealed my sword snuggled in the sand. Far below, I saw my horse dragging his reins as he nipped the heads off of tall grasses. I pursed my parched lips and managed a weak whistle. The gelding raised his head and watched me slide down the dunes, spear and sword aloft.

TREVOR

BEKAH

We had ridden for days in near silence with Trevor, his mouth twisted in a grimace that was part shock and part sneer, responding to my questions with nothing more than, "Yes, my Lady," or "No, my Lady." He would not discuss the men or the weather, not to mention our meeting Graham again, or the tactics for our upcoming engagement with the enemy. Ducking his head, he only offered, "Whatever you think, my Lady."

Within a half-day's ride of Muirray we encountered one of Graham's scouts who reassured us all was well. They had had a quiet winter of restoring the buildings and repairing gear. There had been no sign of the enemy, though several wanderers had passed through bringing the news that areas to the south that had been under siege were overthrown and taken. I instructed the scout to return to Muirray with word that we would be there soon with fresh provisions and supplies. I asked him to give Graham my greeting and say I was anxious to see him again. As he rode away, Trevor's sullen expression shifted to one of longing.

"If you wish to be rid of my company," I said, "go on. Go with him."

"My Lady," he said, looking away.

"You have been like a scolded boy or a rejected suitor since we started out. It is clear that you opposed my sending Ywain away.

And I have asked you many times not to call me 'my Lady.' My name is Bekah."

Trevor did not speak. He merely nodded and would not meet my gaze. The hare I held in a bundle tied to my belt stirred in my lap, its twitching nose nuzzling my inner thigh. Hooded, Lilith dozed on my right arm. The mid-day sun beat down, making the horses move with lazy complacency.

"Oh," I said with more anger than I intended. "Go. Get away from me. Catch up with the scout and accompany him back to Muirray."

Trevor spun his horse, spoke a few words to the men behind me, then spurred away. A short, high-pitched whine stirred the still air. Lilith screamed, thrashed to fly, and her jesses slipped from my grip as my startled mare reared. The hare clawed my legs as I fought to stay astride.

Trevor flew from his saddle, his foot catching in a stirrup as he fell. His galloping horse slammed to a stop, then whirled back toward us. The Roman arrow lodged in Trevor's bouncing chest danced in time to the horse's frantic hoofbeats.

Calming the mare, I raised my hand to halt the men, signaling one of them to follow Lilith where she had risen in blind flight. A second whistling hiss sounded and Lilith fell, spiraling from the sky in a whirl of freed feathers. As I dismounted, I released the hare with a fervent prayer. It cowered for a moment, its eyes stunned by the sun, then sprang straight up, impaled by a third arrow. I had no time for anything except to shout "Fight!" as I drew my sword. The enemy spilled from the trees and engulfed us as I ran for my mare.

OPEN ARMS

BEKAH

Ywain, my beloved, there is no way to tell you how it felt when the night's darkness settled over my shoulders and the sound of swords clashing still echoed in my ears, the screams of the horses and men, of myself hollering until I grew hoarse trying to rally my warriors, trying to give them some reason to fight on, because if we did not fight, we were lost. We were lost anyway, but what was losing if we had not even tried to fight for what was right and just. Inside my head, the clamor, the noise tortured me. Even the smallest breeze stirring my hair kept me awake, kept me flushed, hot and sweating, my fingers curled round the haft of my dagger. When I did sleep, dreams of running kept me from real rest. I raced through unknown woods, clawing my way through brush, branches slapping my arms and face, my feet tangling in undergrowth. My horse—gone. My sword—gone. My warriors—gone. Direction—gone. Sanity—gone. Only running. A frantic, fierce pace, each step taking me closer and closer into waiting arms I could not see but believed were there. Somewhere there was safety. Somewhere there was rest. Somewhere there was peace. Somewhere there was a shoulder to cry on. Somewhere there was someone else's warm pulse to thaw the ice closing off my heart.

Ywain, I ran to find you. I could not breathe. Terror traced each gagging gasp for air, pulling fire from my lungs, my wheezing cry the wail of an old woman in agony, her soul torn open. I ran and ran. Fell. Clambered up. Staggered. Forcing my legs to move, to leap. I ran and ran, and then I saw the arms that waited for me—the wide-open, all embracing, arms of death.

ANGUS

BEKAH

"My Lady, my Lady, please," the soft voice and touch to my shoulder bolted me from sleep, my dagger in hand. It took me a moment to focus, to recognize the young man in front of me. Trevor's son, Angus. Scrambling to my feet, I looked in all directions, searching for the enemy, searching for my men. The woods spun around me, the early morning air a mottled mix of light and shadow. Small birds twittered from the trees. Nearby a stream purled. A doe stood in the shallow water drinking. No one else was near. I lowered my knife.

"Angus, what? Why are you not at Lynnmer? How did you—"

"Forgive me, my Lady." He dropped to one knee and held out his filthy hands in supplication. "I could not stay at Lynnmer even though you told me to. I followed the men, keeping far enough behind so you would not send me back. I had to come, to be part of the—"

"Oh!" I collapsed, my legs going out from under me as if another Roman arrow had found its mark. "Angus, your father."

"I know." Tears seeped from his eyes. "I saw it all. I tried to get to him, to you, but the battle—"

He stopped, not able to go on. I reached up for him and he sat, lowering his head to my lap. I let him cry and stroked his hair. He was as close to a son as I would ever have. The bird song ceased. The drinking doe threw up her head, then bounded away. Angus lifted his head and we both held our breath.

He whispered, "That is why I woke you. They followed us. We must go on."

Angus helped me to my feet and brushed helplessly at the debris clinging to my skirt. I took his hand and said, "Did any of the others—"

"I do not know, my Lady. I saw you kill the tall ruffian, the one who struck away your sword. And when you ran, I ran. I did not look back."

Nodding, I raised my head to find the sun and get bearings. Was there any sense in trying to get to Muirray in hopes that Graham had held on? Or should we head north for Lynnmer? Angus squeezed my hand and pulled me southeast. Ah, his brave heart. I motioned toward the stream, and we walked hand-in-hand to the water. I knelt to splash my face and drink. When I rose, the man who had ordered my death stood before me, his hand on the hilt of his sheathed sword. Angus gasped and jumped in front of me. With a mother's gentleness, I moved him to my side, never taking my eyes off the sparking ones of the dark stranger. We stared, each daring the other to look away.

Finally, in a rough way, his tongue tripping over the words of my language, he said, "A woman who seduces the wolves is a woman to be feared."

"Do you fear me?" I asked, wiping the water from my face.

"Yes," he said, and then laughed as if he did not mean it. He raised his arm and a bevy of men appeared from the trees, weapons drawn.

I laughed. "All this for a woman and a boy?"

He spoke in his own language, the words an order. I bent over as if to fix my boot and put my hand to Rowena's wide belt where I had tucked my dagger before I drank. When I rose, a man with a length of thin leather reached for me. I hissed and slapped him. "No one ties me. I am not a dog," I said.

The dark one laughed and waved the man away. He gestured to me, a polite bow, suggesting that I walk ahead of him. I took Angus's hand and moved forward. The men whispered until the dark one commanded, "Enough!" In the silence, I heard his footsteps behind me, felt his breath on the back of my head. He smelled of sweat and blood, of turned dirt and overripe mushrooms, but beneath that there hung the faint, sweet scent of bergamot.

When we reached their horses, I saw my mare tied to another's saddle. Blood seeped from gashes on her chest and rump. A long ragged tatter of skin hung from her hock, and she lifted her hind leg and set it down over and over. I said her name and she turned, her eyes dull and lifeless, but her ears perked forward and she nickered. I placed my hand on her shoulder and buried my face in her mane.

"Thank you," I said to the dark one.

"You are welcome." He placed his hands on my waist and lifted me into the saddle as if I were as light as a babe-in-arms. Then he nodded at Angus, cupped his hands and boosted the lad on behind me. Untying my mare, he handed me the reins and said, "I trust you not to run."

Shouting commands, he swung onto a faded yellow gelding with an ugly head and disappeared. His men mounted and surrounded me. They took us back the way we had come. At the site of the battle, they stopped. The riders in front of me moved aside to reveal the full scene. Angus clutched my hips and buried his face against my back. His shuddering cries rocked me.

I screamed. A long wailing cry of vengeance. Clouds of ravens rose. The wolves at work ceased their feast and skulked away. Far off, a small speck fluttered feathers in the mid-day breeze coming up from the sea. Lilith. I tried to count the corpses fallen like deadfall in all directions to see if anyone might have survived, but tears veiled my vision.

I urged my mare forward, but one of the men reached over and grabbed her reins. He glared at me, shaking his head no. Wiping my eyes, I said to him, "I want to go down and offer prayers for my people." He shook his head again.

"Please," I said. "At least let me do this much."

He did not understand. Jerking the mare's reins from my hands, he led her and the circle of men surrounded us again. Helpless, I shrieked and wailed, beseeching the Goddess, demanding to know why she had deserted us. The men kept to their imprisoning ring, but moved back. They did not know whether to stare or look away. Angus wrapped his arms around me and whimpered. I screamed until I had no more strength. Then, silent, I rode the last miles into Muirray.

DOYLE

ᛒEKAH

Gutted a second time, Muirray smoldered. The dark one's men were pulling bodies from the wreckage and throwing them on stone boats to be drug away. I could see the work Graham had done over the winter to rebuild and blessed him for his dedicated effort. In the middle of the stone enclosure in front of the fortress, the dark one issued orders. In a corner, huddled against the wall, a group of my men raised their heads as we approached. The gallant cry *Bekah* rose above the noise of the hoarde of workers. The dark one turned to watch Angus dismount and help me from the saddle. Someone took my mare. My men's cheer sounded louder, becoming a victory chant. I stood in the shattered gateway, leaning on Angus. The men tried to rush to me, but the dark one's soldiers forced them back with threats and blades. I raised my arms to them, asking for quiet.

The dark one walked to me, motioning for someone to take Angus over to the captured men. I held tight to him and said, "Let him stay with me. He is but a boy."

"You saw the slaughter you caused?" he asked.

I nodded and said, "Please. Tell me your name."

"I am Antonius Augustus. Your wise one calls me Doyle," he said. "You should prefer that since you refused to know my true name when we met the first time."

"Wise one? The one who interpreted for me," I said.

"Yes. He is the one who urged me to learn your words."

"So, he is a traitor," I said.

"If you choose to think that, then he is." Doyle gestured that we should sit. He picked up an overturned bench and righted it in the shade of the wall. I sat with Angus standing close, his hip against my shoulder. The dark one faced me, his eyes weary and sad.

"I ask you now to surrender," he said.

"I do not know how to do that." I tried to pull dirt-stained hair away from my sticky face.

"It is easier than you think. You say to me, I will cease fighting. I will take my men and go home."

"I have no home," I said. "This was my home. You have taken it. Ruined it."

"You know what I mean," he said, his soft voice turned hard.

"Will you let me speak to my men?" I asked.

He hesitated, his large hand scrubbing at the dried sweat on his stubbled cheek. He nodded that I could go to them, but gestured that Angus would have to stay. I walked the long steps across the inner yard. The guards stepped back, and one by one, my men, many of them bleeding with untended wounds, came to kneel and receive my blessing.

We converged in a cluster and I asked, "Graham?"

"Wounded, I know. Escaped, I think," one man said.

"Any others?" I asked.

"Perhaps a few. Not many. I am sorry, my Lady. We were prepared. We—"

"You did your best. This you must know. I owe you my life. All of you have my heart. Whatever happens now, each of you must decide for yourselves. I have no power to— I mean, I cannot—"

"Bekah," Doyle said. "Come here." It was a request, not a command. I walked back and stood before him.

"I want your answer now. Will you surrender?"

"No," I said.

"No?" His eyes flared his surprise.

"No."

He pulled his sword and gestured to a guard to bring one of my men. I moved to Angus's side and took his hand. Doyle said to the unarmed man, "Will you swear to lay down your weapons and go home to your family?" The man stared at Doyle, then looked at me and swallowed.

"You must do what is right for yourself," I said.

He looked back at Doyle and said, "I will stand by my Lady." He screamed my name as Doyle cut his throat. Angus choked and tried not to vomit. I did not close my eyes. I stiffened my back, raised my free hand to the sky and offered the man's spirit to the Goddess.

When I had finished speaking, Doyle gestured for the man to be dragged away. "Well?"

"No," I said.

He motioned for another one of my men to be brought. He asked him the same question. I told the man the same thing I had told the first one. He said, "I will stand by my Lady." Again the slash of Doyle's sword split the silence. He asked me again, "Well?"

"No," I said.

He murdered my men. The smell of blood overpowered the salt air. A widening red-black ring darkened the dirt before me.

I slumped in the hot sun. Angus held me up. The last prayer I uttered had been little more than a croaked whisper. Doyle's eyes turned blank as stone. Mine were on fire from the burn of held back tears. "Well?" he asked one last time.

"No," I said.

He knocked me to the ground and grabbed Angus by the hair. His sword winked back ominous light. I heard Rowena, a voice I had not heard in a long time, say, "Bekah, there is another way." I raised my hand to stay Doyle's strike. Pushing myself to my knees, covered in the gore of my dead men, I said, "If you spare the boy, I will yield to you."

Doyle shoved Angus away and hurled his sword. It spun through the suffocating sky to crash against the wall. The echoing clang brought the men who had served as guards to attention. Like a hawk-threatened covey of quail, they clustered tight and silent. I crawled to Angus and held him against my blood-soaked breasts.

"Take them down to the sea," Doyle said. "Strip them and make them bathe. Then give them something clean to wear and something to eat."

His voice, hard and weary, grated against the air. Then he walked away, his left hand, the one that had held his sword, twisting with a fierce clenching and unclenching at his side.

ANOTHER WAY

BEKAH

A guard directed Angus and me into Muirray and up the steep stairs that led to my tower room. Though the flagstones had been swept and most of the debris of the battle had been cleared away, the smell of smoke and death permeated the air. Inside, despite the blaze of a setting sun, it was chill and quiet. Outside, the clamor of many voices at work faded and settled as evening approached. Angus wore a ripped pair of pants and a too-small shirt, but looked as if he might live. His sea-clean hair curled to his shoulders, and he kept smiling at me as if to reassure me that all would be well.

At the closed door, the guard pounded three times. Doyle answered unarmed and without armor. He looked smaller. He had washed his face and hands, and a ruddy glow pulsed from his fresh-scraped cheeks and jaw. Staring at me, he stepped aside and motioned all of us into the room.

The wreckage of my belongings had been shoved aside to make room for his things, including a thick pallet overlaid with blankets. The windows were open to the sweet breeze coming off the sea and the crimson cast of the sun sinking into the water. The guard held out my dagger and my belt saying something that sounded accusatory. Doyle took them, shook his head, and laid them next to his own knife on a low table near the pallet. Doyle spoke to him and the guard took Angus's arm.

"No," I said. "Please. He is all I have now."

"He will be just outside the door. You have my word he will not be harmed."

Tears brimmed in Angus's eyes. I held him and whispered, "If they try to take you away, call out. Do not worry about me. No matter what you hear. I will be fine."

He nodded and walked before the guard out of the room. Moving to the nearest window, I leaned out to see the gulls that I heard crying. The stone outcropping where Lilith had loved to perch was within an arm's reach. I stretched my hand toward the memory.

"Do not," Doyle said, coming close.

"What? Did you think I was going to jump? I am not that desperate."

"I believe you are wearing one of my shirts." He surveyed the well-worn white garment that hung past my knees and over my fingertips.

"It is what the guard gave me." I held my hands to protect my child-swollen belly.

"Where are your boots?" he asked.

"Taken. I assume they thought that without them I could not escape," I said.

Doyle reached over to brush back the hair that had fallen over my eyes. His finger lingered for a moment on my cheek. I looked up at him.

"What?" I stepped away until the wall met my back.

"I was trying to decide if you are more beautiful when you are angry or when you are subdued," he said.

"As if that matters," I said.

"It matters a great deal," he said. "If you had been ugly, I would have cut your throat and been done with you."

When I said nothing, he turned away and busied himself lighting a candle and a brazier set with wood and coals. He drew the scorched and tattered window coverings to keep out the cooling air. Then he sat on the only chair and stretched out his long legs. As if settling in for an evening by the fire, he kicked off his boots and threw them toward the door where they fell side-by-side next to his sword and armor.

"When does the child come?" he asked.

"You should know," I said. "It is the result of your slobbering curs."

He crossed his legs and arms and stared at me, his lips held together.

"And this." I turned my back and pulled the light garment off over my head.

I gathered my hair and brought it across my shoulder, then stood and waited, my flesh quivering. The small fire cracked and popped. The candle blazed brighter. I counted his footsteps as heartbeats exploded in my ears. A warm hand settled against my scarred back like a butterfly settling on a thistle. Another hand settled on my arm as if to turn me into an embrace.

Collapsing, my head to my knees, I pounded the floor with my fists. A great whine seeped from my throat, and I ground my teeth to keep the agony inside.

"Bekah," he said, covering me with my makeshift dress. "Bekah, do not."

He moved away, then came back and knelt beside me. "Please." He touched my hair. He spat out an oath and rose. Then nudged my hip with his bare foot.

"Get up. Get up! I swear I deal with you better when you have a dagger in your hand."

I struggled to my feet, shaking. Tears dripped from my chin

as I covered my swollen breasts with my arms. Doyle picked up the garment at my feet and tried to drape it over my shoulders. I kissed his arm and he froze. I took his hand in both of mine and I kissed his palm and kissed his wrist. I turned his hand over and kissed his weather-roughened skin. I kissed each finger with slow attention. Then I placed his blessed hand between my breasts where my heart leapt and danced. I held it there, making him feel the life beating in my veins, then I lowered his hand to the taut bulge beneath my navel.

"The child will be a boy. Since you ordered my defilement, he is of your doing. You have taken my husband. You have taken my home. You have taken most of my people. You have taken my dignity and my sanity. Why not take me?"

Doyle did not blink, or swallow, or move. His hand melted into the mound of the child beneath my flesh. Then his free hand sought the back of my neck and rested there. In his grip, I began to glow and grow warm. My trembling ceased and I looked up at him.

"I will ride by your side," I said. "I will beseech my people and those of other tribes to lay down their swords and submit. I will beg them to save themselves and allow the change you bring to come in a peaceful way. There will be no more bloodshed. No more dying. Only rebirth. I yield to you, Doyle, if you will have me as I am."

I waited, looking at his softening eyes. When a slight tremor hummed in his hands, I stood tiptoe and brushed his smooth cheek with my lips. I whispered near his ear, "Is there any other way?"

THE DAGGER

BEKAH

I did not give Doyle time to think or act. Still standing tiptoe, I kissed him as a girl kisses a boy. Then I kissed him as a maid kisses a suitor. His lips flickered. I touched them with my fingers. They were dry. Taking a deep breath, I eased the contours of my body against his and brought his lips to mine. I kissed him as a woman kisses a man. His shoulders slumped beneath my hands as I moistened his lips with my tongue and kissed him again. He sighed. It was the sigh of a child returned to his mother's arms.

With a gentle sway backwards, he made room for us to breathe, but he kept his hips united to mine by holding my rump in his hands. My feet no longer touched the floor. Hard nipples stiffened more in the cool air that swirled between his chest and my breasts. I took my time tilting back my head so I could see his eyes. Light that had not been there before glimmered in their depths. A hint of irritation battled hesitation, but around the melting round edges delight flared. Without trying, a tentative smile blossomed on my mouth.

"Doyle," I said, murmuring his name like a prayer. "Please. Heal my wounds. Your passion stabs me. I know you want me. Take me. But, please, as a man who desires me, not as a victor who means to demean me."

His delight ignited and burned away the irritation and hesitation. His pulsing hands slid to my waist. Closing his eyes, he drew me to his chest. His embrace was that of a drowning man. Not frantic or scared, but deep, trusting, and unable to let go. My lungs buckled in the unexpected crush, and I fought for breath as he kissed my head and shoulders. He whispered words I did not know. Curses. Endearments. Pleas. Promises. Yielding, I let myself go.

Doyle placed me on the soft pallet and walked over to set the bar on the door. He undressed. His eyes did not leave mine. He knelt in front of me and kissed the tops of my feet and my ankles. His lips trailed up my calves and hovered at my knees as his hands persuaded my legs to open. I reached out to touch his head as he kissed the tender inner skin of my thighs. I began to burn, tendrils of heat and pain flicking far inside, making me arch my back. He parted me with his tongue, teasing and playing and demanding until I could not prevent the escape of a guttural cry trapped in my throat. Writhing from the pain and pleasure, I grabbed him by the hair to pull him away. He kissed his way across the unborn child and levered himself on knees and one hand. He suckled one breast while tormenting the other with his thumb and forefinger. My thighs clenched around his knee, my hips rising and falling, the slick pressure of soft lips against taut skin making me throb until I cried out again, my hands clawing his shoulders and back. Nipping my neck and ears, he slipped a finger inside of me and reached up, finding the spot high against the bone where I smoldered.

He whispered at my ear, his tongue flicking the lobe, "Again. Bekah. Again. You are so hot. So willing. Do not hold back from me. If I am going to take you, I want all of you."

His fingers pushed and nudged a small circle as he kissed me, his tongue probing. I felt the sweat on his face with my fingers. I smelled the harsh musk of his armpits mixed with fleeting wisps of bergamot. The scream that began between my thighs coursed through my stomach and chest and exploded. Doyle put his hand over my mouth, hushing me, whispering, "All right. All right. All is well. Let it go, Bekah. Let it all go."

His stiffness searched my splayed legs. He touched and withdrew, touched and withdrew. With each inquisitive test, he touched harder and pushed farther. I planted my feet wide and lifted my hips, opening myself. As Doyle eased into my wetness, I felt myself rise like a spark from a fire.

I floated away, out the window that looked down at the sea, across the wind-troubled landscape, over the trees brightened at times by a shy, cloud-draped moon. I found the rocks guarded by a lone horse and an anguished man on his knees. Settling in the brush, igniting the night, I said, "Ywain, forgive me for what I am about to do."

The intensity of Doyle's building agony brought me back. With silent flowing rhythm, he moved within me and I within him, our bodies sealed together with sweat. His heart battered my breasts, his hands gripping my shoulders, his forehead pressing mine. When I felt the first twinge of a shudder in his loins, my left hand dropped off the pallet to the table. My fingers searched for what my eyes could not see. Our hips pulled apart, then drove together, the momentum sucking me into a tumbling blackness like an undertow. Doyle lifted his head, poised to explode, his thumbs digging into the sides of my neck. Raising my left arm, I slammed the dagger into his back. Withdrew it and stabbed him again.

THE FALL

BEKAH

Squirming out from under Doyle's body, I unbarred the door and peeked out. Angus cowered in the corner within reach. The guard lazing against the wall partway down the hall, jumped up.

"All is well," I said, breathless but calm. I gestured for him to stay there and pulled Angus up and into the room. I barred the door.

"Hurry," I said to him. "Help me."

"My Lady." He gawked at my nakedness.

I searched for the shirt and shrugged it on. "Here," I said. "We must get him out the window. Help me."

Angus shifted his stare to Doyle's inert body wearing the protruding hilt of the dagger.

"Angus," I ordered. "Now."

I wrapped my belt around my waist, pulled the dagger free, wiped it on Doyle's discarded tunic and secured it at my waist with my belt. Grabbing Doyle's feet, I nodded that Angus should get his arms. We turned him over.

"My Lady," Angus said, "His eyes are open. He lives."

"Not for long," I said. "Do not look. Hurry. This window. If we are lucky, he will hit the sea and be taken away."

We half-carried, half-pulled the body across the room. The noise brought the guard to the door where he pounded three times. Angus and I struggled and lifted the body to the sill. The guard pounded again. With combined effort, we shoved, and Doyle disappeared into the black mouth of the night. I listened for the sound of his weight hitting the rocks, but heard nothing except the roar and crash of the water far below.

The guard jammed his shoulder against the door.

"A moment," I said with a patient tone knowing he could not understand the words.

I put Doyle's discarded overshirt on Angus to cover the bloodstains on his own. "This is what you must do. Stay the rest of the night in the hall. Do not let the guard enter. You know what to tell him. I will leave the door unbarred when I go. Before dawn, pretend you hear me call and come in. Bar the door. Then follow."

"My Lady," he said. "There is no way down the cliffs."

"Yes, there is. Only I know. I will leave sign for you. That is why you must wait until you have light. I am riding to Lynnmer to find Graham and rally new men. You must stay and wait for Ywain. He will come. Hide. When you can get away, climb to the top of the Tor to the west. You will find the path. Watch from there. When Ywain comes, he will need your help."

"My Lady." He plucked at the extra long sleeves.

"Go," I said and shoved him into the guard's arms, then slammed and barred the door once more. I held my breath and listened. Angus said, "She was afraid I would get cold. He is sleeping now. They were— They had— You know—"

I could imagine Angus miming to get his message across. I heard the guard grunt, mumble and walk away. I heard Angus slide to the floor with his back against the door. I put Doyle's tunic around my shoulders like a shawl and tied the ends. I looked at his boots, but knew I would go better without them. Taking his sheathed sword, I slung it over my back, fastening the belt for the scabbard across my chest. Blowing out the candle, I stared into the dying coals in the brazier. My body tingled; my hands trembled. Taking a deep breath, I mouthed a prayer of thanks to the Goddess, pushed back the window coverings, clambered onto the sill, found the small square of stone that had served as Lilith's perch with my fingers, and jumped. I clawed the stone as I fell, searching for a handhold. There was none in the darkness. My feet hit the ledge I knew was there and I forced myself forward with arms outstretched. As I kissed the cliff, its sharp rock grinding against my belly, I felt the warm trickle of Doyle's seed slipping down my thigh. Forcing myself not to cry, I held my breath and listened for any sound above in the tower. When I was certain no one had entered the room, I squatted, then sat, then felt for the narrow path the rainwater had carved in the stone. Feeling with my bare feet and holding myself back with my hands, I began my slow-sliding descent. Whenever I rested, wedged against the rough stones, I cut a bit of cloth from Doyle's tunic and left the snippet for Angus to follow.

ENCOUNTER

ᛒEKAH

I reached the bottom of the cliff to find the tide high. The sea surged inland and smashed against the rocks, the sandy beach I used to walk obliterated. I made my way by clutching stone with raw fingers and toes. When I heard a wave building, sensed it rearing above me, I turned my back, held my breath, and gripped harder. The unsettling thought of encountering Doyle's body forced me to hurry despite my near blindness in the dark.

Jagged forms gave way to smoother boulders. In places I trod on pebbles and sand, but I kept close to the cliff so I would not lose my way. Often I paused to listen, straining to hear over the roar of the water, in case Doyle's men guarded the shore.

Beginning its slow ascent, the moon cast a pale shimmer on the water. Ahead of me, something white appeared, then faded in a rising mist. Shivering, cold, wet, death hovering, I could not stop or turn back. I had to go on no matter what confronted me. The image shimmered again, then disappeared. My feet found packed sand. I rushed ahead and plowed into a dark figure with outstretched arms.

"Bekah," it whispered as I choked on a scream. "I heard you call."

"Keenan?" I gasped grappling for my dagger. "You heard me call?"

"Yes," he said touching my arm.

"I call you a traitor," I said.

"I am too late then?" he sighed. "Doyle is gone."

"Given to the Goddess and the sea. Move away, Keenan. Let me pass."

"Bekah, you cannot hope to succeed. When his men find out, they will regroup and come for you."

"Let them come. Graham will help me rally a new force. I have to get away." I brushed off the hand that held my arm.

"Ywain—"

"What do you know of Ywain? Have you turned him against me too? No, I saw him. Spoke to him. He remains loyal. He will come back to me."

"Then you both will be lost."

"So be it," I said. "Move aside."

When he did not budge, I hissed and raised the dagger. I felt his smile and heard his thought: "Little good that will do."

"I care not if you are man or spirit," I said. "You are in my way."

"All right," he said.

He clucked his tongue, and two horses emerged from a gap in the stone behind him. One was a dappled gray. One my white mare.

Wrapping my arms around her neck, I said to Keenan, "I do not know whether to curse you or thank you."

"You have already done both." He cupped his hands so I could mount. "Doyle was a good man, Bekah. Like you, bound to his higher calling."

"I do not doubt Doyle's integrity, but it does not matter. He was our enemy. With him dead, the others will be easier to rout."

"No, Bekah. You have only given them reason for vengeance. Their number increases each day. Can you not see it is hopeless?"

"I see only this, Keenan. My fate is sealed. No matter what I do, I will die. It is for me to choose how."

"I cannot ride with you," he said.

"I would not want you. I no longer trust you. I do not believe the Goddess guides you any longer."

"The Goddess works in inscrutable ways," he said placing his hand on my knee.

"Who are you to tell me how the Goddess works?" I said pulling the mare in a circle.

"No one," he said. "I am no one, Bekah, except an old man who has loved you and protected you since you were a child."

"I do not need your kind of love. Neither do I need your protection. You betrayed me."

"No, I was trying to save you. Save all of us."

"Well, you failed," I said.

I jammed my naked heels into the mare's sides, and she spun north. Following the white foam of spent waves, I pushed her into an all-out gallop.

CAPTURE

YWAIN

I rode with my sword sheathed and the spear tied to the side of my saddle under the stirrup, its point gleaming in the sunlight, its shaft streamers fluttering near my gelding's rump. The heavy cross thumped against my chest, making my head ache. Drifting in and out of true awareness, I could not tell what was real or what was dream. I had not seen the hand that threw the spear that killed Gordan, but I knew that it had been Doyle's. His precise, powerful throw had changed the course of our lives. Though I lived, I felt as if I had died in the battle trying to reach Gordan and had been reborn in some strange way. My bones did not feel connected to my flesh. My flesh did not feel connected to my heart. My heart did not feel connected to my head. Every spot on my body ached as if I had been kicked and beaten, thrashed and stabbed. Only one thing remained clear to me: I had done what Bekah had asked me to do. Now, I had to return to her. Her face floated behind my closed eyes. I saw her streaming wet and shivering, bent over the neck of her racing mare.

Voices roused me. Surrounded by mounted men, my horse had stopped. Weapons drawn, the men argued, one pointing to the cross hanging from my neck. Another to the spear secured under my knee. I recognized the men from the night at the Doyle's campfire. I shifted my weight in the saddle to sit up straighter.

Someone yelled, striking me from behind.

Smoke. The shuffling of men and horses. The soft twittering of robins as they bid good-bye to the day. My head was in someone's lap, a hand held to my bleeding cheek and ear. I tried to rise, but the owner of the hand patted me and said, "Stay. Keep your eyes closed. It is better if they think you unaware."

"Keenan?" I whispered. "What is going on?"

"I came with them from Muirray. They trust me, but they are trying to decide what to do with you. You wear Doyle's cross and carry Doyle's spear. They wonder if it is a sign that they are meant to follow you now that he is gone."

"Doyle's gone?" I asked.

"Dead," Keenan said. "But they do not know that. They only know he has disappeared, as well as Bekah and the boy. They think you had something to do with it."

"How could I—"

"Shhh. One comes," Keenan said.

I lay still, hearing the conversation. Keenan kept his voice level and calm. The other man sounded puzzled and contrite, then angry and frustrated. He stomped away, issuing orders to the camp.

"What?" I asked.

"He asked me what he should do, and I told him he would have to choose for himself," Keenan answered. "He is trying to decide if they should retreat, or stay and try to hold Muirray."

"Retreat?"

"Ywain. Muirray fell again. Most were killed. Doyle spared Bekah and the boy."

"Boy?"

"Trevor's son. Angus."

"Graham?"

"Not certain, but Bekah made it sound like he escaped. She headed to Lynnmer to find him."

"She came to me in vision asking me to forgive her. For what?"

"I do not know," Keenan said. "Shhh. Listen."

Somewhere a man pissed in the bushes. A horse stomped and snorted. The robins had ceased their sweet chatter. Sounds of cooking and settling in were set against the clang of sword and shield.

"Keenan, I must go," I whispered.

"No. You are in no shape. If you try to escape, they will kill you. They are sending two runners, one returns to Muirray with a command to pull back. They are afraid of Bekah. They think the place evil. The second goes south to ask for orders from Doyle's superior. Until they find out, you will be safeguarded. They do not want to make a mistake," Keenan said.

"What do I do? I need to get to Bekah."

"You wait. To do anything else means your death."

LAST CHANCE

BEKAH

I spent my mare the second day, but still I drove her north in a stumbling jog that rattled my teeth. Between the succor of prayer and the nightmare of visions, I managed to make Lynnmer. The yard was empty, not even an animal stirred the summer dirt or broke the eerie silence. I slipped from my horse and led her to water. As she drank with gulping sighs, I saw Gwendolyn drifting from the house, her skirts trailing. Dropping the mare's reins so she could graze, I ran into my sister's arms.

"Bekah, I have been waiting. I knew you lived. I saw you on a cliff hanging above the sea. Quickly, come in. Let me get you something to eat."

"Not yet. Where is Graham? Where are the girls? We have no time to waste. You must go north. Graham must help me gather another force. He has to—"

"He is not here, Bekah. Nor the girls. Come in now. You have to rest," she said.

"Not here. How can he not be here? I came all this way—Where—"

"Bekah. Please. I sent everyone north the day before yesterday. The girls are safe with Alanna. Graham has to—"

"Come with me and fight. I need him. You had no right to send him away. Gwen! How could you send him away?" I yelled pushing away from her.

"Because he has no arm with which to fight!" she hollered. "I doubt even that he will survive the journey."

"He cannot die. He has to help me. He has to—"

"Bekah! Look at you. Bloodied. In rags. Barefoot. Barely able to stand. Stop it. You have to stop. Give up. Come with me to eat and rest. Then tomorrow we will go north. Your daughters are waiting. You have to think of your daughters—"

"I am thinking of my girls, of their future, of our future. Without the dark one at the door, we can go home."

"Are you crazy? You have no home. Muirray is gone. Lynnmer will fall. All that we have known disappears in front of our eyes and still you cannot see. It is time to stop. Admit defeat and find a way to go on with what is left."

"I will never admit defeat." I pulled Doyle's sword from the sheath on my side. "This will see me to victory with the Goddess's help."

"The Goddess's help? Oh, Bekah, she will no longer help you after what you have done. Defeat surrounds you. Defeat hangs from you like a shroud. Defeat screams at you in the voices of all the men you had slaughtered and the ones who were slaughtered for your sake. Defeat eats with you and sleeps with you. Defeat wakes you at night and sits on your chest. Defeat devours the child inside you."

I shook, a deeper trembling than the one caused by hunger and lack of sleep. A horrible howling assaulted my ears. The scent of bergamot and dead flesh filled the air. The taste of blood filled my mouth.

"You took Ywain from me when he was all I had," I said.

"That is ridiculous," Gwen said.

"I saw you with him in the garden. In his embrace. You bewitched him and—"

"Do not be an idiot, Bekah. He was waiting for you. Concerned for you. We were talking. Nothing more. He loved you. He was trying to find a way to keep you safe, as well as allow you to follow your destiny."

"You took him away from me," I said, barely speaking.

"I did not. You sent him away. Not I. You are the one who sent him to his death," Gwen said, cutting the words off with sharp emphasis.

The smallest of tears squeezed from my left eye. I blinked it away, squinting in the bright light of mid-afternoon. I raised my face to the sky and called out to the Goddess. There was no answer. Only a heavy buzzing like the sound of a bee trapped inside an empty water jug. I swallowed and looked at Gwen. She stood waiting. Her hand reached out and open.

"Please. Bekah," Gwen said. "No more. Come inside with me."

She stepped forward to take my arm, her determination to seal my fate in defeat strong in her eyes. I stepped back, setting my feet, and raised Doyle's sword.

THE PAIN

BEKAH

When the pain came, it crept in through the cracks of my skin, through the seeps and holes in the protective armor I had tried to build around my heart. It was mine to suffer; mine alone. No one else was responsible for the agony. I was reaping what I had sown. I alone knew what I had done, rightly or wrongly, to make the pain come to me like a thief in the night, stealing the last of my joy and releasing sorrow like a flood so that every pore of my being was suffused with discomfort.

I would suffer then. That was all there was. All I felt in the dark hours alone with myself were the old injuries and the solemn vows broken. Weakness and tears, labored breathing racked my lungs trying to alleviate some of the torture. Does torture seem too strong a word when it felt like the inside of my body was pushing to be released, to come apart, to explode to let the sorrow out and allow the hurt to burst through?

My trembling and the sickness of my breath was so obnoxious that anyone would think I had drunk too much wine, that I was nothing but a sniveling coward incapable of anything but suffering. But it was the child coming too soon, and the pain of his dying in the cold, dark and lonely place where I went after the enemy struck down my sister and I managed to sever the neck on one man and slice into the chest of another before I found my rearing mare and vaulted onto her back.

    Now, no one was left. My husband gone. Poor Ywain sent away mistreated and abused because I would not, could not believe the truth of what he was saying and my sister innocent in all ways. Yet my anger and jealousy roared to the surface like volcanic spew, red hot and scalding, the agony of betrayal and defeat. Even knowing that Gwen was right, that I had been mistaken about her and Ywain, could not help me save her from fate. The enemy arrow had flown true, colliding into her back. She was down before her eyes registered the horror of what had happened. Leaving Gwen there near the garden for the ravens and wolves, knowing no one would come to touch her, give her the blessings of transition to the next world revolted me. Anger, rage, and the sickening, inconsolable sound of my own weeping gripped me as I gouged the mare to escape. All would have feared my wrath except there was no one left after my unwise undertaking. Hopelessness. Helplessness. My husband gone. Ywain sent away to die at the hands of the enemy. My sister lying in her own blood among the wildflowers, her hand reached out in supplication. My daughters sent away far to the north where I hoped they would be safe from the terror of the war, not only the one raging around us, but the one raging in my soul. The fire that could not be quenched. The smoke and ash and embers of our burning world. Even Pet punctured by the enemy as he leapt snarling as Gwen fell. The servants screaming, fleeing, scattering with the winds to seek shelter somewhere. No one left. Only the mare.

    Miles later, unfollowed as far as I knew, I sheathed Doyle's sword and kept on riding. I could not think of the birds pecking out my sister's eyes, the ants and flies coming to claim her blood, the scavengers that would wait until nightfall, then come to tear the flesh from her beautiful bones. She would haunt me forever.

Destroy the last ounce of courage I had hibernating in my heart. They would all haunt me.

How long did I ride? Hours and hours that stretched into days until I reached the ruin of Muirray, the stone fortress on the edge of the sea where my husband had brought me as a bride, where my daughters had been born, where we all played in the sand and surf of the tiny cove graced by the flight of the gulls. There had been happy times; there had been peace. But they were so long ago that the memory shimmered at the edges of my mind like a mirage. I turned the mare loose to graze the briny grass growing up between the rocks and climbed the winding stairway to my old room, a square haven jutting out over the roar of the surf crashing on the rocks below, windows on three sides open to the air and sky, a place where Lilith and the sea eagles liked to soar, so close at times that I could have reached out and touched their slow wings with my fingertips.

The heavy draperies drooped, pulled and torn by Doyle's men as they searched the room after my escape. The mice and rats had gnawed the coverings on the pallet, their droppings littering the floor like black seed pearls glistening in the sun. I thought of carrying water, of cleaning and scrubbing, of trying to make my tiny room a home again. But the thought wearied me. What would it matter now if I tried to live a frugal life or died in squalor? Surely I would die. There was nothing left to keep me alive, not even the child who did not move inside of me. With no food and little water death had come to him before me.

I raised Doyle's sword to hack down the remnants of the draperies and tapestries, cringing at the rust-colored stains on the blade and the artistic design of blood splatters on the shirt I wore as a dress. I was destined to wear Doyle's ruination until my death, destined to wear the mark of my rage and hopelessness. Fury built inside me, my blood seethed as I hacked and slashed at the fabric, ripping and tearing it from the windows and walls, tears boiling from my eyes, so scalding they singed my face as they fell.

Spent, I spread the draperies on the pallet to cover the vermin scat and lay down, my body instinctively curling around the sword, my hand still clutching the haft, my face turned toward the unadorned windows, the open sky and sea, the blood-red reflection of the setting sun smearing ranks of clouds that gathered on the horizon. Everything turned bronze and gold, then scarlet. The sighing of the surf, the screaming of the gulls, the slow tentative beating of my heart, and Ywain's last unspoken words echoing in my ears: I will return, Bekah. I will come back to prove my love.

REUNION

ᛒEKAH

"My Lady. I saw you ride in. I came as quick as I could." The voice outside the room stirred me from a drowning blackness.

"My Lady?"

"Go away," I said, and succumbed to the swimming waters.

An insistent tapping on the door brought me back to a room flooded with light.

"My Lady. Are you all right? I took care of the mare. I brought you some water and some meat. Please open the door."

"Go away," I said and covered my head.

Vicious pounding dragged me up from a deep, unmoving sleep. Another sunset smudged the walls.

"My Lady. You have been there for three days with nothing to eat or drink. If you do not unbar the door, I am going to climb the cliff face to get in. If I fall, my death will be on your head. Open the door. I beg you. Open the door."

Naked, I crawled on my hands and knees toward the voice.

Grappling with the wall, I found the bar and tried to lift it. My strength failed and it fell back in place. I slumped to the floor.

"Please, my Lady. Try again. Do not give up. Do not give up on me. There is no one else. I have only you. Please."

I fought again to stand and this time the bar crashed down. The door shoved open, and Angus took me in his arms and held me a moment before half-dragging me back to the pallet.

"Look at you." He tried to smile. "A skeleton. Almost a corpse. If you die, I will be very angry. What is wrong? Why would you not open the door?"

He saw the bundle at the foot of the pallet; a bloody package wrapped in Doyle's tunic. "Oh," he said and looked away.

"I need you to take it to the top of the Tor. Can you do that for me?" My unused voice rasped against the walls of my throat.

"Yes. But only if you will drink some water. Will you?"

"Yes," I said. "Ywain did not come?"

"Not yet, my Lady. I have kept a careful watch. When the men retreated, I was so happy. I knew you would come back. Did you find Graham safe at Lynnmer? Is he coming?"

"No one is coming, Angus. We are alone."

"When you are stronger, I will take you north." He took off the outer shirt he still wore from my night with Doyle. "Let me help you put this on."

He lifted my flopping arms and shoved them through the sleeves. He tied the front opening over my shrunken breasts. He tried, without success, to gather my thicket of tangled hair behind my back.

"I am going to get you some water," he said. "Do not bar the door again."

"Angus," I said.

"Yes, my Lady?"

"I need you to do two things more."

"Yes?"

"At the top of the Tor there is a gigantic, gnarled dead tree."

"Yes, I know. I have sat there many nights."

"Put the child there in the tree's arms. Forty paces to the west of the tree there is another like it, only it lives. Dig deep at the base and bring me a handful of the root. Can you do this?"

"Yes, my Lady."

"If you follow the trail north a half day, you will find a place where thirteen oaks grow in a circle. Stand in the middle and face the place where the sun rises. Go in the opposite direction. If you look, you will see the faint trace. It will lead you to a hut deep in the woods."

"Who lives there?" he asked, fear coloring the question.

"No one. Not anymore. It will be safe. Do not worry. In the farthest room. Back in the cave behind the hut. You will find a trunk. Inside. Some clothing. Bring me something to wear. And look for a chalice. It should be there still."

"How will I know what clothing to bring?" he asked.

"You will know. Go now," I said, lying down.

"You promise to drink the water I will bring," he said.

"I promise," I said.

He leaned over and touched my cheek. I watched him pick up the bundle and go to the door. He stood there a long moment staring at me. I tried to smile.

I heard him return and opened my eyes long enough to see him with a cup in hand. He helped me sit and I choked down a few swallows. He had brought a cloak, which he spread over me, taking care to tuck my feet under the folds.

"There is smoked fish on the table," he said. "And water."

I nodded.

"Remember your promise to me," he said.

I nodded again, then heard him close the door and descend the stairs.

FOREVER BOUND

YWAIN

Keenan and I rode into Muirray side-by-side. The silence stunned me. The fresh morning sun did nothing to brighten the sad remains charred by fire and torn by battle. We had woken two days before in the camp of Doyle's men to the same kind of silence. It was the silence of defeat; a quiet desperation still filled with longing. Keenan had looked at me and shrugged. The men and horses were gone. Our horses remained, tied together at the same tree. Doyle's spear leaned against the trunk. The coals of the previous night's fire still glowed and food had been left for us. We ate, waiting. When no one came, we saddled our horses and headed north. Now we were met with the same uneasy scene, as if we were the only ones left alive.

Raising his hand, Keenan signaled me to stop. A boy was running from the trees that guarded the base of the Tor. He waved his arms, calling out. He fell in a great rolling tumble, bolted up, and ran again. When he reached us he was out of breath, but his eyes danced and he jumped up and down.

"Angus," I said.

"Yes. Yes. I have been waiting and waiting. I knew you would come. My Lady said you would. She made me stay and wait for you. She said I would know you because you would be carrying a spear." He pointed to the object in my right hand. "But," he said, gasping, "I would have known you anyway. No matter what."

Keenan and I laughed. "Of course you would," I said, dismounting.

"And how is our Lady? Is she inside?"

"Oh, no. She has gone away. But she made me stay. She said if I followed her this time she would kill me. But she was smiling. She said I had to wait for you—and tell you—"

"Catch your breath, Angus. It is all right. We have time. Tell me what?"

"That you were to go to the circle of stones by the spring where you first took her," he said, a great blush sweeping up his cheeks.

I laughed again and pulled him into a crushing embrace.

"Do you know where she means?" he asked.

"Of course," I said.

I boosted him up behind Keenan and handed him the spear. "Will you carry this for me?" I asked.

"Yes," he said, grinning.

We did not push the horses hard, but neither did we linger. I had feared that though I knew the place with the circle of stones well, I would not know how to find my way back. But the passage was easy. The day was fine, brimming with bird song and sunshine. We walked, then trotted, then walked again as if guided by an unseen hand. As we rode, Angus spilled out the story of the battle, his father's death, Doyle killing the men, of Bekah's strength and resolve. When he reached the part about her being sequestered with Doyle, my guts twisted with intense pain. Keenan rode close to touch my shoulder. Angus's voice rose as he described his descent of the cliff and the way he had hidden until night, then made his way up the Tor. He told of nightmares and strange sounds, of an old woman who came and taught him how to snare small birds to eat and find water under the moss on the north side of the rocks. He told us about Bekah's return and taking her dead child and placing it to rest in the arms of the great tree. When he was spent, when he could tell no more, he sighed as if he had set down a great burden.

"You did well," I said. "Thank you for everything that you have done."

"I did it for my Lady," he said.

"Yes, I understand," I replied.

In the gloaming we reached the place where Bekah and I had first come together. Keenan stopped, far from the circle, and motioned that I should go on. He slid from his horse, helped Angus down, then took my reins. Bekah's white mare came prancing up from the spring, her high tail held to the side, a ragged whicker sounding from her throat.

"We will wait here," Keenan said as Angus handed me the spear.

I walked into the quiet. A soft mist rose from the knee-deep grass. Movement caught my eye and I turned to watch a pair of wolves slink into the growing shadows. On the highest stone, a raven perched, its head swiveling to watch my passage.

Bekah lay on her back in the middle of the circle. She wore a long dress that shimmered cream and blue. Her bare feet faced west. Her hair was loose and spread about her like a halo around the moon. Her hands clasped the hilt of a strange sword held on her breast. The weapon's bare blade ended at her thighs. A chalice coated with milky fluid lay by her side.

"Ywain," I heard her say. "Do not grieve. Take the sword I hold and the spear you have brought and go north. Your wife and son wait for you. My daughters as well. Take them and Gwen's sons and Angus as your own. When the enemy finds out that I am gone, they will not follow. They will leave you in peace. Do not mourn. The Goddess gives way to another, but she will return in time. I beg you, do not bury me. Leave me to the open sky and stars. Leave me to my peace."

I knelt and touched Bekah's lips, but she had no more to say. I pleaded for the sweet release of tears, but none came. I unclasped Gordan's brooch from my shirt and pinned it to her dress.

When I could force myself to leave, I took the cold sword from her cold hands. Picking up the spear I had laid in the grass, I walked away.

Angus stood where I had left him, holding our horses and stroking the neck of Bekah's mare.

"Keenan's gone," Angus said. "I turned to speak to him and he was gone. My Lady?"

"Also gone." I handed him Doyle's sword.

He stumbled against me and wept.

THE HARE

BEKAH

I am Bekah. Now you know. I swore that I would swallow poison before I allowed the invaders to take me again, allow their hands of filth and greed to touch me. I sipped the sleeping drink in the circle of stones and lay down. My soul endures. In death, as in life, I will work to keep the enemy at bay, keep them from marauding, slaughtering my people, taking away the life we have known and our close knit connection to the land and the animals who show us the right way to live. They do not know that my spirit, the spirit of all women, will haunt them, force them in dreams to face desires unknown by those who would wrest the balance of power and equality from our hands, we who have held it in such good sway for centuries. They do not know the havoc they wreak on the earth, the sacred places we have long gone to for sustenance and strength. They do not know that their way will destroy and demean, take all that humanity has striven to gain, and sell it for the sake of control and power. They do not know what they do.

Someday, in the far distant time to come, the earth will weep, seeping her life's blood into the rivers and streams, her forests will fall, her skin will be broken, her heart wrenched from within. All this horror wrought by the ignorant hand of Rome. I say again, they do not know what they are doing. But they will. And when the knowledge comes, it will be too late for them to save anything.

See why I never laid down my sword no matter how futile the fight, or how sheer the numbers of lives lost, the countless times I fled, or, like the hare, disguised myself to go into hiding, to dig myself deep underground to stay safe. Even when my bones are there, rotted into the earth for all time, they will feel my wrath and shudder from the knowledge of my power. They will never rest easy; they will roll in unsavory sleep, the weight of what they have done burdening their shoulders. Long after they think I am gone, I will be remembered. The world will cry out for me to return. And I will return. The ancient ways, the sacred ways of the Goddess, the ways that knit us close to the land will come again. And then, all that they have wrought will be for nothing. The balance of woman and man, of animal and earth, of human and divine will return. For this I gave my life. For this I sacrificed all that I had known and loved. For this I was willing to commit myself to eons of coldness and darkness so that when the light returns, all will know. All will know and understand and finally be saved. The Goddess lives on.

Woman, this much I can tell you. Follow the pathways of the hare. Learn to hide. To disguise yourself. Be fleet and wary. Learn to run, with lungs that know no pain, and a heartbeat which races faster than thought. Be safe. Take your light underground, into the labyrinth, into the secret spaces. Nurture it here. Tend it well, with care, keep the flame burning, the warmth of hope will save you. The light of love will guide you. Look always above you and to all sides. The hawk is quick on the wing. The wolf wily and fast. Be aware. Do not sleep. Danger is everywhere you turn. Trust no one. Not even the lover who comes with sweet words and tender touch. He too harbors the ill that has undone us. There is no escape in the end, but you can prolong life, keep the light from going out, if you follow the pathways of the hare.

Large ears: hear everything. Big eyes: look everywhere. Long legs: run fast. Fertile: breed often. Soft and simple and sweet natured: this is the disguise to wear. No one will know that beneath the cloak of fur the dagger is unsheathed and ready. Heed the hare. Spill her blessed blood on the stone to honor the Goddess. Carry her close beneath your beating heart. Release her to run when the time is right and see well how she guides with the direction she chooses, with the erratic racing of the feet as she flees. This way. This way. Follow her to safety. Or follow her into the dark heart of battle. Either way, follow her to victory.

Even if I could not save myself, I must now save you. If you listen, you will learn to be silent. Only in silence can you hear the voice of the Goddess who speaks through the wind in the grass, the breeze in the trees, the rush of water over stone, the push of root against earth. She is there. Everywhere. Speaking to you. Take time to be silent, to listen. No one else can show you the way, only she. Honor her by walking everyday in the pastures, upon the rocky hills. Follow the pathways of the deer and the hare. Look beneath the surface of everything, for there is hidden the secret that was known long ago, but forgotten. Underneath the earth where the hare hides, the soil sparkles, sunlight reflecting off the surface of that lost wealth. Search. You will discover the gift that was given in the beginning. You will find the misplaced key that opens the door to the Otherworld where she still walks in radiance.

I am Bekah. Know my story. For in knowing me, you will know yourself.

ACKNOWLEDGMENTS

For the healers who gave me guidance: Celinda, Chris, Nancy, Valerie, Julia, Suzanne, Sue, Barb, Dave, Beth

For my beloved Carlos, with gratitude for holding me on the nights when the dreams and visions were too much to bear, for being a willing listener as well as an astute advisor on the attributes of men and the primal elements of warfare.

For my lovely mother, Joan Wagner, my intrepid agent Elizabeth Trupin-Pulli, and my incredible readers: Natalia Brothers, Paulette Jiles and Lee Arellano.

For Sonya Unrein with special thanks for her design and publishing expertise.

NAMES AND PLACES
From the Celtic, unless otherwise noted

Bekah: a short version of Rebekah, which is Hebrew for *bound*, or *beautiful snare*

Ywain: young warrior

Lilith: from the Hebrew, a female demon In rabbinic legend Lilith is Adam's first wife, who, supplanted by Eve, becomes an evil spirit A famous witch in medieval demonology

Gordan: upright man

Alanna: harmony

Jenna: white wave

Morgan: dweller by the sea

Keenan: sharp or wise

Gwendolyn: white-browed

Graham: stern faced

Maureen: the Celtic form of Mary, which comes from Miriam, meaning *rebellion* in Hebrew

Nola: white shoulders

Wallace: stranger

Rowena: white skirt

Trevor: prudent

Doyle: dark stranger

Antonius Augustus: a fictional, not historic, name From the Latin of Roman times, *Anthony* means *flourishing* and *Augustus* means *imperial* or *magnificent*

Angus: of great virtue

Muirray: my own spelling of Murray, a great body of water In honor of my friend William J Murray

Lynnmer: My own creation, *lynn* is Celtic for *lake*; *mer* is French for *sea*

Harpy, a foul, maligned, creature of Greek mythology, part woman and part bird

SOURCES

Daileader, Philip. *The Early Middle Ages, The Great Courses/Ancient & Medieval History*. Chantilly, Virginia: The Teaching Company, 2004.

Duffy, Kevin. *Who Were the Celts?* Barnes and Noble Books, 1999.

Fleming, Fergus. *Heroes of the Dawn: Celtic Myth*. London: Duncan Baird.

Gibson, Claire. *Symbols of the Goddess*. Glasgow, Scotland: Saraban Ltd.

Laing, Lloyd. *Celtic Britain Before the Conquest*. London: Routledge & Kegan Paul, 1979.

Muschell, David. *What in the Word?: Origins of Words Dealing with People and Places*. Brandeton, Florida: McGuinn & McGuire:1996.

O'Neill, Tom. *The Celtic Realm*. National Geographic, Vol. 209, No. 3: March 2006.

Pan Gaia: A Pagan Journal for Thinking People, Special Issue on Celtic Spirituality. No. 42: Sept./Nov. 2005.

Phipps, Carter. *Death and Rebirth & Everything In Between*. What is Enlightenment, March-May 2005.

Scott, Manda. *Boudica: A Novel of the Warrior Queen, Dreaming the Eagle*. Delta Trade Paperbacks, Delacorte: 2003.

Stone, Merlin. *When God Was A Woman*. Barnes and Noble Books: 1993.

Sykes, Homer. *Celtic Britain*. London: Cassel & Co.

ABOUT THE AUTHOR

Laurie Jameson writes and resides at Casita de Luz, a small stone cottage in the Texas hill country town of Llano. For many years, as a ranch wife in the Rocky Mountain West, she wrote poetry and memoir under the name Laurie Wagner Buyer. *Beautiful Snare* is her first novel, the debut book in her Spirited Women Series. Visit Laurie at lauriejameson.com

CPSIA information can be obtained at www.ICGtesting.com
Printed in the USA
LVOW120838030613

336535LV00004B/133/P